The DRAGON WARRIOR

Deanna Cooner, PhD

Stones in Clay
PUBLISHING

The Dragon Warrior

Copyright © 2022 by Deanna Cooner, All rights reserved

Unless otherwise indicated all Scripture quotations are from the Holy Bible, New American Standard Version, 1995 by Lockman Foundation; A Corporation Not for profit, La Habra, Ca. All rights reserved.

No part of this publication may be reproduced, stored in a retrieval system or transmitted in any way to any means, electronic, mechanical, photocopy, recording or otherwise without the prior permission of the author except as provided by USA copyright law.

This is a work of fiction and any similarities to any person living or dead is purely coincidental, other than those historical persons used for the story. Any details used about them are public domain.
The opinions expressed by the author are not necessarily those of Stones In Clay Publishing.
Some extracts that appear to be Scripture quotations are an amalgam or paraphrase written by the author.

Stones in Clay Publishing
P.O. Box 1302
Newcastle, Ok 73065

Living stones, being built up as a spiritual house for a holy priesthood, to offer up spiritual sacrifices acceptable to God through Jesus Christ. 1 Peter 2:5,
But we have this treasure in jars of clay, to show that the surpassing power belongs to God and not to us.2 Corinthians 4:7

Cover Design and Graphics by Mindi Stucks
Book Design by Gary Cooner
Edited by Jeanne Marie Leach
Published in United States of America
ISBN: 978-1-7337093-6-1
Young Adult Fiction / Religious / Christian / General
2022.03.24

Table of Contents

O'Lord,

I bless thee that the issue of the battle between thyself and Satan has
never been uncertain, and will end in victory.
Calvary broke the dragon's head, and I contend with a vanquished
foe, who with all his subtlety and strength has already been
overcome.

When I feel the serpent at my heel may I remember him whose heel
was bruised, but who, when bruised, broke the devil's head.

My soul with inward joy extols the mighty conqueror.
Heal me of any wounds received in the great conflict;
if I have gathered defilement,
if my faith has suffered damage, if my hope is less than bright, if my
love is not fervent, if some creature-comfort occupies my heart, if
my soul sinks under pressure of the fight.

O thou whose every promise is balm, every touch life, draw near to
thy weary warrior,
refresh me, that I may rise again to wage the strife,
and never tire until my enemy is trodden down.
Give me such fellowship with thee that I may defy Satan, unbelief,
the flesh, the world, with delight that come not from a creature, and
which a creature cannot mar.
Give me a draught of the eternal fountain that lieth in thy
immutable, everlasting love and decree.
Then shall my hand never weaken,
My feet never stumble,
My sword never rest,
My shield never rust
My helmet never shatter,
My beast plate never fall,
As my strength rests in the power of thy might.

Valley of Vision
Puritan Prayers and Devotion

Troye Family Tree

Buster and Merilee Troye – Patriarch and Matriarch
   Family Story *The Dragon and the Mask*-- Book 1

The children – *   Adopted Children – **
Barbara* – Daughter of Buster and Merilee
   A Gathering of Dragons – Book 2
   Sharon; College Roommate –
   Dr. Daniel Holloway, Barbara's husband
   Michael Donovan, Church Creek Falls City Attorney,
       Barbara's cousin, Married to Sharon
   Hannah, Barbara's daughter
       Hannah's children
        Stacy – *Dragon Warrior* Book 5 – 10 years old
        Henry –*Dragon Warrior* Book 5 – 16 years old
 Zay* – Son of Buster and Merilee
  A Cursed Dragon – Book 3
  Ronnie – Zay's lab assistant
  Marcy – Student lab assistant and later Zay's wife
Rance* – Son of Buster and Merilee
   Profane Dragons – Book 4
   Jenny Gale – Rance's wife
   Nathan – Rance's son
   Emily – Nathan's girlfriend
   Peggy Strand – Jenny Gale's cousin

Alyssa** – Adopted Daughter of Buster and Merilee
Troye's   Book 4
Jason** – Alyssa's brother adopted by
Buster and Merilee   Book 4
Naomi – Jason Troye's date

Other Characters
Mrs. Waithe – Merilee's Bible teacher
Paps - Buster's Army Buddy

The Dragons – Names and Territory

Nisroch – god of agriculture in Nineveh

Belial – god of sexual perversion

Apollyon – led rebellion against the Most High God

Ezequeel – god of pestilence and destruction

Lilith – winged female demon that attacks women and steals children

Ishtar – goddess of war and sensuality

Lahash – god of torture and interference with God's divine will

Lucifer – god that appears as light

Asaubosam – female vampire

Asmodeous – Male vampire dragon of death

Dagon – fish god of Philistines

Rahab – goddess of chaos

Sukkoth-Benoth - god of jealousy

1
Enter the Dragon

BARBARA HOLLOWAY STRETCHED her aching back then relaxed in her chair. The shortage of personnel coupled with an overload of patients caused the hospital to call her for help. She didn't realize until this moment how much she enjoyed retirement. After a sip of coffee, she returned to patient charting. With a sigh, her hand grasp the mouse pointing to data fields.

Before the computer screen captured her attention, a young man walked in the front door. She smiled and prepared to greet him. Then her mouth fell open and her eyes grew large when she saw a huge, familiar dragon hovering over him.

In the last few days, many dragons entered the hospital clinic with patients. Barbara often felt there were more dragons than people. However, this one was the beast of them all—the one who appeared on their farm, the black agriculture dragon with a demon son named Jorkphat. The one to whom Barbara almost lost her life. Nisroch.

Barbara set her coffee cup down as she trembled too much to keep the hot liquid in the cup. The dragon winked at her and dug a claw deep into the heart of the young man.

"Why?" She said in a low voice. "He's too young." Only the dragon heard her question and her analysis of Nisroch's latest victim.

Barbara saw more than heard the deafening roar of the creature. The waiting room full of patients turned their faces toward the big windows and scanned the sky, thinking they heard a clap of thunder.

Nisroch laughed at the weaklings. The laughter of the beast vibrated the chairs and any object on tables. Barbara's coffee sloshed over the rim of her cup.

People set their magazines down and headed for their cars. Panicked people drove wildly to get out of the parking lot. The month of May in tornado alley caused people to be skittish. Most of the waiting patients simply headed toward the basement floor.

One elder gentleman glanced at Barbara. "Come on. That sounds like a tornado's coming!" he yelled as he passed her to get to the stairs with the crowd.

"No, it's not a tornado," Barbara said with a calm voice. "It's much worse."

No one heard her assessment except the young man and the dragon who poured words and actions into the head of its captive prey. "You're right." The young man said to Barbara with a smirk. Then he reached into his jacket and pulled out a 9MM gun. He pointed it at Barbara and began firing.

As the young man emptied the gun magazine with a shaky hand toward Barbara, he spoke a curse with each squeeze of the trigger.

"You're a liar."

"You're toxic."

"You're narcissistic."

"You're a manipulator."

The accusations continued ending with the vilest accusation of all, "I despise you."

Barbara felt no pain from the bullets, the pain in her heart overshadowed the pain in her body. With each accusation, she held up her hand defensively and shook her head."

As the final bullet left the gun machine, Barbara fell to the floor and whispered, "Jesus, help him."

The dragon removed his clawed foot from the young man's head. The monster leaned over Barbara's body and blew his fetid breath over her. The green cloud of heated gas from the bowels of hate covered her as the young boy dropped the gun and fell on his knees.

He shook her and wailed, "What did I do?"

The room soon filled with security and police. The young man fell on Barbara's body and groaned, "I didn't mean it . . . I didn't want to . . . Please forgive me." He continued to cry as the police escorted him to their car.

Dr. Daniel Holloway came into the waiting room to see what was happening. He saw Barbara lying on the floor in a growing pool of blood. He gasped in horror, dropped to his knees, and knelt beside her, taking her hand in his.

"Nooo!" Daniel cried over his beloved wife. Two nurse aides hurried to his side with a gurney. Daniel didn't let go of her hand as they lifted her from the floor to the gurney. With Daniel being the only doctor in town, the charge nurse took control of the situation. She checked Barbara for a pulse. She needed to know which direction to send Barbara—to the morgue or surger.

Stephanie, the charge nurse, felt a tear creep down her face. Barbara Holloway had been her mentor, her friend, and her supervisor. For those relationships, she grieved. She had to keep things moving if Barbara were to survive. A small spark of life throbbed in the exacerbated bleeding body.

Stephanie started an IV and ordered plasma. No one questioned her orders. The waiting room emptied after the shooting. All medical staff worked on their colleague.

Daniel wept like a baby and kept groaning, "Don't leave me."

"Dr. Holloway!" Stephanie spoke firmly to the doctor to get his attention. "She needs surgery now."

Daniel nodded and let Stephanie lead him to the surgical wing. They both knew Daniel couldn't do the surgery, and the back-up doctor was eighty miles away. Stephanie had an idea. She turned to one of her trusted co-workers and said, "Call Dr. Marcie Troye."

The friend nodded and whispered, "Is that a good idea?"

"Do you know anyone else who can do surgery and is available?" Stephanie whispered back.

"She's a pathologist, not a medical doctor, and she's the patient's sister-in-law."

"She's an M.D." Stephanie stated while they wheeled Barbara to a surgical suite.

"For dead people." The other nurse ran alongside Stephanie."

She's also Barbara's best hope. Look at Dr. Holloway. He's mush."

The nurse nodded and pulled her cell phone from her pocket. Since Marcy and Zay did most of the lab work and autopsies at the small country hospital, they were both on speed dial. "What about Zay? Do I need to call him too?"

"We'll let Marcy make that call."

Marcy made it to Barbara's side in record time from the basement lab. Even though Daniel was scrubbed and outfitted in surgical clothing, both Stephanie and Marcy knew he wouldn't be able to help Barbara. Barbara's life hung in their hands.

While the anesthesiologist prepared Barbara, she groaned.

Startled, Marcy saw Barbara whisper, "Come."

Marcy took Barbara's hand to assure her. Before she could speak she heard Barbara's weak voice whisper.

"Dragon."

Marcy stiffened. "How?"

"Brought boy."

"Who?"

"My boy."

Marcy wrinkled her nose in confusion at the last statement.

"What do you mean, *your* boy?"

"Henry!" Barbara muttered before passing out.

Stephanie heard the name. "Is that . . .?"

Marcy answered before she finished the question with a nod, "Her grandson."

2
Quiet Drive

HANNAH HOLLOWAY MITCHELL hummed along with the music blaring from her car stereo at full volume. Even though she couldn't carry a tune in a bucket, the loudness made her sound good. The stars twinkled above her, and the music swayed with magical expressions of love. She didn't want to go home. She wanted to drive off into the sunset and to a perfectly peaceful world.

When she saw her house approaching, she kept driving until she was out of town on a less-traveled road with few houses. She drank in the country with stars so deep they pierced the night with twinkling lights. Alone in this magical world, she sang loud and with the confidence that comes when one knows one is alone. She loved it.

Her journey to the grocery store for milk should have only taken ten minutes, by now, she knew an hour or more had passed since she left the house. She sighed, knowing she needed to turn around and head home She doubted anyone missed her, even now. After dinner, everyone went to their own corners of the house and did their own thing. She finished cleaning the kitchen and leaned against the kitchen cabinet. Her husband, Trey, dismissed himself to his makeshift office. Her children Stacy and Henry plopped themselves on the floor in front of the television.

As the music of Rachmaninoff's *Rhapsody on a Theme of Paganini* filled the car with the rapturous themes, Hannah soaked in the beauty of a star-lit night as a backdrop. She smiled contentedly. It had been months since she'd been alone to enjoy her kind of music. She tired of Britney Spears and Miley Cyrus, and she especially tired of having to read some of the most awful lyrics. Hannah kept a close watch on the trash that tried to claim her children's minds. Tonight, she could enjoy her style of music, which in her mind was real music. She didn't want to go home to the blaring base that would be shaking the house.

While enjoying her moment of wonder and solitude, something strange happened. The stars, the music, the peace of her solitude, the joy of driving her car, all disappeared. Even the music faded. It all left as if a blanket had been dropped, leaving her in total darkness. Even the headlights on her car dimmed. She saw the glimpse of a reflector and pulled into the opening of a gravel road. She stopped the car and strained to see something—anything. Yet, darkness surrounded her . . . until a small canvas of stars appeared for a few seconds. Then the blackness consumed all once again.

With her mouth agape, she continued to stare at the sky, noticing the intermittent glimpse of light peeking through the darkness.

"I gotta get home," she muttered to herself, her heartbeat pounding in her chest with an accelerated speed. She headed toward home and prayed she hadn't traveled too far. Her foot grew tense and heavy on the gas pedal.

A loud thump beat on the roof of her car. She jumped and almost drove into a ditch. With shallow breaths her eyes focused on the road, barely lit by her dimming headlights. With relief, she drove into the driveway and saw Trey, her husband standing near the garage.

"Where have you been?" Trey asked with a raised voice and shaking hands.

Hannah stammered with disconnected words and trembling. This along with her body tremors in the middle of a warm evening frightened Trey. He pulled her to himself. "I've been so worried."

Hannah melted into his chest and felt a dampness on his shirt. She ran her hand over his chest and took a deep breath. Her fear melting.

"I'm sorry, I went to get milk," Hannah answered, trying to calm her quivering voice.

"For an hour?" Trey could no longer contain himself. His controlled voice gave way to his panic and anger.

Hannah nodded. "I needed some time alone and drove out to the country and admired the stars."

Trey sighed and put his arm around her shoulder. "You know I understand; I just need to know you're okay." He kissed her on the side of her forehead. "Are you cold?" he asked.

She shook her head. "No, why?"

"You're trembling."

"It got dark and I got scared." She smiled and put her arm around her beloved husband. They walked inside the house. It was time for the family to join in the living room for their nightly ritual of reading another chapter in their current novel and from the Bible.

Trey opened the family Bible. He determined the best way to calm Hannah was to stay in their regular routine. "Stacy spoke to her mother with a smirk as she walked into the room." Hanna didn't notice.

Hannah poured herself a large glass of water settled into her chair and pulled a throw over trembling body. The thirst exceeded the fear. "Where's Henry?" ten-year-old Stacy asked.

Hannah and Trey exchanged an all-knowing parental smile of teenagers. "Probably with his friend, Cory Frye." Trey teased. Stacy blushed, "I like him, he's cute."

Hannah managed a slight smile at Stacy's comment.

"Okay, let's read; Henry may not be home for a while," Trey said and winked at Hannah. She pursed her mouth in a tight smile, keeping her recent, fearful experience quiet. She didn't tell Trey that Henry's absence made that fear gurgling in the pit of stomach growl louder.

Trey read, "*Cursed is the man who trusts in mankind and makes the flesh his strength, and whose heart turns away from the Lord, for he will be like a bush in the desert and will not see when prosperity comes. But will live in stony wastes in the wilderness, a land of salt without inhabitant.*"

"That sounds bad." Stacy wrinkled her nose.

Hannah took a sip of coffee and nodded. "It is a bad place to be. My mother would describe it as the place one lives when the dragons overtake a life."

"Mom, do you think the dragons Mimi talks about are real?"

"I know she does," Hannah answered. "I'm not sure."

"Your skepticism in your mother's experience appears to be fading." Trey chided.

Hannah turned the corners of her lips upward into a mock smile and said nothing. Instead, she rose to answer the persistent and nagging jingle coming from her cell phone.

3
What is Truth?

SIXTEEN-YEAR-OLD HENRY MITCHELL sat in a cold isolated room, sobbing like a small child. He groaned, "I'm sorry." No one heard, and worse, no one cared. No one to comfort except a small circle of light piercing the ceiling of the interrogation room. The stream of light so small a pencil lead would cover it.

Zay Troye stood in a small room adjacent to Henry. He prayed with a fiery passion seeking to pierce heaven and earth to bring the power of the Holy One in to Church Creek Falls.

"Hello, Zay," Came a familiar voice from his childhood. He looked up and saw his old high school buddy Jeff. He smiled a bit and stood to shake hands with his friend.

Jeff grabbed him by the shoulders and pulled him into a tight hug. Jeff whispered in Zay's ear, "I'm here and I want to help."

Zay nodded at his old friend as he pulled away from the hug. "Do you work here?" he asked.

"In a way. I'm the district attorney."

Zay took a deep breath and sighed, grateful he hadn't said anything that would endanger Henry. "How can you help?" Zay asked with a furrowed brow.

"No need to be cautious . . . Jeff continued to drone while Ezequeel, a dragon, covered the words Jeff spoke by a contented growl.

The beast spoke to Zay, "Let me introduce myself, I am Ezequeel, the god of pestilence and destruction." With that, the dragon roared and released a plume of flames over Jeff. "We will destroy the Troye family once and for all," the beast bragged.

Zay ducked his head and took his eyes off the horrid apparition. "Greater is He that is in me than any ugly dragon," he whispered.

"What?" Jeff asked. "What about a dragon?"

"Oh, nothing. It seems our family is constantly attacked by dragons," Zay answered.

Jeff laughed aloud and patted Zay on the back. "Come on; I'll let you see that nephew of yours."

The moment Henry saw Zay, he jumped up and ran toward him, hugging him and sobbing.

Zay held tightly to him. "Your mom and dad are on their way," he said with a stern tone.

Henry pulled back. "Please, don't be angry at me, Uncle Zay, I didn't . . . I mean . . . I wouldn't . . ."

"You shot your grandmother," Zay raised his voice at his nephew.

Henry slumped down in the stiff-backed chair and ducked his head. "I know, and I don't know why."

Zay sat down in the other chair. "I do."

"You do?" Henry raised his head and looked at his uncle.

Zay nodded. "You couldn't help it."

"Have your parents told you about your family history?"

"Mom said her great-grandfather help build the town and built the first church."

"That's right, his name was Robert Troye, and he did battle with a mean man."

"Phillip Donnigan?"

"Yeah. And he wasn't only mean, he was pure evil."

"How? And . . . well . . . what does it have to do with my situation?"

Zay smiled and patted Henry on the hand. "It's because of that history I know you're telling the truth."

The door opened and Hannah and Trey entered.

Zay had to leave. He headed toward the hospital where his sister lay in critical condition with her life in his wife's hands. *This is not a good situation.*

Watching the gut-wrenching scene of a confused family the dragon Ezequeel roared in delight. Their pain and agonizing in it made the creature stronger. He released another plume of flames from a huge maw, brighter, hotter, and bigger. Then he saw it; that small stream of light. It revealed the prayers of the beast's enemies were being heard. It struck fear in the dead soul of a fearsome beast. The beast looked closely and saw the small stream growing. He knew he had to act fast before the Troye family formed a group of prayer warriors against the dragon horde.

Daniel felt a cold wind settle over them. He shuddered with the familiar scent of evil in the room. "Another battle?" he murmured.

"I think so," Marcy answered with a shiver as she and Stephanie pulled four bullets from Barbara's body. Two in the arm, both superficial. One on the right side barely missing the intestine and the fourth from her head. It slid by the skull severing some facial nerves. Barbara's face would most likely be paralyzed on one side.

Daniel watched the two women, knowing they were capable of saving the life of his beloved wife. He spoke to no one in particular he simply needed to express his thought. "I don't think I have the strength for this battle, it's . . . it's too close to my heart."

"You know what Barbara would say." Marcy winked at Daniel, hoping to alleviate the tension.

"Yeah, she would say, 'we need to sharpen our swords and bow the knee to the commander in chief of our army.' Did she ever tell you about our first date?" he asked Marcy.

"Yes, she said she was a little brat back then."

Daniel laughed. "She was." He gazed at her sleeping figure, praying for her to awaken. "I told her I was going to marry her on that day."

"I bet that went over well," Marcy smirked

Daniel nodded with a slight grin. "Those were feminists' days; she didn't like the male gender too much. He paused a moment. "The only reason she went out with me was her love of horses. You should have seen her ride. She was like a dream in slow motion. I was impressed."

Daniel reminisced and Marcy gave thanks for his distraction. She chased a bleeder in Barbara's left quadrant. Daniel grabbed a hemostat, clapped the bleeder, and swabbed the blood.

"It was a good day, sometimes when you can't stop the pain; you have to remember there is a plan."

Daniel sighed. "Lord, you promise a way of escape. I know you are faithful, but . . ." He stopped his prayer.

Marcy finished it for him. "God. How long must this go on? Why do you let wicked people enjoy their family, You seem intent on letting the devil destroy us? God. I don't understand!" She almost screamed. "Leave us alone!"

Ezequeel the dragon hovered over the surgical table. The beast mocked Marcy, "Yeah, Most High God, leave them alone."

Daniel's physician memory muscle must have kicked in because he took control over the surgery. "We don't have to understand; we only have to trust."

"How? Look at the damage the bullets did to Barbara's body?" Marcy said through gritted teeth as she chased bleeding vessel. "I'm not use to blood." She whispered. "I work on those whose blood no longer flows through their veins." Marcy talked to herself as sweat poured off her brow. She needed the panic release as she worked to save her sister-in-law.

"I don't know." Daniel answered unaware of the actual conversation. He became a well-respected surgeon instead of a blubbering husband. "I know that whatever is happening, God will use it for good and His glory."

Ezequeel roared, releasing a stench of rotting flesh in the room. "I will destroy your whole family before that happens." The monster roared.

An angel of God stood between the monster and God's children.

Neither Daniel nor Marcy heard the threat. They wrinkled their noses at the pungent smell.

"Eww, smiles like death in here," Stephanie remarked from across the room.

Marcy heard and she prayed Daniel didn't. She recognized the stench of a dragon, and it truly did smell like death. *Please God, don't let this woman die, she still has work to do.*

Daniel stroked Barbara's arm as the surgery was completed. "She's going to be okay," he said, looking at Marcy and Stephanie.

"Yeah, other than some loss of facial muscles, she'll be fine. Her time on earth is not finished."

Daniel pushed her to room 203. Marcy walked beside him.

"I wonder what Henry's motivation for this was?" He mused to himself.

Ezequeel wrapped his reptilian body around the couple. "Me! I'm the motivation. I am destruction."

Belial, the meanest dragon of them all, roared with pleasure. "Don't fail me. Crush this family into oblivion." The beast roared in Ezequeel's ear.

Ezequeel knew it was a command, not a request. The beast shuddered a bit when even the cold blood of a dragon froze for a moment in the veins of evil hatred.

4
So Many Patients

DR. DANIEL HOLLOWAY pulled his lab coat over his street clothes as he walked through the corridor of offices into the patient area of the Church Creek Falls hospital. He straightened his lab coat before he entered the small workroom behind the nurse's station. The lab coat may be a bit old-fashioned, he liked having a garment over him, and being the only M.D in town, he set the standard.

The nurses wore badges declaring their education and responsibility level, and most of them followed his example and wore their lab coats.

The extra layer of germ protection probably didn't protect them from the nosocomial infections which inhabited this place, still it looked more professional to him. He pushed his hands into the left pocket of his lab coat and found a sweet surprise. He pulled the single, wrapped, candy truffle from his pocket and smiled as he unwrapped it and popped it in his mouth. Pockets held gifts given by patients in gratitude.

The candy reminded him of sweet, young Addie he treated a few days ago when she had a terrible earache. He grinned when he saw the sprouted grain seed in her ear.

"Addie, have you been playing in the grain bin?"

The rambunctious ten-year-old nodded her head with a toothy grin.

Daniel handed her the seed after he flushed it out with an ear lavage. "Here's the first of this year's crop." He smiled.

Addie turned to her mother, "Can I have a candy?" she asked. A strange request. Her mother handed her the wrapped truffle. Addie slipped it into Dr. Holloway's pocket.

Daniel pretended he didn't see her do it. He knew Addie would ask if the candy tasted good the next time she came in with one of her many 'accidents.'

The quiet chatter of nurses, lab techs, and the office personnel came into his hearing range as he approached the nurse's station, the center of the hospital floor. It started as a passage from one area to another forty years ago.

Today it served as a central hub to the four wings of the small hospital. Here any worker could reach the required patient handout forms on any one of the multiple computers lining the desk. Over the years, patient care took a secondary place to record keeping. Audits ruled the hospital. The staff adapted, only the extra office employees liked it.

He rounded the corner and saw his beloved wife, Barbara, hovering near a student nurse, pointing out the necessary information to needed in the patient chart. Her recovery from the shooting incident fascinated him. Even though older patients often recovered faster than younger ones, it still amazed him. He watched for a few minutes with a grateful heart for her presence. As he reached the nurses' station, he passed the door opening to the waiting room. The room was full.

"What's going on? I've not seen that many people here in years." Daniel nudged Barbara with the question.

"You have a full load today," she answered him with snipped-off words then returned to her student.

Daniel knew this was code for, "Not now, something's wrong." It wasn't her words, rather the way she used them. After nearly forty years of marriage, the couple developed a silent code of communication, especially around other medical personnel or patients.

He clicked on a few keys of a vacant computer and looked at his patient load for the day. He printed the schedule. It was almost empty. He held it up toward Barbara and mouthed the words, "What's up with this?"

Barbara slapped her forehead and instructed the student to get up from the computer. As soon as Barbara sat down, she flew through a few keystrokes and then rose to continue with the student. She pointed toward the printer. Daniel retrieved the new list; every fifteen-minute slot was filled.

"Are we in the middle of a pandemic?" he asked aloud to anyone listening. A nurse near him answered, "Not exactly, more like a *feardemic*?"

"Fear of what?" Daniel wrinkled his brow and let his gaze fall through the glass into the crowd of people in the waiting room. His mouth agape, stared at the number of people in the waiting room.

Barbara stepped beside him and gave him a gentle poke in the ribs. "Hurry up." She said. He didn't respond. She followed his gaze and caught the sight that had paralyzed him.

She grasped his arm. "It can't be." She felt moisture gathering in her eyes and the feel of a jackhammer in her chest as her heart began to beat with a panic attack.

Daniel nodded. The man in the waiting room wearing a black suit with an orange and turquoise tie smiled at the two of them and gave them a mock salute with a rotten, toothy grin.

"Da—" Barbara began.

Daniel took her hand from his arm where her nails were digging into his flesh and turned her away from the window. He walked her to the little office behind the registration counter and sat her down.

Another nurse called to Daniel, "Dr. Holloway, we need you bad," she pleaded.

He put his hand in the air and motioned to her with his palm. "Give me a 2mg. Valium please."

The nurse complied and handed him the medication.

He put it in Barbara's hand. "What's this?"

"Valium."

"No, that makes it worse. We've got to stand firm."

"Why is that thing here?" Daniel asked.

"What thing?" the nurse who'd given him the pill asked.

"The man out there in the black suit with the orange and blue tie."

The nurse scoured the waiting room. "I don't see anyone fitting that description, Dr. Holloway."

"Would you call the city attorney and ask him to come here?"

"Sure,"

Michael Donovan, the city attorney and cousin to Barbara, entered the hospital back door and headed directly for Daniel's office.

Daniel and Barbara greeted him with wide eyes and drawn faces.

"What's up? It sounded urgent," he said as he entered the office.

"Look at the waiting room," Daniel told him.

"Discretely," Barbara added.

In a few minutes, Michael came back, pale-faced, and slumped into a chair next to Barbara. "When?"

"We just saw it a few minutes ago. What do you think?"

"No good."

"What do we do?" Barbara groaned as she held her forehead in her palm.

Michael took her other hand and tensed up. With a slack jaw and his right hand grasping his chest, Michael choked out one word, "Help."

Daniel recognized the body language. He pulled Michael to the floor and started chest compressions. "Heart attack!" he shouted to Barbara.

She pulled an emergency cord and called for a crash cart over the intercom. A full team of cardiac specialists whooshed into the room, each getting right to work and none of them speaking.

Soon the team had Michael stable again.

"Get him to CCU!" Daniel shouted.

As the team took Michael to the Coronary Care Unit, a man came walking up to Daniel's door. He stepped inside the frame of the door and grinned at Barbara.

She screamed.

Daniel turned and looked at the man in the black suit with the orange tie. "Get out!" he shouted.

The man changed to an orange, horned image with a black body and green teeth. He glared at Barbara and said, "See what you did to me?"

Barbara held her hand over her open mouth, repulsed by the vision and unable to turn away.

"Now you know why I'm here. I'm getting my revenge, starting with that soldier boy. He's on his way to meet his master, and I'm afraid his exit will not be pleasant." The creature laughed. "And this is just the beginning."

With one voice, Barbara and Daniel whispered a word they hadn't spoken since their college days, "Jorkphat."

5

Loss and Gain

THE RAINDROPS TAPPED on the bay window and then trekked their way to the bottom where they pooled on the patio. Sharon leaned her head against the back of Michael's favorite wingback chair. He liked to watch the wildlife, the grandkids, or even the rain through the bay window. The five-acre plot of ground on the outskirts of Church Creek Falls where Michael and Sharon spent most of their life served as a respite from the evils of the world they faced each day.

Neither had retired from their duties. Michael served as the city attorney, while Sharon managed the pregnancy crisis center she and Barbara started many years ago.

The days Sharon spent in the hospital maternity ward as a charge nurse gave her much pleasure. She loved bringing new life into the world and seeing a new family grow. Of course, the department brought much sadness. The maternity ward was either the happiest place in the hospital or the saddest. She remembered every baby that died under her watch, as well as the grief of the parents. At this moment she understood that grief better because she no longer watched and empathized with those in grieving, she grieved over the loss of her beloved Michael.

The heart attack shouldn't be a surprise. Michael had been short-winded ever since that dragon monster, Mammon, tried to choke the life out of him. He'd been a strong and able soldier both in the physical army of man and the spiritual army of God. The battles fought in the spiritual realm took a big, physical toll on his body.

Sharon wiped a tear from her eye and sighed. *At least he died peacefully surrounded by the people he loved.*

Barbara sat in the chair opposite Sharon and watched the raindrops. Their friendship traced back to college days when they first met as roommates.

"God said He wouldn't give us more than we can bear," Sharon stated.

"Without a way of escape so that you will be able to endure it. God is Faithful." Barbara finished the verse from 1 Corinthians 10:13.

Sharon took her gaze from the window and tipped her lips in a slight smile at Barbara. "Thanks for coming," she said, wiping a tear from the corner of her eye and pointing toward the rain tracking down the window. "That shows you what's going on in my heart."

Barbara responded with a pat on the hand. "Death is both a blessing and the worse blow to the heart."

"How's Buster and Merilee?" Sharon asked.

"Daddy's taking it pretty hard. He thinks it should have been him." Barbara ducked her head and watched her hands fold over each other.

"It's not time for Buster yet . . ." Sharon's voice trailed off. Then with a slight jerk of her head, she turned back toward Barbara, "Do you think Jorkphat did this?" Sharon almost screamed.

Barbara moved from her chair toward Sharon. "That monster doesn't have this kind of power. Remember, Christ came and died and took away the power of death so it no longer holds us slaves to fear of it."

Sharon relaxed a bit. "Then why is it here?"

"I don't know."

"The vile thing may be looking for someone to inhabit. Church Creek Falls has its share of possibilities."

Barbara nodded. "Ain't it the truth."

The music played quietly as the townspeople filled the church auditorium. Michael lived his life as a lawyer. The people filling the church were there for the man, not his occupation. Michael—who helped many of the townspeople through times of financial disparity or loss, or helped them gain advancement in life was a favorite son of the community. Michael was a man who gave to whomever whatever was needed.

The city paid him a meager salary. His cousin Rance Troye taught him to make wise investments. As a result he left his widow, Sharon, in a good financial state.

Michael's two sons lived honorable lives in the same manner as their father. Sharon would be able to live her life without the worry of money or family. Her daughters-in-law adored her, and the grandkids loved being around their Grammy even though they were no longer children.

Barbara's daughter, Hannah, walked to the podium and sang a favorite song of Michael's. After the eulogy, she sang a song of Psalms and then closed the service with a beautiful rendition of "It Is Well with My Soul."

Sharon remained quiet throughout the service. After all the friends and relatives paid their last respects, Sharon stood before the casket with the body of her beloved.

She tapped his hand and said, "I'll see you soon, babe." Then she kissed her fingers and laid them on his lips.

She walked out to the portico where the crowd stood with bowed heads in reverence.

All except one—the sneering black creature with an orange chest.

Sharon gasped when she saw him. "Get out!" she screamed. Without realizing it, she faced one of the leaders of the town when she shouted.

With a startled look, he backed away and headed toward his car. His wife followed with a dazed expression.

The mourners stared at Sharon. Some looked like they were going to leave too.

Buster stepped up to speak to the crowd. His older, weak voice couldn't reach above the din of the startled mourners.

Jason stood beside his dad and spoke in his deep, resonant voice to the crowd. "Dear Friends and Neighbors. Sharon and I are grateful for your presence to help us celebrate the life of our beloved Michael Donovan. His loss leaves a great hole in our hearts and sometimes grief explodes when we least expect it and in ways not within our character. However, your presence and patience help to bear that grief."

As Jason spoke, he didn't look at the black creature pacing in front of the people, attempting to get his attention.

When Jason finished, the people nodded.

The creature growled, "The worst is yet to come." Then they laughed with a roar.

The Troye family heard the growl. Others looked up in the sky and ask if it was thunder while a few seemed oblivious to the mocking of an evil monster.

Rance noticed a few people looking in the direction of the creature. *Maybe they saw the evil too.*

Barbara and Daniel held hands tighter as they witnessed a horrific sight alone, and they both knew it was meant for them. As the black creature growled, the dragon known as Nisroch grew from the body of one of the mourners and hovered over Hannah and her family.

The claws of the dragon held tightly onto Hannah's head, and the serpentine tale draped over her husband, Trey, and their two children Stacy and Henry.

The dragon consumed the vision of Barbara and Daniel. "You are about to learn what my kind can do. You are going to see what happened in the beginning with the woman, Eve, and the man called Adam."

"What do we do?" Barbara whispered to Daniel.

He shrugged his shoulders, and Barbara saw the fear that bound his voice and his body. She pulled on his hand; he reluctantly followed.

Michael felt the warmth of the bright being standing next to him. "Can you help them?"

The being gathered Michael in his powerful arms and led him away from the earthly scene. "It is not your concern. You have fought your battle, and it is now time for your rest."

Michael soaked in the warmth of the being. It embodied a love unlike anything he'd ever known, and all things earthly disappeared from his sight.

"It is time for you to meet the lover of your soul, your Savior."

Michael felt his stomach lurch with excitement. Soon, he would see Jesus face to face. Nothing else mattered.

The next day the waiting room filled again. "What's going on?" Barbara asked as she deposited her belongings in the Director of Nurses' office. She pulled on a lab coat and entered the medical floor to help the nursing staff.

She didn't have time for this. The hospital's annual audit approached faster than a speeding train. Two nurses called in sick, leaving them short-staffed; and with the Director of Nurse's job empty, the responsibility of preparing for the audit and managing staff fell to Barbara.

Barbara didn't want Hannah to see her in that office for fear of her daughters reaction. Some of the nursing staff noticed Hannah's growing disdain toward Barbara.

None wanted to become involved, except Shannon Wright. She loved being Hannah's confident and encourager. She liked to talk and reveal details on any employee conflict to anyone who would listen.

Barbara knew Shannon fed Hannah any negative detail she could find on Barbara. Nonetheless, she was helpless to stop employee chatter.

Barbara pulled up the computer screen to see patient check-ins. The screen moved so fast with new admissions she couldn't keep up. There needed to be a plan put into place. She looked around and saw three nurses and two customer service reps handling the unusual mass of people.

"Mandy and Gracie, you pull the ones that are here for clinic visits."

At the pleading of Hannah's friend Mandy, Hannah returned to help.

Melody asked Hannah to staff surgery.

"I'd rather help Mandy," Hanna said. "Gracie likes to do the hospital; can we trade?"

"No problem. Come on, Gracie, let's get busy."

Mandy divided the patient list. "I thought you liked surgery," she said to Hannah.

"Yeah, I do, I just don't want to spend that much time with my mother." Hannah went to the waiting room door and called her first patient into a treatment room. A busy day began.

Shortly after, Daniel came through the hallway and met Hannah. "Hi, sweetie, how are you feeling today?" He smiled at his daughter.

"Don't call me that at work," she snarled at him.

"Sorry, you're right, not very professional," he answered with a smile and kept moving toward the first treatment room. Before he entered the room, he pulled up the patient's record and read the vitals and complaints of the patient. The name shocked him, Mr. Jorge Fha.

Mandy entered the lab with her hands full. "This is just the beginning." She said as she set the samples in their proper places.

Marcy Troye looked up from her microscope and nodded, "Busy day?"

"That's a mild statement. Have you found some phenomenon going on to cause this influx of people?"

"Yes, I have."

"What?"

"I don't know yet; it's bewildering. Zay has gone to collect soil samples from farms and animal DNA."

"Do we need to start with some precautions?"

Marcy shook her head. "Not yet, we don't think it's contagious; we think it may be environmental."

"What do you mean?"

"There's something in the environment causing the illness and isn't bacterial or viral, so it must be chemical," Marcy answered, and under her breath, she whispered, "Or spiritual."

Buster and Merilee Troye sat at the kitchen table. They could hear the stomping, growling, and screaming.

"The mask?" Merilee asked.

"That and more. I hear the bracelet from Barbara's dragon encounter screaming too," Buster responded.

"But—"Merilee started. Buster put his hand over hers and nodded.

"You think it hears us?"

He shrugged his shoulders and shook his head.

"What do we do?" Merilee grasped his hand.

Buster pulled his Bible closer to him. He turned to Psalms 83 and read.

"O God, do not remain quiet; Do
not be silent and, O God, do not be still. For
behold, Your enemies make an uproar and
those who hate You have exalted themselves.
They make shrewd plans against Your
people, and conspire together against Your
treasured one. They have said, Come, and let
us wipe them out as a nation. . . They
conspire with one mind and against You they
make a covenant.

"Oh, my God, Pursue them with
Your tempest and terrify them with Your
storm. Let them be ashamed and dismayed
forever, and let them be humiliated and
perish, that they may know tha You alone,

whose name is the Lord, are the Most High over all the earth."

The sound of a thousand bat wings filled the house with the screaming of Ishtar, the goddess of war.

"I don't know what's happening, Buster, it's more than we've heard before." Merilee stared at the ceiling and whispered, "It's really loud."

The two prayed as was their custom every night. They kissed, put in earplugs, and went to bed. As sleep covered them, the noise abated, and they heard no more.

Aww, the sweet aroma of prayer reached the nostrils of the Holy One. He sighed and smiled. All the realm of heaven lit up with His smile.

"Prayers are coming forth," The angel Raphael stated to Jophiel.

Michael listened as Paps taught him about his new home. "I miss praying." Michael moaned as they watched the realm sparkle with joy.

"So, pray," Paps said.

"Really?" Michael wrinkled up his nose as he asked. "Is it necessary?"

"Always. We left many loved ones on earth, and they are still at war even though we are at peace. Remember how Ben Hur and Aaron held up Moses's hands while Joshua fought the Amalekites?"

"Yeah," Michael cracked a grin.

"Well, we have to hold up the prayers of our people as they fight the same dragons."

Michael shuddered. "Thank goodness those things aren't here." Paps laughed at his comment.

Jophiel, a cherubim angel stepped into the conversation. "They're not gone. Your family still fights them, and your wife is even now being consumed by them in her grief at your loss."

Michael slapped his forehead. "How could I have been so insensitive?"

"It happens to us all when we first arrive; that's when we learn to be supporters rather than warriors," Paps said.

"I don't understand."

Paps looked at Jophiel. "Do you mind if I take him? I love this part."

"Sure," Jophiel answered. "If you need anything—"

"I know; you're just a thought away," Paps answered and saluted the messenger of God.

"Where are we going?" Michael asked.

"To the altar of incense. You're gonna love it."

Sharon sat beside the bay window. The rain was gone, and sunshine filled the window on this bright morning. "I wish I felt as sunny as it looks," she moaned.

With a full, hot cup of coffee, she sat down and prayed, "Lord, I'm selfish today. I hurt and I need to sit with you. I can't even form a thought to pray, I need you so badly."

The Holy Spirit indwelling in Sharon wrapped arms of comfort around her lonely heart.

She sighed and began to sing a song she heard at a Dennis Jernigan concert. "If I could just sit with you awhile, I need you to hold me."

Paps ran. Michael wanted to slow down and observe the beautiful scenery. However, Michael tried to do both. When Paps slowed down, Michael ran into him. "Oops, sorry."

Paps didn't answer. He stood there with a silly grin on his face and his hands resting on his hips. He took a deep breath.

Michael did too. "That smells good," he said in reverence.

"It's the prayers of the saints. Our prayers are in there too. When there's a spike in the flames, it means there's fervent prayer coming. A blaze is a group of prayer warriors. I think it's the most beautiful sight in heaven."

"Welcome Paps and Michael," a soft yet overpowering voice spoke their names, or rather, the secret names He had given them when they entered His realm.

Michael's jaw dropped, and his voice disappeared.

Paps bowed. "Our Father," he said.

"I see you are enjoying the sweet aroma of my children's prayers," the Father said as He surrounded the two without moving.

"I hear music too," Paps replied with the voice of a child discovering something for the first time and relating it to his parent.

The Father smiled. He looked at Michael. "What about you Michael, what do you see and hear?"

"I hear my wife, Sharon, singing," Michael muttered.

"Yes, My son, Jesus is holding her and comforting her. He is giving her assurance that she will see you again."

Michael fell on his knees and tuned his ear to the soft strains of her voice. "Is she well?"

"She is, My Son is preparing her for a battle without you."

"The dragons . . . again?"

"Yes."

With a down turned face, Michael stood and asked, "What? Why? I don't understand."

44

"It's not yours to understand, my child, it is yours to trust."

"How?"

"Paps, can you tell him?" The Father said.

Paps smiled from ear to ear. "Absolutely."

"Michael, we have the opportunity to come here and pray too. Just because we have left sinful earth behind doesn't mean we forget everything. We forget the hurt and the pain. Here at the altar of incense, we offer our prayers for those still fighting the war with the dragons."

"She has fought so bravely; why must she do it again?" Michael pleaded with the Father.

The Father answered, "Her battle will allow many to see Me, know this, my child, My Son, Yeshua, will fight the battle for her because she trusts Him."

"What can I do?"

The Father pointed to the altar. "That is the healing balm."

Michael stared into the flame and watched it smolder and almost die only to have it flame in bright and high arcs. A hand touched him on the shoulder. Michael rose and turned toward two beautiful women standing next to him.

"We'll be here to help too."

"Thank you." Michael felt a tear of appreciation form in the corner of his eye. He recognized the women from his time on earth.

"Hello, Mrs. Waithe. You are looking young and spry and Peggy, you are more beautiful than ever."

Michael wrapped his arms around the two women in a greeting hug.

In unison, they said, "Welcome home."

6

Accidents and Mysteries

HANNAH SLUMPED IN her chair and took a deep breath. "Man, what a day," she said to Trey. "Smells good. What'cha cooking?"

"My old standby, spaghetti."

"Anything would taste good right now, I haven't had anything except vendor food all day, and that was a bite between patients and charting."

Trey joined her in the den handing her a glass of ice water.

"You are the best." She sighed.

"Why was it such a busy day?"

"I have no idea."

"Are people really sick?"

"Some are, there's been a multitude of accidents from extremely serious to just a scratch. They all involve blood, so everyone comes to the emergency room."

"What kind of accidents?" Trey asked as he pulled her well-padded work shoes from her feet and put them in the salt bath he prepared.

"How do you think of these things?" she asks as she feels the hot saltwater bathing her swollen, aching feet.

"I'm married to the most wonderful woman in the world, I have to take care of her." He smirked and smiled. "And most important, I love you," he said and then kissed her.

"Good thing you went into something more practical than a medical career."

"You mean farming?"

"Yeah, we all have to eat."

"Speaking of . . . it's time for slaughter. Do we have room in the freezer?"

"If we share with Zay, Rance, Alyssa, and Jason."

"What about your mom and dad."

"I'm not sharing anything with them." Hannah leaned back on her chair and closed her eyes.

Trey opened his mouth to challenge her exclusion of Barbara and Daniel. Before he could speak, Hannah spoke.

"We lost Derrick Martin today," She whispered.

Trey looked up at her. "Please tell me you misplaced him."

"No, he died."

"No!"

"I know, he was only seventeen—a baby."

"What happened?"

"Motorcycle accident. There wasn't much chance of saving him. He lived for about five hours after we got him. It was bad. Mom said it was a blessing he didn't live." Hannah said through gritted teeth. "That woman can make me so mad."

Trey leaned back in his chair and rested his face on his fist. "He's my friend," he whispered without acknowledging Hannah's rant.

"I quit my job today."

Trey still focused on Derrick and didn't hear Hannah's words. At least not at first, when the words found their way into the labyrinth of his occupied mind, Trey sat up. "What? Did you say you quit your job?"

Hannah nodded.

"You just got the job."

"I know, I can't work with mom."

"There's only one hospital. I don't think you can avoid her."

Hannah sat up in the chair with wide eyes. "You're right." She smiled, dried her feet, then grabbed her phone.

Trey had learned soon after their marriage that he married a spitfire with a determined spirit. Rescuing her was easier than trying to stop her. Whatever plan entered her mind, she'd pursue it until complete defeat or complete success. He felt a sigh of relief when he heard her talking to the chairman of the hospital board. She was asking for her resignation to be nullified.

Marcy walked in the back door, pulled her work clothes off, and put them in the washer. This was her habit since seeing microbes under a microscope in college. She slipped into her robe hanging near the washer and pushed her tired feet into her comfy house shoes.

"I think tonight is an eat-out," she called to Zay.

"I'm already ahead of you." He held up a bucket of chicken.

"I hope you got some of their good coleslaw."

"Always."

They sat at the table munching on the food. After a few minutes, Marcy ventured the question swimming in her mind. She felt afraid of the answer. "Did you find anything?"

Zay shook his head. "Some strange things about the soil, nothing to cause the sickness. There's a gross-looking fungus growing in the soil in every field, although there are no microbes that would cause human diseases. I don't understand it."

Nisroch wrapped a spiky tale around Jorkphat. "You're learning."

"I'm just beginning. Those people will think Phillip Donnigan was a saint."

"Who are you planning to inhabit?" Nisroch growled.

"The princess of the Troye family, Mrs. Hannah Mitchell, her husband Trey, and those beautiful children, Stacy and Henry."

"I thought you were getting smarter; you can only take over one."

"Yeah, and that one will take over the others." Jorkphat petted the tail of his handler.

"Hannah!" Nisroch blew a puff of smoke as he spoke the name. "Very good."

Rance ran the numbers again and again. It couldn't be, there had to be a mistake. Alyssa heard his frantic banging on the keys.

"Hey, hitting them harder doesn't change the results." She shouted as she looked for more records. His groaning and banging getting on her nerves.

"What are we gonna' do?" Rance rose from his desk and entered Alyssa's office, formerly Michael's.

"We work it out." She ducked her head and pulled the palms of her hands over her forehead pushing her hair back.

"Nothing's going to change tonight. Let's go home." Alyssa agreed, flipped off her computer, and gathered her purse and jacket.

Mammon laughed out loud. Jorkphat kicked him. "They can hear you, you stupid dragon."

"Did you hear that?" Rance asked Alyssa.

"I did and I'm ignoring it, who knows what's behind that sound."

Rance nodded and helped Alyssa put her jacket on, "come on, let's get out of here."

Jason Troye stood at Naomi Wilmington's front door holding a bouquet of roses. He pressed the doorbell. Maybe it the nerves of a first date that made time stand still. He rang it again. He could see lights and hear voices. Still no answer. He knocked. The door swung open. With a loud gasp at his date's appearance, the hand holding the roses dropped to his side with the red flowers dangling. Her hair was mussed framing a face of palpable fear. An odd crimson design covered the front of her cream lace dress. She didn't speak when she flung the door wide open, looked at him with mouth agape and turned back into the house. Jason followed, dragging the bouquet with him.

"What's wrong?" he asked, following her into the kitchen. She pointed to the kitchen floor. Jason gasped and dropped the flowers on the floor. "What?" He muttered. Then his military training kicked in and he knelt beside Naomi's mother; a knife protruding from her abdomen. His grabbed a towel and put pressure on the wound.

"Have you called an ambulance?" he shouted at Naomi.

She shook her head and fumbled around the room looking for her cell phone. It sat on the kitchen cabinet. With a shudder she dialed 911. "Please, help my mother; she's bleeding."

While Naomi kept repeating the phrase without listening to the dispatcher on the other end of the phone, Jason became aware of Naomi's father standing a few feet away, hiding in the shadows. Mr. Wilmington stared at the bloody body of his wife, waving his hands at Naomi and screaming at her, "No, no, no, what have you done?"

With Naomi becoming more anxious and loud, Jason ignored them and instructed Naomi's dad. "Press down here, hard," he said. Then he took the phone from Naomi, gave the address and asked for an ambulance and the police.

While they waited, Jason spoke to Naomi with as calm a voice as he could muster amidst the chaos, "Can you tell me what happened?"

"She was cooking dinner and Naomi stabbed her." Mr. Wilmington accused his daughter, "See, she holds the knife that killed her mother."

The red stain on Naomi's dress flashed brighter as her face drained into a pale shade of pink. Her words were muffled and scrambled by her sobs.

Jason turned back to her dad. Mr. Wilmington continued to shout and wave his hands in the air, repeating the accusation against Naomi. Jason ignored him since his words were nonsensical. Jason heard the ambulance sirens closing in. He sighed with relief and rose from Mrs. Wilmington's side to allow the paramedics room to work.

"I came in here," Mr. Wilmington said, "and saw Naomi bending over her mother, holding that knife and covered in blood." He burst out in tears. "My daughter stabbed my wife."

The paramedics heard the last statement as they entered the house with a gurney.

Jason stepped back and let them work. Naomi reached over to pull the knife from her mother. The paramedic caught her hand and firmly said, "Don't! Let the doctors do it."

It took a while before the police arrived after the EMT called the incident to the police. The statement Mr. Wilmington made was reported, so the police questioned Naomi. Or rather they tried. She couldn't stand still and she kept muttering. Mr. Wilmington repeated the phrase, "My daughter stabbed my wife." With no other options the police arrested Naomi and took her dad to the hospital. Jason stood in the middle of a bloody kitchen as everyone except Sheriff Johnson departed.

"Somethings not right," Jason muttered to himself.

"What?" Sheriff Johnston asked.

"The knife."

"What about it?"

"Her dad said he found Naomi holding the knife, it was still in her abdomen."

"That's where it was when I arrived. What do you think?"

Jason harrumphed. "I think he really saw Naomi holding the knife."

"Why would he accuse his daughter?"

"Shock at the scene, his mind created a scenario that didn't fit the reality."

"Are you a psychiatrist?"

"No, a veteran with lots of trauma experiences.

"Why would his mind create such a scene?" The sheriff muttered to himself.

Jason heard the question and muttered, "To cause a wedge between parent and child."

"Did you see anything else?" The sheriff asked Jason.

"No more than what you saw." Jason looked around. So much blood everywhere.

The sheriff got his name, address, and phone number. Then he asked Jason what he was doing there and once again, what he saw.

Jason cooperated, and when he finished giving the information, he asked, "What's going to happen now?"

The sheriff took Jason by the arm and walked him out of the room. "We let forensics do their job now. Do you need a ride?"

Jason shook his head and walked out of the house and to his car. Before he pulled away, he heard a tap on his car window.

Sheriff Johnson. "Did you see the flowers spread around the floor?"

Jason rolled his eyes. "Yes, I brought them for my date."

"Quite a date you had tonight." The sheriff smiled at him then told him to be sure and stick around. Jason nodded.

7

Where Did it Go?

THE MOMENT RANCE walked in the door, Jenny Gale saw him, "What happened?"

Rance smiled and pulled her close to him. "You know me too well." He kissed her on the side of her head in her hair.

"That's right, don't ever try to hide anything from me because I'll know."

"Alyssa and I have been working on the city budget."

"Well, that's enough to make anyone miserable."

"Under normal circumstances, there's something amiss, and neither one of us can find it."

"What do you mean *amiss?*"

"It would appear someone is embezzling city funds. We're supposed to report our audit findings to the mayor and city council tomorrow, and we have nothing."

"That sounds like a good thing." Jenny wrinkled her nose.

"It should be. Where did all the money go?"

"Okay, this is a conversation for you and Alyssa. I have some other bad news for you."

"Oh no, what is it?"

"The dog died."

"Aww, I love that dog. How?

"I don't know, I went out to feed him and . . . and . . ."

"And what?"

"And his body was scattered all over the yard . . . like a wild beast got him."

"What did you do?"

"Came in the house."

"So his carcass is still out there?"

"Yep, I ain't cleaning it by myself."

"Okay, we'll get it after dinner."

Alyssa Troye felt content in her singleness. After spending months alone with Christ through study in a mysterious cabin where no dragon could enter, no human man could meet her standards. Her brothers and pastor often gave her pep talks, which she loved. Their advice flowed from their hearts of love for her and their desire to give her a meaningful relationship. They all knew how Matt lured her into a human trafficking situation. She still had a bald spot on her head where she escaped from her captor, leaving a piece of her scalp in his hand. Still, they hoped for her to find a solid relationship with a godly man.

Alyssa longed for a human companion; However, it needed to be someone trustworthy. For that to happen, she had to learn to be alone and trust her judgment. After all, she went willingly with Matt.

Pastor Kevin told her to trust who Christ made her to be. He even helped her discover her spiritual gift of discernment. Ha! What a laugh. Discernment. Really?

Then that same comforting voice whispered in the recesses of her memory, "You were willing to search for the answer."

Willing, yes, not discerning?

She knew the answer would come from her Bible. She hungered every day for even a few moments alone with her Lord.

Several of her friends said she was afraid of being alone and didn't trust anyone to stay with her. She would patiently listen to their amateur psychoanalysis with a faint smile. Behind that smile, she was rolling in laughter. She spent months in a cabin surrounded by dragons and never felt fear of being alone.

Alyssa tipped her head and chuckled. *I was never alone; my Lord was with me every minute.*

No! Being alone wasn't Alyssa's problem. She didn't have a problem. She was a forty-something-year-old maid and content. She doted on Stacy and Henry, her great-niece and nephew. She didn't need children.

What she needed was the direction in life to fulfill her heart's desire. Her family would be shocked if they knew her deepest desire. She wanted to establish a home and a ministry to help victims of human trafficking recover. Two big obstacles stood in her way—credentials and money. She had neither. Therefore, it remained a dream and not a reality.

The idea of money brought her back to the city financial problem she and her brother Rance worked on for the last week. It appeared Zay or Marcy took and hid city funds. She couldn't bring herself to say 'embezzled' because she knew neither of them would do that. The facts pointed to them.

While muddling over her problem and personality, Alyssa prepared her dinner and ate most of it. That was when she heard it. She dropped her fork because she knew exactly what caused the sound.

"Lord, hold me tight," she said out loud as she rose from the dining table and peeked out the front room curtains.

There it was, or rather, there *they* were. However, this time there was no hedge of protection. She saw dragons. Hordes of them, they were entering every home.

"I guess I do have discernment because the people can't see the evil coming into their homes. Lord, what do I do with this?"

Prepare for battle came the quiet response from the pages of her Bible open to Ephesians 6. "We battle against principalities, powers, and rulers of the darkness of this world, and spiritual wickedness in high places."

If people could only see the ugliness of those principalities and rulers of darkness. They wouldn't make dragon stuffed animals, they would pray for protection from the vile creatures. She took a deep breath and sighed, "Lord give me direction."

8
Plot of Demons

NISROCH KEPT A long serpentine tail wrapped around Jorkphat, even though the demon wrestled against his elder.

"Quiet!" Nisroch growled at Jorkphat. "Belial and Ezequeel will be here soon."

"Belial?" Jorkphat stammered. "Why?" Jorkphat stopped resisting Nishroch's tightening of his tail around him.

"The dragons' victory approaches!" Nisroch shouted.

Jorkphat let out a foul smell of Sulphur. "I've heard that before," he spouted with disdain.

"This time the dragon force comes together to destroy that little hamlet known as Church Creek Falls."

"Then why am I here?" Jorkphat sneered.

"Because, my little demon, you will get the pleasure of tormenting your enemy."

Jorkphat looked into Nisroch's eyes with a firm glare, "Barbara?" He snarled.

Nisroch nodded. "You will join with Ezequeel to cause her more pain and grief than she has ever known or will know again."

"That Troye family. . . they still pray. How do I get past them?"

"You will not be seen. The pain you cause will not be attributed to us this time. And the Supreme One is giving one of the Troyes over to us to torment."

Jorkphat snickered. "She must have done something really bad." He hissed the word with a delightful smile on his smoky face.

"I don't know, I only know we are going to enjoy this. Belial brings the instructions. I give you a warning, even when the Supreme One gives us an assignment, He will turn our evil to their good and His glory."

"Then why are we doing His bidding?" Jorkphat snarled.

"We have no choice, other than to do our best."

"At what?"

"The destruction of the flesh, He turns over to us."

The area filled with a purple haze. Nisroch loosened his grip on Jorkphat.

Mammon followed Belial into the dark space of evil. All the dragons great and small including Beliah bowed to the one called Apollyon, Satan, Lucifer, and the Accuser, Tempter, Angel of Light, Prince of the Power of this World, and The Dragon of Old who deceived the whole world—the one they called the devil.

The dragons in the realm of evil raised their heads, opened their mouths, and sprayed the air with foul-smelling flames of hate and destruction.

Apollyon stood behind Belial, the appointed commander for their mission, and took in the smell and the flames with a smile.

"Today, you will be given an assignment. Unleash your evil for there will be no stopping the flow of our destroying flames this time. No prayer, no Bible, no strong soldier will defeat us. We will prevail and destroy the little garbage bags of life called humans."

Again, the dragons raised their heads and blew their plumes of flame in the air.

Jorkphat, the demon child of Nisroch and his human wife, watched and whispered, "Showoffs."

Belial continued his speech. "Even the Supreme One is tired of them and He has given us free rein to move through them with destructive force. Soon the earth will be free of them, and we once again will reign—equal to the Supreme One.

This time there were no shouts or plumes of fire shot into the air. Only total silence filled with hope for truth, and fear of failure and judgment. Belial sensed it.

"Our judgment has been determined long ago. If the Supreme One is willing to let us desiccate his beloved humans, then we must have been restored to our former glory in His kingdom. We are now the children of the Most High!"

Again, the plumes of smoke filled the air.

Belial stepped down in the midst of the dragons and whispered an assignment to each one. "You must not share your assignment details, you carry them through no matter what you see. Understood?"

The dragons roared in agreement.

"What about me?" Jorkphat asked Nisroch.

"You are my son; we will find you a habitation."

"Barbara?"

"No, she is stronger now than in her young years. Too strong for you. You will get your revenge as will the dragons."

"Who?" Jorkphat snuck his way up to Nisroch's face and whispered his question.

Nisroch answered, "Stacy, Hannah's daughter."

9
It's Time to Tell

JASON SIGNED THE visitors' chart. He didn't know Naomi very well. Their first date ended in a knife attack on her mother. Still he felt an obligation to visit her in prison. The clanging doors closed behind him, and he shuddered. He entered a room where Naomi sat.

She saw Jason and smiled. "This is a surprise; I didn't think I would ever see you again," she said with a big grin when he sat down opposite her.

"You owe me a date."

"Are you claiming it?"

He smiled and grew serious. "How are you doing?"

"As well as can be expected. It's a county jail. Have you heard anything about my mom?"

Jason furrowed his brow. "I thought your dad would be giving you those reports."

"He told me he no longer wants me in his life. He loves my mom. She is his world."

Jason ignored the last comment and answered Naomi's original question. "She's getting better. The knife went into her spleen, that's why there was so much blood; one can live without a spleen—"

"But not without blood. Is she going to be okay?" Naomi leaned toward Jason.

"I think so. I'll go visit her before I come back next time. Do you have a lawyer?"

Naomi shook her head. "I have no money, and my daddy, he . . . well . . . he's disowning me. I don't know." She ducked her head and sniffled.

Jason heard her muffled sob before she regained control and looked back at him. "I never thought my daddy would desert me."

"He's confused; he doesn't know what to do. I believe he loves you. He can't understand why you'd stab your mother."

"I didn't!" Naomi looked Jason straight in the eye. "I didn't stab my mother, I found her like that."

"Then—"

"Then who? That's the question that has me locked up in here."

Jason shook his head and looked around the room. He put his hand over his mouth. "I think I may know what happened."

"Really?" Naomi raised her shoulders and sat up straighter in her chair. "That's the best thing anyone has said to me in a week. What do you think?"

"If I tell you, then I will get locked up. Give me some time," Jason said and patted her on the back of her hand.

"Why are you helping me?"

"Because you need it," Jason answered.

Mammon watched Jason. For a moment, he suspected Jason saw the green sparkles of his scales. After Jason left, Mammon crept around Naomi and stared into her eyes, searching her heart. Even though a dragon can't read a human's heart, sometimes the eyes betray the thoughts of their mind. Mammon was looking for evidence of the Master in Naomi.

"Ah-ha! She does not belong to Him," Mammon roared and laughed at the discovery of this disciple of his leader, Lucifer. "We are going to have some fun, sister."

The police officer came to get Naomi. "I'm glad you had a visitor," he said to her.

Naomi smiled at her keeper, Todd Williams. They had been classmates through their school years and had even dated a few times.

"Not many people in this town like me anymore," Naomi responded.

"Your mother was a popular woman."

Naomi nodded, "I know, it was hard to live up to her image."

"Stop right there, I don't want to hear anything about your relationship with your mother. Understand?"

Naomi didn't understand. Todd pointed to his badge. She suspected he was telling her anything she said to him might end up as evidence against her.

"I didn't do it, you know." She responded.

He smiled, "I didn't think you did."

Jenny patted the last mound of dirt on the grave Rance dug for the dog. "Are we going to get another one?" she asked.

"Do you want one?"

She nodded.

"Then yes."

"What do you think did this?" Jenny asked as they walked back to the house.

"I honestly don't know. It was too torn up to be a coyote, maybe a mountain lion," Rance answered.

"Or a dragon," Jenny added.

Rance didn't disagree. Their conversation ended with unrest and fear in their minds and hearts.

Later at the dinner table, Jenny said, "I don't think I can survive another bout."

"I know." Rance picked at his food with his fork.

"What do we do?" Jenny took a bite and chewed on the tasteless food.

"Stay in the Word," Rance said.

As soon as they finished their meal, Jenny pulled the Bible out and sat it on the table. "Where do we start?"

"Matthew 13—the parable of the sower."

"That seems a strange place to start."

"Ever since my dad found that first dragon on the farm, they would taunt us with a phrase. 'The planting of the seed is singular, but the harvest comes in multiples.'"

"I thought Alyssa explained that."

"She did, but if that was a dragon that tore our dog to pieces, we need to understand a lot more about that phrase." Rance took his wife's hands.

At that moment their teenage son, Nathan, walked in the door and joined the conversation.

"What's going on?" Nathan asked his parents as he filled a plate with food. "Humm smells good, Mom."

He sat his six-foot-plus, football-player frame down beside his mother and gave her a hug.

"That was nice," she said.

"I needed it too," he said before stuffing his mouth with food.

"Why?" his dad asked.

After swallowing and taking a drink of water, Nathan set his fork down and leaned his elbows on the table. "There's some freakish stuff going on out there—worse than our dog getting run through a shredder."

"Like what?" Nathan's mom asked him.

"There are fifty-two students in my class."

Rance and Jenny Gale, Nathan's parents, nodded at the statement.

"Of those fifty-two, thirteen failed their ACT, fourteen failed to complete the required classes, ten have moved away, five have lost a parent or sibling in the last few months, and three have had serious accidents."

"That is weird."

"So, only twenty-three will be eligible for graduation, and only nine of us will be going to college." Nathan stuffed another bite of food in his mouth, chewed, and partially swallowed before adding, "And, all scholarships have been revoked."

"What?" The look on his dad's face told Nathan that he understood the consequences of his last statement.

"Yeah, Church Creek Falls has been black-balled somehow."

His mom looked at his dad and pushed the Bible toward him. "Matthew 13. I think we need some direction."

68

His dad took the Bible, opened it to the section she mentioned, and read aloud.

Jesus sat by the seaside and multitudes of people gathered. He spoke in parables.

Behold, a sower went forth to sow some seeds; some fell by the wayside and the birds came and ate them. Some fell on stony places without much soil, they sprung up quick, but when the sun hit them, they were scorched and soon withered. Some fell into thorns and were choked out, but there were some that fell into good ground and brought forth fruit, some one-hundred times, some sixty times, and some thirty times.

The disciples asked Him why He spoke in parables. His answer, 'because you have been given the ability to know the mysteries of the kingdom of heaven, but to them it is not given. For those who have been given much shall have more given, but to those who do not have, it shall be taken away what he has. So, I speak in parable because those you are seeing, see not, and those who are hearing, hear not, neither do they understand."

"That sounds harsh," Nathan said.

"There is an explanation," his dad answered. "The people have joined with the idols of dragons."

"What? Where does it say that?" Nathan jumped from his chair and stood behind his dad reading over his shoulder.

"I guess you could say those who do not see or hear have a heart of wickedness so their heart has become gross, their hearing is dull, and their eyes are closed," his dad explained. "If they see and hear with their heart and understand, then they can be converted, and Jesus may heal them from dragon evil."

"That sounds more like my Sunday School lesson." Nathan smiled.

Rance winked at Jenny Gale.

"Nathan," Jenny said while clasping Rance's hand. "There's something we need to tell you."

"The Troye family has been given in abundance," Rance started.

"I know, Dad, we're rich. Probably the richest family in town."

"That's not what I meant."

"We've seen and heard things that others in town haven't," Jenny clarified for Nathan.

"Really, what?" Nathan pushed his empty plate away and gave his parents his attention.

"I think this passage is talking about the blessings of the disciples to see and know Jesus as God, as the Messiah."

"Okay." Nathan nodded. "I still don't understand."

"Let's look at the explanation Jesus gives for the parable, starting with verse Nineteen." Rance took the opportunity to teach his son. "When one hears the word of God and understands it, then comes the wicked one. "Nathan, do you know who the wicked one is?"

"Sure, it's the devil," their son replied.

"Right, do you understand what Jesus is saying in this scripture?"

"When one understands, then the devil comes to them," Nathan said.

"Good," Rance said, and his mom smiled.

"Look at what the wicked one does," he urged his dad to continue.

"He takes away the Word that is sown in the heart. The seed sown by the wayside illustrates this. The one who hears the Word and shouts with joy when he receives it and is on fire to preach and teach the word. He does well until he meets trouble, and then he becomes offended by the Words of God. This is the person who is planted in stony ground and never puts down any roots. The one who lives his faith by his emotions."

"Okay, I get it." Nathan felt a bit restless at this explanation. "So why did you say this passage is about a dragon?"

His mom scooted the Bible over to her place at the table. "The next seed falls in a thorn bush."

"Well, good luck on getting a crop out of that one," Nathan spoke up. "Have you seen that patch of grass burrs in our yard? Don't go out there without shoes."

"And don't wear those shoes in the house," His mom grinned.

"Touché, Mom. Tell me what it means."

"The person who becomes a Christian and is planted in the thorny ground will be choked out by the lure and things of the world. Things like wealth and beauty, fame and fortune."

"That's rather deep, isn't it?" Nathan stroked his chin.

"Are you making fun of us?" Rance asked him.

"No, I mean it, that's a simple example with some deep meaning."

"That's the definition of a parable."

"Where's the good guy in this story?" Nathan asked.

"The last seed falls on fertile good ground," Jenny Gale said, "and puts down a deep root and bears much fruit, some more than others, but all bear fruit."

"What's the fruit?"

"The visible evidence of good seed." Jenny answered.

"What?" Nathan wrinkled his brow.

"You see, the next verses tell how the enemy plants bad seeds that will not bear fruit among the farmer's good seeds. When they come up, they have both good and bad seed." Rance explained.

"You mean like on Papaws' farm when the wheat comes up, and there's Johnson grass mixed in with it," Nathan says with confidence.

"Exactly." Rance slapped the table. "Son, you're going to get an A in this course."

The family laughed.

"So," Nathan continued the study. "I assume it's the same at harvest. You get as much of the Johnson grass as you can early, everything you miss is tossed out the back of the combine."

Rance chuckled. "Yeah, that's basically it, however, when you talk about people, the bad seed that produces no seed will be bundled up and tossed into a fire."

"Hell?"

"Yeah, I think so," his mom added.

"How do you recognize the bad?" Nathan asked.

Now came the part neither Jenny nor Rance wanted to face. The time had come to tell their son their encounter with a dragon.

Mom and Dad gave each other a look before his dad answered. "Son, it's time we tell you something you need to know. Those who follow the dragon will be condemned to follow him into the lake of fire."

"Huh! Dragon? What you talkin' about?"

"It's time to develop your eyes to see and your ears to hear," Rance said.

"Cool!" Nathan gave them a toothy grin.

"No, son, not cool. Don't ever think it is cool to see and hear a dragon."

His mom shivered, and his dad reached over and put his arm around her.

"Mom, what's going on?"

"Your mother faced a horrible dragon, and the monster damaged her.'

"Mom, I'm sorry." Nathan fell on his knees in front of her and took her hand.

"I'm okay, son. It's not your fault. Still you need to hear my story."

Ezequeel, the dragon of violence, hovered over Nathan Troye with delight. "You're right, dear boy, it is spiritual. And I'm the spirit that's going to take you down." With a deep growl, the monster tilted a spiky reptilian head down—all the way down to Nathan. The monster laughed and belched smoke into his face.

10

Dragons Gather

ZAY AND MARCY pondered over the soil samples collected from several farms and around town. They observed the common and expected elements in the soil, such as layers that make up a soil's profile, the color of well-aerated soils, iron compounds, texture and structure, or the proportion of the soil separates that make up the minerals common in forming soil.

They noticed the overabundance of blocky or rough cube-shaped granules. These were types of soil common in clay soils, Church Creek Falls land had little clay. A little bit would have been normal, however the soil samples collected by Zay were almost all bulky, and the elements weren't right for that type of soil.

Marcy raised her head from the microscope and pulled off her glasses. She rubbed her eyes. "Zay, come look at this."

"I noticed it too. It's in all the samples. What are you thinking?"

"This type of soil comes from constant expansion and contraction of the clay minerals."

"Yes."

"Do you think the dragons could be . . . you know. . . burrowing underground?"

"They *are* serpents."

"The clay particles could be their waste?" Marcy wrinkled her nose.

"Still, there has to be something here to indicate why people are getting sick in such huge numbers."

"Could it be bacteria forming in the soil?" Marcy muttered and the two of them pondered the importance or lack of importance of their findings. Marcy shivered, "Did you feel that?"

"No, what?"

"The same cold I felt in that psychiatric hospital when the beast was near."

"Do you think—"

Belial decided to step into their world for a brief moment and give them a scare. They didn't need any more information.

"Whoa!" Zay dropped a petri dish. "Did you see it?"

Marcy nodded. "Please God, not again."

"I don't think it's after us." Zay stepped close to Marcy.

"Then why?"

"To let us know it's here."

"You think that monster is causing this?"

"Absolutely."

"That monster—"

"Is trying to kill Church Creek Falls . . . again!"

"Yes, and I think he is using us to do it," Zay said and pulled a records book and a financial ledger from below his desk. "Look at this."

"Our experiments and expenses?"

"Now look at the city budget for us."

Marcy read the numbers and compared lines. "We're being set up!"

Belial laughed out loud, causing a belch of smoke and stench to fill the lab where Marcy and Zay worked. They put their hands over their faces and ran from the lab, slamming the heavy door behind them as quickly as possible.

"What. . .?" Marcy coughed out the beginning of her thought.

"Evil stinks, and I think the worse the evil, the worse the stench," Zay said as he peered through the small, rectangular window in the lab door. "There's a cloud gathering in there."

"Glad we didn't find anything to be contaminated," Marcy said between sips at the water fountain.

Zay grinned as he locked eyes with Marcy, "It may be to our advantage."

Marcy's eyes grew wide, and she nodded in agreement. "Let's go."

Zay put his hand over his face and went back into the lab to retrieve the journals. As he entered, he shouted a prayer to make sure the dragon would hear him. "I hate evil! It's a vile monster that defies the law, mocks the one true God, defies nature, and spreads misery.

"Teach me to look on Jesus on His cross so I can know the loathsomeness of sin. Show me the shame and agony so that I may recognize the stealthy dragon and tear it away from my own heart and the heart of my people. Only at Your cross can every evil trap be shut."

When he exited the room, he coughed and spat for a while.

"Those unusual soil granules are formed by sins," he told Marcy.

"You're right it *is* the dragon's waste with a specific purpose."

A superhighway formed in Church Creek Falls when the tunnels were built. No one tried to explain them and their speed between certain locations.

Alyssa Troye found the narrow, almost invisible tunnel to a cabin in the woods, which was not part of Church Creek Falls origin or any earthly origin. The cabin rescued her from a dragon horde seeking to send her into a hellish existence when she prayed for an escape.

The entrance is found only by those seeking the knowledge and the safety of the Holy One. The Troyes called it their prayer closet because the dragons weren't allowed to enter. The cabin welcomed any who came into it looking for a refuge from a time of trouble. Other than the Troye family, few entered, and then only in times of desperation.

"We're witnessing desperate times," Zay told Marcy.

Marcy nodded.

Zay called the family to meet at the farm. They would go into the tunnels together with Alyssa leading the way. Zay and Marcy agreed they needed to share their feelings of uneasiness with the family. They needed confirmation or comfort. The city-wide influx of disease and accidents hung over their heads every day as they completed lab tests on patients. They couldn't prove their theory, without the interference of the dragons, they would be able to discern the truth at the cabin.

"Zay, do we have the right knowledge, or are we—"

Zay put his arm around her, and she leaned her head into his chest. They stood there for a long moment, resting in the comfort of the embrace of the only person they could trust—each other.

Zay stroked Marcy's hair. "This is why I called for the family to go to the tunnels. There's a crafty wisdom among the city leaders, and it isn't the kind of wisdom that God gives. Let's gather the family to the cabin and tell them. The wisdom that comes from my dad comes from his years of experience."

Marcy pursed her lips and nodded. "And study," she added. "Okay, I agree. Let's go to the cabin."

"Mom, I'm so sorry, I didn't know what you went through," Nathan whispered to his mother, Jenny Gale.

She took his hand. "It's okay, I didn't want you to know until you could understand it.

Rance put his arm around his wife. "She's a strong woman," he spoke to his son while he gazed into the eyes of his beloved. "I almost lost her to that awful dragon."

"How do you fight a dragon?" Nathan stood and paced with his fists clenched.

"Stay strong and courageous in the face of the evil. We have one who fights the battle for us," she said to her son.

"After the story you told me of your capture and captivity, I want to blast those evil things to hell," Nathan growled through clenched teeth.

Rance smiled at his son, "I understand son. I felt the same way. At the right time, they *will* be blasted to hell. Jesus told us that in Matthew in His first sermon."

"He did?"

"Yes, hell is made for the dragons. God never intended for humans to go there. He made a way for humanity to be with Him as His family."

"Then why do we tell people they can go to hell?" Nathan asked.

"Because some don't want to be a part of God's family." Rance answered with a smile.

"You mean like Hannah is with Aunt Barbara, her mom?"

Rance's smile faded at the mention of Hannah's growing enmity against her mom. He hoped Nathan had not seen the cruel way Hannah spoke about her mother. Jenny Gale watched Rance and waited for his answer to their son. He nodded with pursed lips.

"Son," Rance addressed Nathan. "The family unit was the first place of worship God gave us. He designed it for each family member to have a role in the family and to strengthen the ability to teach children about Him as well as protect them from the dragons."

"Do you think the dragons can do more harm to Hannah?"

"Yeah, I do."

"That could explain what happened with Henry, couldn't it?" Nathan stared at his dad waiting for an answer. Rance didn't want to answer the question, even though the same though entered his thinking when Henry took a gun into the hospital and shot his grandmother.

"I think so, son."

"Do you know what Henry said to her while he was shooting her?"

Rance pursed his lips, "Yes, and I'm pretty sure those were words he heard his mother, Hannah say."

"Did Mimi tell you what he said to her?"

"Yes."

"What do you think we should do?" Nathan asked his parents.

Jenny Gale answered with gentle words, "What can we do?"

"Fight the dragon?" Nathan said. "How?"

"Prayer and fasting. That's how I got your mother back." Rance said raising Jenny Gale's hand to his lips and kissing the back of her hand. She smiled at him and leaned her head on Rance's shoulder. "We need to join Barbara in this fight for her daughter."

Nathan sat down beside his dad. The family sat at the kitchen table together, pondering the steps being taken to separate the family.

"Division makes us weak." Jenny Gale broke the silence. "What do we do now?" Nathan asked.

Rance's phone rang. "Zay asked the family to meet at the farm. Seems he and Marcy have some evidence they want to share with us."

"Evidence? Of what?'

"Don't know. Guess we'll find out when we get there." Rance gave Nathan a gentle and loving scruff on the back of his neck.

Nathan took his mom's hand. "I'm so sorry."

"I'm here, aren't I?" She smiled. "It was hard, but we overcame. Your dad battled as much as I did, and we both overcame the monster."

Nathan pursed his lips and nodded. When the family arrived at the farm, he saw his cousins Stacy and Henry.

Henry looked like a whipped dog.

Nathan felt instant pity for him "You okay?" Nathan asked as he joined his cousin in the front yard.

"It helps that you're not ashamed to be seen with me."

"Hey cuz, I know you, and I know you love our grandmother as much as I do. I don't know what happened, but I know you."

Henry raised his chin at Nathan. "You know what's happening? Why we are all here?"

"Probably dinner . . . if I know Grammy Lee." He used the familiar term of endearment the family used for Merilee.

Henry smiled. "I think we are going on some kind of trip too. You know anything about that?"

"A little. My parents told me a story about a cabin. I think Aunt Alyssa found it. We may be going there."

Hannah approached Henry and Nathan, her cousins, with a smile. "Come on, you guys, we're going on a family picnic."

Nathan winked at Henry, "told ya."

Hannah's smile changed to a frown when she saw her mother, Barbara Holloway, standing in front of the kitchen window. "I wonder what mischief my mother is causing now" she groaned.

Nathan and Henry ignored the remark and kept walking toward the house. "When's your trial?" Nathan asked Henry.

"There won't be one."

"Really?"

"I pled guilty, so it is up to the judge for sentencing, no trial."

The cousins arrived at the food laden table set in the picturesque patio. Merilee and Alyssa brought out loaded bowls of food and set it on the table.

"Mom, this looks great." Alyssa said to her mother Merilee.

"Look up in the sky," Merilee whispered.

Alyssa followed her finger and gasped. "So many! What's going on?"

"I think the dragons have called a council meeting at the place they first invaded us."

11

The Cabin

THE FAILED ATTEMPT by the dragons to break up the Troye family trip to the cabin with an extravagant display of futility faded when the family settled in the cabin Alyssa found almost twenty years ago.

Do you think there could be any significance to the dragons gathering at the same place they first appeared fifty years ago? Zay asked his dad, Buster.

"I think they're attempting to divide the family. That way we are easier to manipulate and be deceived. It hides information, when we are each seeking our own way."

"I agree, and I have some information," Zay added.

Zay and Marcy explained their findings of the soil contaminant. They speculated it could be causing some of the illnesses—both physical and mental—in Church Creek Falls. The heavy soil compounds they found were mostly clay particles compacted together. The problems with crops were obvious. The clay was causing poor drainage and restricting water movement to the roots of the plants.

Alyssa pulled a gardening book and a Bible from the bookshelf of the cabin. She read the parable of the sower from Matthew 13:20-21. *"The one on whom seed was sown on the rocky places, this is the man who hears the word and immediately receives it with joy; yet he has no firm root in himself but is only temporary, and when affliction or persecution arises because of the word, he immediately falls away."*

"What are you saying?" Jason asked.

"If what Zay and Marcy are saying about the soil being a source for the rise in illness and accidents, could it be the dragons are using it to persecute the town?"

"Or hide God's will?" Alyssa pondered.

"When clay soil is wet," Zay stepped in to explain, "it becomes heavy and sloppy and almost impossible to work. It can even become hard like concrete and store some bad elements, making the land acidic with destructive salts and salinity."

"Still not getting the connection to the dragons," Rance said.

"This area doesn't have clay soil," Zay said.

"You just said it did," Henry said.

"Yes, it does, but it's not supposed to," Marcy said.

"So, you're saying the dragons are bringing the clay?" Buster asked.

Zay and Marcy nodded their heads and continued to explain, "There is little in clay soil to cause healthy bacteria and worms in the soil to keep crops flourishing."

"Then how is this soil causing people to want to kill each other?" Hannah asked with a skeptical look on her face.

"That one is easy; the clay soil releases toxins into the air when the farmer tries to remove it from his land. If this is on every farm, the air is full of the dragon's blood."

"How do we defeat that?" Hannah asked with a snarky voice.

"We need to capture a dragon and get a biological sample," Zay said.

"Why?" Nathan asked his first question with a note of disdain.

"To stop them," Zay answered. "Besides, Marcy and I have used a dragon for lab samples before."

Sharon remained quiet during most of the discussion since she was the wife of Michael, Buster's nephew. She could not remain silent any longer. "I remember that dragon, you didn't capture it, and you found it in an underground steel bunker."

Barbara snickered at Sharon's reminder of their college days. They were roommates and were the first to see the cursed dragon lying on the ground. Daniel took Barbara's hand and stroked it.

"Michael and I found that dragon and we thought it was dead." Daniel added. "We called Dr. Weinstein and he took it. Until it was given to Zay for research, we didn't know what it was."

"I don't think that can happen again." Barbara laughed.

"You judge everybody by what you want." Hannah sneered at her mother.

Barbara's mouth fell open to speak. Daniel squeezed her hand and she turned her face away from Hannah. She leaned on Daniel's shoulder and whispered where only could hear. "Why, does she do this?"

"I've heard the most unbelievable stories about these dragons in the last few days, and now you're telling me you want to capture one?" Nathan rose and said to Zay.

Rance put a hand on his son's arm. Nathan sat back down.

Trey stood. "I've been working this farm for more than ten years, and I've seen and heard Nisroch torment Buster."

"I spent months listening to those monsters chasing me," Alyssa spoke up.

Jason leaned over with his elbows resting on his knees. "I've seen the carnage of those beasts."

"I don't want my children hearing these stories or seeing them. Please stop." Hannah moaned.

Henry rolled his eyes at his mother and said nothing.

"I saw one of the beasts with vicious claws digging into Barbara's head." Sharon moaned, ignoring Hannah's request.

Nathan stood again and paced around the room. He pointed at his dad. "You said you didn't want to tell us about the dragons, but we need to know."

Silence settled over the group after Nathan's comments. The younger generation nodded their heads. Buster and Merilee Troye's grandchildren huddled around the dinner table watching their grandparents.

"Why the long faces?" Merilee asked.

"Zay wants to capture a dragon and we're scared." Nathan answered. "What's going to happen to us when we have to face these dragons?"

Henry added to Nathan's question. "Are they coming for us?"

Nathan looked to each of the three generations setting around the table before he answered Henry. "I guess it's our turn to do battle."

Hannah pulled Stacy closer to her side and patted Henry on the shoulder. "I'm not doing it. I didn't cause this fiasco, and I'm not playing a part in your stupid drama." She stood and started toward the door.

Trey took her hand and pulled her back down. "Be quiet." he whispered in her ear." She huffed and returned to the room and listened to the rest of her family's diatribe before dinner, even though the talk of dragons stole her appetite.

Merilee called on Buster to offer thanks for their dinner and this cabin, free from dragons. "No matter what trouble awaits us, we are safe in the arms of a Savior who knows how to keep evil under darkness."

The group followed the matriarch's command. Soon the clatter of passing bowls filled the air, and normal conversation replaced the horrific realization of a coming battle.

"Jason, how is Naomi?" Alyssa asked.

"I finally found her a lawyer. She's wilting with grief. At least she is out on bail now."

"Where is she staying?"

"With me."

"Well, that date escalated quickly." Nathan winked.

Jason ignored the teen's comment. "I know who stabbed her mother, I don't want to say anything."

"Why not?" Nathan blurted out.

"It was a dragon."

"Why Naomi's mom?" He questioned without any reservation in the conversation.

"It wasn't just Naomi's mom," Daniel answered.

"That night there were five other stabbings," Hannah said.

"Wow, how did you know that?" Nathan said with his mouth full of food.

"That's how many the hospital saw; there may have been more."

"Were they all as serious as Naomi's mom's?"
Hannah nodded.

"They were all the same type of wound," Daniel added. "Serious but not life-threatening with medical attention given promptly. "

"That's strange," Nathan said.

"That's not the strangest part, either," Daniel added. "None were believers in Christ."

Silence filled the room, and the group stopped eating for a second as if they were all pondering Daniel's statement. Barbara broke the silence with her evaluation, "I think the dragons were showing off."

Hannah rolled her eyes at her mother. "You always have a theory, don't you?"

Barbara opened her mouth to address her daughter; instead, she turned away from Hannah and addressed Merilee. "What do you think, Mother?"

"I agree, it's more than showing off. It was intimidation."

"How so?" Nathan asked.

"Those who do not have faith in Christ already belong to the dragons, they can do to them as they please. So, they demonstrated their power by injuring their own."

"Sounds familiar," Hannah muttered. The family either didn't hear or ignored her remark. Trey pinched her thigh and glared at her. She hushed.

Barbara continued. "Even though the injuries were dramatic and not life-threatening. There were enough to keep all medical personnel busy through the night."

"Did anything else happen that night?" Nathan asked.

"Naomi's dad accused her of trying to kill her mother," Jason said.

"That was the day you yelled at me," Barbara said, looking at her daughter.

"It was a tense time," Hannah answered.

"I know we were all under stress."

Merilee rose from the table, "Anyone ready for dessert?" She handed out saucers of warm chocolate cake. She gave each of her children a wink as she served them. "This makes everything better."

Buster cupped his hands under his chin and watched his wife serve their offspring. He noticed Zay's furrowed brow, Hannah's tight lips, Trey's constant observance of Hannah, Rance, and Jenny Gale holding hands and leaning into each other. Alyssa conversed with Jason and shook her head. And Nathan encouraged Henry.

Buster knew the war with the dragons wouldn't end until the only Warrior able to defeat the dragons returned to earth with a sword of judgment. He also knew more of his family would suffer at the whim of those dreadful dragons.

Right now, the look on Hannah's face and her demeanor revealed to Buster her thoughts were not her own. She changed. She would have never spoken to her mother with such harshness before the multiple attacks.

Buster loved his granddaughter Hannah, and he adored his daughter, Barbara. He wouldn't choose one over the other, he could see there could be a showdown. Barbara was strong in her faith. Hannah was strong-willed and knowledgeable.

Hannah hadn't looked into the eyes of a dragon and watch the monster give her body over to a demon. Hannah didn't know true evil. Buster could see the dragon feeding its hatred of Barbara into Hannah's heart.

He recalled the memory of Barbara when she decided to be a feminist. Daniel and Michael changed that when they rescued her from a marriage to a demon.

Buster noticed Trey kept a tight hold on Hannah. He wondered if Trey would be able to rescue Hannah in the same way Daniel did.

Dear Lord, I taught them, now I pray you give each of them the full armor against the dragons so they may be warriors against the evil.

12

Attack

NAOMI'S TRIAL ENDED almost before it began. The witnesses from the other five stabbing victims related similar incidents. The irony of the attacks came in the simultaneous timing. The defense attorney presented the five case files. No evidence could be presented for Naomi's guilt other than her dad's comment at the scene.

Jason, the other prime witness, stated the knife was still in Naomi's mother when he arrived, not in her hand. The police report supported Jason's testimony.

Once the known facts were all presented, the jury reported more confusion. The case ended in a mistrial. The judge ordered the prosecuting attorney to have evidence that is more substantial before presenting the case again. Reasonable doubt changed the course of Naomi's future.

Testimony revealed all five victims suffered with a strange fungus. Since the incident, the families of the victims experienced deep family conflicts. Accusations flew between families like geese flying south for the winter. The constant barrage of insults led to families separating: fathers from sons, and mothers from daughters.

When the authorities arrived, a frantic Naomi stood over the body of her bleeding mother. She looked to her dad for help. Instead of help, she heard him screaming at her. She stared at him as he raised his hands in the air and brought the back of his hand across her face.

The sting of the backhanded slap faded in the pain of his words. "You killed your mother!"

Horrified, she shook her head. "Dad, please help" she pleaded with him. The more she pleaded, the more anger he expressed.

He raised his hand to slap her again.

She curled her face into her chest, put her hands in front of her face, and winched.

He stopped. Dropped his hands to his side. "Why did ya do it?" he moaned as a gush of tears soaked his face. He lifted the head of his beloved wife and buried his face in her neck. Naomi didn't understand what happened. She lost both parents to that strange event.

After the trial, Jason and Naomi went to the Honey Tree for dinner. Naomi remained solemn during the trip, even though Jason held her hand as he drove. She stared out the window until they arrived.

Once they settled at a table, they studied the menu. Jason watched Naomi over the top of his menu. He followed her gaze to the top of the window behind him. The silence of the moment broke when Michelle came to their table.

"So happy for you, ma'am," Michelle cooed as she prepared to take their order.

Naomi smiled and thanked her.

Another couple passed their table. They stopped and gave their blessings as well. One gentleman identified himself as the father of one of the other victims.

"How has it been for your family?"

"Hard. Our daughter recovered, made accusations then left. We haven't heard from her since."

"That seems to be a common theme," Naomi told Jason.

"What do you mean?"

"My dad won't talk to me."

"Your dad was distraught that night, his mind muddled at the scene."

"I mean, he won't speak to me even now. What should I do?"

"Go see him."

"I can't, not now, I'm still hurt by his words."

Jason wrapped his hands around hers. "It's okay. Give it time."

A loud ruckus at another table in the restaurant roused the attention of the diners. A woman stood with mouth agape and arms flaying in the air as she screamed harsh words and profanities at her dinner mate.

The lady receiving the tirade paled, her eyes wide. Not saying a word, she dodged jabs from another dinner companion.

"Looks like she spilled hot food on her," Jason said.

Naomi stared in disbelief. "Jason . . . look, that's a steak knife in the screaming woman's hand. What is she doing?"

Jason stood and shouted at Naomi, "It's a dragon!" Then he sprinted toward the women.

The whole place froze at the horrific sight and sound of the woman berating her friend, accusing her of sleeping with her husband. Her words kept coming louder and louder. She raised her hand with the knife in it. Jason saw a dragon gripping the woman's shoulders.

Sukkuth-Benoth's bloody claw grasped the skin on her back. The dragon pierced Jason's gaze and said, "I am the dragon of dissent. I reveal the wickedness in the black hearts of these arrogant humans."

Jason reached for the woman's arm, moving it seconds before she attempted to plunge the knife into her friend.

"Let her go!" Jason shouted at the monster and punched the ugly reptile in the jaw."

Patti, one of the restaurant's owners rushed out of the kitchen with a firm grip around a strange black object. She hit the monster on the back with the book. She opened it and with all her might pounded the scaly reptile with it.

She shouted, "And Jesus rebuked the devil, and he departed out of him: and the child was cured from that very hour. Then shall he say also unto them on the left hand, 'Depart from me, ye cursed, into everlasting fire, prepared for the devil and his angels.'"

Patti kept screaming until the woman fainted and fell to the floor. Jason caught her before she hit the floor and helped her sit in the booth.

The dragon stood over Patti with an open maw, revealing spear-like fangs, dripping his poison drool over her. She held the Bible over her head and shouted, "I know you, and what a wimp you are! Leave this place because Christ lives here!"

The dragon spread his wings and lifted his bulk through the ceiling with a scream.

Jason and Patti watched the creature leave. Patti took Jason's hand, "Thank you." He nodded.

The women in the booth said in unison, "What happened?"

The filled restaurant buzzed with murmurs of disbelief and horror. All patrons watched the scene and heard mumblings, nevertheless no one could describe anything. The raging woman stared at her hands and the cuts on them. Her friend sobbed and her hand over her mouth.

One of the men shouted at Patti, "What were you doing swatting the air with that Bible?"

The rest of the clientele added hushed nods.

Patti looked around at the horrified faces of her customers. "Sometimes it takes the Word of God to calm a person," She answered.

The man smiled and shouted, "Amen."

Patti headed back to the kitchen with a smile as she hummed a tune.

Jason hummed with her.

"What are you humming?" Naomi asked him with a broad smile.

"It's a song my dad sings all the time, it's called *Wonderful Words of Life*. Patti's humming it."

"Yes, you're singing it. Do you know the words?"

"Sing them over again to me, wonderful words of life, beautiful words, wonderful words, wonderful words of life," Jason sang to Naomi.

She watched him as he sang every note. "That's pretty. What does it mean?"

"It's the words of the Bible."

Naomi's smile faded. "Oh."

Patti poured herself a tall glass of water and instructed her waitress. "Give water to everyone; they'll be thirsty."

The girl nodded as she downed her glass of water.

"The strangest thing about those monsters is the thirst they cause," Jason said.

Naomi took her glass of water and said, "I'm ashamed to admit it, I got a glass of water before I knelt to check on my mother. Why?"

"The monsters are condemned to live in a waterless desert, so they sap the moisture from us when they're near us. That's why we have to have the Living Water of Jesus Christ in our lives before we can face them," Jason answered as sat.

"Jason, what monster?"

"The one—"

"What did you see?" Naomi tilted her head. "I saw you run to the woman's aide, you, um . . . you shouted something when you went to help her."

"I did?"

Naomi nodded. "You yelled, 'It's a dragon.'"

Jason smiled and gulped the last of his water.

"What did you mean?"

"Just what I said, a dragon was attacking the woman with his lies and making her believe them."

"Huh? I didn't see anything except a crazy woman screaming and another crazy woman batting the air with a Bible.

"Not everyone can see evil because it disguises itself."

Naomi ducked her head and pushed her napkin around on the table. "What is a dragon?"

He could see Naomi trembling, and her voice teetered on the edge of a good cry.

"They are supernatural beings intent on the destruction of humans."

"I thought supernatural beings were our spirit guides to help us be healthy and happy."

"That's what they want you to think."

"How do you know they aren't"

Jason sucked on the straw in his water for a few minutes before answering Naomi. "Did you see what just happened?"

"I saw some people acting crazy, I didn't see a dragon."

Her quivering chin turned hard and her lips firm. Jason didn't answer.

"So, what are you trying to say happened?" She prodded Jason with a raised voice.

"Dragons are evil and only . . ." He stopped. His words weren't right.

"Only?" She repeated.

"There's evil in the world."

"Well, duh!" Naomi leaned back in the seat and crossed her arms.

Jason kept drinking his beverage. *Lord, give me the right words to show You to her.*

"Naomi, I believe a dragon is a fallen angel or the demonic spirit behind a man-made idol."

"What's that?" Naomi looked at Jason with wide eyes.

"There was a time when one of the chief angels, known as arch angels, decided they wanted to be equal with God. So, they rebelled."

"That sounds like a movie plot." Naomi gave a nervous snicker.

"I know, the lead angel known as the devil or Satan is the prince of the power of the air, in other words, he owns the airwaves, and he loves to be adored and loves to tell his story. However, he can't let people know he is real because he is in the supernatural realm hidden from man. He uses media like movies, music, video games to brag on his powers."

Naomi sat back in her seat and covered her mouth with her hand.

"Are you alright?" Jason asked her.

She removed her hand to reveal the laughter she was suppressing. "Do you realize how corny you sound?"

Jason smiled, "Yes, I do, I assure you it's serious, not corny."

"Okay." She snickered. "So, you think you see dragons?" She could hardly contain herself.

"You did battle with one, you should know," Jason said.

Naomi quieted and leaned toward Jason. "How?"

"I don't know; I only know that it was a dragon that stabbed your mother."

Naomi gasped. "Oh, no! And I really liked you."

"What's wrong?"

"You must be crazy. There was no dragon in my house."

"You wouldn't have seen it."

"Of course not, it's a mythical creature." Naomi chuckled and twisted her glass around on the table.

"Think about it; what happened that night?" Jason took her hands in his.

"That night just before you arrived, I did see something."

"What?"

"A twinkle, like stars."

Jason knew her deceived heart would not accept the truth. With a gentle tone of voice, he asked her, "What do you think it was?"

"I don't know, I felt it more than saw it." She smiled.

Jason knew she mocked him. He nodded. Then he heard the woman who'd been shouting at her friend apologize.

Her seatmate worried with her hands and said, "You accused me of sleeping with your husband." The distraught woman ducked her head, "I couldn't have done that, and you know it. I've known you for three years."

"Yeah, so?"

"Your husband has been dead for five years."

Jason winked at Naomi, "The lies of a monster feel real, even though the facts can't support the lie."

The two women hugged.

Jason stopped them at the door and handed them a business card. "Please understand; there are forces at work in our town, and they don't care about the truth or who they use. Your best weapon is prayer and Bible Study." He then gave them a card that read, *Barbara Holloway, 806-555-3786.* "Call her, she will help you understand and prepare."

"Prepare?" The two women said at the same time. "For what?"

"More attacks like the one you just experienced." The distraught woman patted his hand and thanked him. Then she asked to speak to Patti. Jason rejoined Naomi.

Soon Michelle brought them both a lovely plate. "We haven't ordered yet," Jason said. "It doesn't matter, this is Cook's special tonight, and its complements of the two ladies you just helped."

"If Cook made it, it will be special. Thank you." Naomi said as her mouth watered at the smell of the delectable meal—the cure-all for anxiety and craziness.

Jason chuckled. "You dodged a jail sentence, we watched a woman try to kill her friend, and we're eating a gourmet meal."

Naomi ignored him as she put her first bite of food in her mouth, closed her eyes, and said, "Mm . . . that's good."

"Yes, it is." Came a chorus of angels surrounding The Honey Tree singing to the Master.

Nathan Troye, the son of Rance and Jenny Gale, sat across the room near the back door, watching the drama play out before him. A bead of sweat trickled down the small of his back, and his heart pounded in his chest. He saw the dragon with his own eyes. Still in a state of shock, he took the water glass from the waitress and his classmate, Emily.

"Thank you," he said and gulped it.

She stood there waiting with a pitcher to refill the glass.

"Did you see it?" he asked her when he set his glass down.

"The dragon?"

"Yeah!" his eyes lit up.

"I see glimpses of it. I haven't seen the whole thing. What I see is actually quite pretty. It's like jewelry."

"It won't seem that way when you see more of it."

"Did you see all of it?"

Nathan shook his head, "I don't want to either."

Emily started to leave, and Nathan reached out and took her hand. "Would you like to take a ride after work?"

"I'd love it. My shift ends in fifteen minutes."

"I'll wait." Nathan took his water in smaller drinks now as he smiled at the prettiest girl in Church Creek Falls.

Belial struck Sukkoth-Benoth across the snout as he flew from the restaurant.

"You idiot!" Belial roared.

Sukkoth-Benoth, a dragon of jealousy, stared at Belial with smoke coming from his clenched maw. "I did my duty, just like you commanded," Sukoth-Benoth growled at the master, knowing it would bring a beating. Still, the satisfaction of talking back to Belial was greater than fear of Belial's heavy, clawed foot.

"Yes, you did, did you learn about your subject before you attacked?"

"I did, I saw that woman's heart filled with love for her husband."

"Yeah, her *dead* husband."

Sukkoth-Benoth closed the smoke erupting from the monster's spiked head.

The heaviness of failure took the snout to the ground. The monster felt idiocy creeping up the spiky backside that would soon be covered in wounds from Beliah.

Naomi slowed her eating long enough to ask Jason, "What can we do about those creatures if they are attacking the whole town?" She tried to hide her smirk.

Jason nodded, pushed his plate back, and brought his glass to his lips. He relaxed in the booth they occupied and shook his head a couple of times before he answered. "My dad has offered sanctuary to anyone who desires it."

"What do you mean by *sanctuary?*"

"We know a place where the dragons cannot enter."

Naomi's eyes widened. "Where?"

"I can't tell you; we have to take you there."

"Isn't there an address?"

"Not one of this world."

"Are you dreaming?' Naomi chuckled.

"No," Jason answered in all seriousness. "Anyone who wants to travel there may, the problem is that one has to stay there until the battle is complete."

"What battle?" Naomi wrinkled her brow and leaned in toward Jason.

"The war has been won, the Lord is patient. He doesn't want anyone to perish, so He allows anyone to come to the safe place He has provided."

"What?"

"In the Bible, it's called the New Covenant and can be found in Jeremiah 31:31."

"What does it say?" Naomi asked.

"Behold, days are coming, declares the Lord, when I will make a new covenant with the house of Israel and with the house of Judah, This is the covenant which I will make with the house of Israel after those days. I will put My law within them and on their heart. I will write it, and I will be their God and they shall be My people."

Naomi leaned back in her seat with a sigh. "This doesn't help me understand what happened to my mother and that woman or my dad."

Jason took Naomi's hands in his own. With tender words, he said, "It means, things will get worse before they get better."

13
Battle Plan

THE COUNCIL OF dragons gathered over Church Creek Falls. Each dragon found his place, some in the Fifth Realm, and others in the Seventh Realm. Many of the dragons were accompanied by the demons known as Nephilim they fathered with human wives during the days of Noah. The dragon fathers commanded the demon children with missions of deceit and destruction.

On this mission, they all followed Belial, the head commander. Belial served Apollyon, the dragon who led the rebellion against the Most-High God. When the whole council found their place in the dragon's lair known as Sheol, then Apollyon arrived.

When Apollyon, the highest god of all, arrived at the gathering, the smoke of their admiration rose, and they blew fires of feigned loyalty. Even with thousands of dragons blowing plumes of fire in the air, the arena of dragons remained dim.

The demons bowed beneath the wings of their commander and sires. Apollyon gathered dread from the dragon horde as if the beast harvested them. Apollyon held their lives in one claw and with the other claw, he would rip and slash through their scaly bodies with no reason. His blackened heart filled with pride and hate and sought only his own will and whim.

Apollyon directed the dragon's senses to the sound of discordant strains coming from the homes of the awful humans. They listened to rebellious teenagers shouting at their parents. They saw adult children saying terrible things about their elderly parents.

Belial spoke to Apollyon, "You know Moses said anyone who speaks ill of their parent is worthy of death."

Apollyon set his yellow eyes on Belial. "You're right. Did you know the Holy One repeated it?"

Belial growled, "Does that mean we can take those?"

"Be careful." Apollyon shook a claw in Belial's face. "Use that seed of hate in their hearts to do as much damage as possible. Nurture it with planted false memories of abuse. Keep the seed of hate growing until the family is completely destroyed. Unless the adult child repents of disobedience to that fifth commandment, we will have them---forever." He laughed loud and long.

It filled the ears of the demonic horde with delight. Then they all roared. Above the din of discordant worship, the noise of a single, tiny voice broke through.

"Turn Your Eyes Upon Jesus."

The beasts belched large plumes of fire and brimstone while the demons shouted with hate-filled slurs at the sound coming from Barbara Troye Holloway's bedroom. Even in the weak notes of repressed tears, the thread of music reached the horde of dragons' ears like a fingernail across a blackboard.

Belial roared, "Who is that?"

Nisroch stepped forward in slow, measured steps and growled, "It's Barbara Holloway."

Belial reached for the whip of lightning and thunder and slashed Nisroch across the snout.

"*Why!*" The brute shouted with a roar that caused the other dragons to tremble and the heavens to thunder.

Hannah heard the thunder and prepared herself for the padding of little feet. Her Stacy came running into the room where she folded clothes and jumped on her.

"It's okay; it's just thunder."

Trey entered the bedroom. "Not a cloud in the sky," he mused.

Hannah pointed to the South. "I wonder what that is?" she whispered.

Trey followed her finger and saw the wisps of agitated black clouds floating around each other as if they're fighting. "You think—"

"Hannah put her finger to his lips. "Shh."

Trey nodded.

"What do we do, Mommy?" Stacy asked.

Henry entered the room with the rest of his family and sat on the edge of the bed. "Yeah, what do we do, Mommy?" he asked, his voice dripping with sarcasm.

"Nothing." She smiled at her daughter and sat down, pulling her close to her side.

Trey sat on the other side of Henry.

"I hate to say it," Henry mumbled to his dad, "that sound scared me, I don't think it was thunder."

Trey nodded. "I know; it feels different than a thunderstorm."

"I want to go to Grammy's house," Stacy cried.

"Why?" Hannah asked her daughter.

Stacy backed away from her mother and answered with a soft voice, "Because she has a basement."

"Oh," Hannah replied with a smile. "I don't think we're going to have a tornado. At worse, it'll be a rainstorm, and the thunder and lightning will be the entertainment."

Hannah pulled Stacy close. "Mommy and Daddy are here with you, and we will never leave you." She kissed Stacy on the head.

After a few minutes of non-activity, Stacy asked her mother, "What if we leave you like you left Grammy?"

"Which one of you idiots was supposed to take care of that woman and her bag-of-goo offspring?" Belial roared, causing a firestorm to engulf the arena where all the servant dragons gathered, and the demons hid under the belly of them.

Nisroch's snout bled the green gaseous goo of a dragon's blood from the slash from Belial's whip.

Belial then wielded the lighting whip across the faces and tails of the dragons, wounding them all. He kept lashing until the anger was spent. Then he heard the comforting words of young Stacy accusing her mother.

"My plan is working," the huge beast mused and settled onto his throne to enjoy the fracturing and destruction of the Troye family. Apollyon raised his vile head in victory. "I never imagined that little fifth commandment could be such a strong weapon against the Holy One's children."

The lighting streaked from one side of the sky to the other, lighting up the Mitchell house and causing the whole family to gasp.

"I've never seen lighting like that before," Trey stammered as he closed the curtains to block out the eerie lighting.

Stacy whimpered with her legs curled and buried her face in her mother's side. Trey joined Hannah, Stacy, and Henry on the couch and watched the weather report.

"Did you hear what Stacy said?" Hannah asked Trey.

"No, what?

"She said I left mom."

"Well, haven't you? All you do is complain about her."

"I haven't left." Hannah's voice diminished as she spoke the words. Trey watched her face soften. Then she asked Trey a question, "Do you think my children will leave me?"

Another light flashed across the Mitchell's backyard.

"It's Mom," Hannah said.

"What?" Trey wrinkled his eyebrow.

"She brought this on us."

"I don't understand what you're saying."

"Has mom ever told you how evil she was?"

"Hannah, your mom isn't evil," Trey said soothingly, trying not to frighten the children.

"Mom, what did grandma do?" Henry asked.

Hannah forced a weak smile and kissed the back of Henry's hand. "She didn't do anything. I was talking about something else."

Trey gave Hannah a serious 'shut up' look. The family sat in silence.

Belial's anger dissipated. The whip of electric lighting left its mark on all except the demons.

Nisroch whispered to Jorkphat, "Stay put. If Belial learns you failed . . . then. . ."

Jorkphat shuddered and crouched under Nisroch. The wounded dragon tail wrapped around the swollen and streaked belly.

Nisroch groaned a little when Jorkphat moved.

Belial heard him. "Do you think I'm through?" Belial snarled through a smoky maw.

Ishtar stepped up to Belial's altar. "My lord," the female consort of Belial whispered. Her voice calmed him for a second. "If you lay stripes on your army, how will they be able to carry out your orders?"

Belial sat on the throne built from the bones and blood of his victims. The beast raised a lip and allowed the smoke in its belly to escape. It looked over the dragon army, whipped and bleeding. No smoke or roaring greeted the beast. Instead, only moans of pain could be heard. The evil anger of a high-ranking beast left the dragons wounded.

"Demons!" Belial roared. "Step to the front."

The demons crawled out from under their master's wounded bodies and approached the throne with heads down. When a demon horde commits atrocities against the children of the Supreme One, that demon grows into a more intense vision of horror. The more horrific demons demanded the highest regard.

Belial saw the demon with three heads: one a serpent, one a man, and one a lion. Another demon stood before him on the back of a lion with a serpent tale.

Another had the muscular body of a man with the feminine face of a woman. Everyone presented grotesque in their shape and all were filled with hate.

Belial stood in front of them, ready to command them. The monster snickered. Their hate would serve the cause.

"What proposals do you little wimps have to help Hannah Mitchell destroy her family?"

The demons only spoke when Belial called on them.

The last demon called presented a proposal to destroy Hannah and her family. "My master Rahab, known as pride and violence, suggests building the pride of victimhood in Hannah against her parents."

Belial laughed.

Ishtar touched the side of Belial's snout. "It's a good idea," she whispered.

"Is there a working plan?"

"Yes, my Lord, we will instill Hannah with pride."

"How is that going to help?" Belial questioned the servant.

"It will be a pride that leads to violence . . . sharp angry words that cut out the heart of those who love her."

"Interesting," Belial mused. "This should be fun to watch. After all, Moses did say one who speaks evil of a parent is worthy of death."

Ishtar purred with a toothy grin, "And The Holy One repeated it."

Hannah's actions allowed the dragons to destroy the family Belial hated. The monster raised his spiky snout upward and shouted, "Death! Painful death to the Troyes!"

The dragon horde and their demons joined the chorus, and soon the discordant music of untuned metal instruments filled the arena with words of hate, rape, and violence.

Belial whispered to his consort, Ishtar, the queen of heaven, "At least these bags of goo are too stupid to see us working on them."

"All except the Troyes," the gross owl whispered back.

The mention of the family raised Belial's fury. "That is why they must be destroyed. They keep reading the Supreme One's Book."

Rahab, the monster of chaos, pride, and violence rested on the back of the couch where Hannah Mitchell read to her young daughter. Rahab conjured a long-forgotten event in Hannah's childhood. A time when Barbara read to Hannah a story of mirth and fantasy. Her mother had stopped in the middle of the story and started another book.

Hannah wanted to hear the rest of that story. She decided to read it for herself, if she could find the book.

Rahab worked extended claws into Hannah's scalp, planting the memory with the emotion of losing trust in her mother. She added a bit of distortion to the memory for interest.

Your mother threw the book away because she knew you wanted to read it. She was mean to you.

"The moon is always round . . ." Hannah read the favorite story to her children. She'd read it so many times she could almost recite it from memory. The story taught an important life lesson.

That thought led to the book about fairies she loved as a child. She remembered how her mother stopped reading it and threw it away.

Now as her childhood memory floated in her mind, she wondered what that lesson could be. It's just a story.

She continued to read, "No matter what happens, the moon is always round." It didn't even make sense to her anymore.

Her mouth read the words, her mind settled on the still-born baby sister. A baby sister that only existed in a wish list she formed as a child.

"God is not always good," she muttered to herself.

Trey must have heard the words and answered, "The moon is always round."

She smirked and threw the book at him. "You finish." She rose and went to their bedroom.

Trey cradled Stacy on his lap and continued to read.

Henry sat across the room reading his book, he stopped reading, closed his book, and asked his dad, "If God is always good, then why is momma always mad?"

Trey ran his fingers through his hair. "I don't know. Let's give her some time. She'll get over it."

"I hope so," Stacy said. "I don't like it when she's mad. It scares me."

Trey nodded his head. *Me too.*

Rahab, the goddess of chaos, raised her broad, scaled wings and flapped them over the Mitchell family. "This is going to be fun."

14
Vampires?

THE MOON SHONE brightly over Church Creek Falls. The only light given to the three young men strolling through the city park. They laughed and snorted at their silly jokes. Over their laughter, they heard a loud thud.

Then all three of the tall, lanky, teen boys tripped. As they sat in the grass looking at each other with wide eyes and gaping mouths, they heard a moan and then a hiss.

"Snake?" Cory whispered.

The three stood and squinted their eyes, searching for a snake. The hiss came again, this time much louder. They stared at each other and shrugged their shoulders.

Then Cory pointed at Shawn's shirt.

Shawn looked down and saw blood trickling down his chest. "I've been bitten," he said with a flat tone of disbelief.

Derrick reached toward Shawn and saw his hand covered in blood. He wiped it on his pants leg. Still, the blood pooled in the palm of his hand. He looked at Shawn.

Cory watched the lifeblood drain from their faces in seconds, and they crumpled to the ground in slow motion.

Cory ran toward the houses on the street. He reached Shawn's home, whose dad served as a city police officer. He banged on the door, gasping for deep breaths of air for his starving lungs. As he rapped on the door and rang the doorbell at the same time, he tried to ignore the stream of blood pouring down his arm with each hard heartbeat.

When police officer Burke reached the door, he checked the peep hole for irritated visitors. He saw no one. He opened the door with kept his right hand ready to slam it shut. In his left hand, he held a loaded pistol. He expected to find one of the town drunks, instead, he saw a pale, young man lying on his front porch in a pool of blood.

He called for an ambulance and his supervisor. While waiting, he recognized the boy as Cory, a friend of his son, Shawn. He knew the boys were together. He opened the door wide and stepped out to examine the area. He called Shawn's name.

The ambulance arrived within minutes. Officer Burke stayed nearby, although he walked the perimeter of his home looking for the other two boys. His heart pounded in his chest.

"Oh, God, please," he begged through clinched teeth.

The EMTs worked with supernatural energy to revive Cory. "We've got a pulse," the EMT pumping Cory's heart said to his partner. "Let's get him to the ER."

Officer Burke didn't wait for them to finish loading Cory into the ambulance. He took off across the street to the park, following Cory's blood droplets on the pavement coming from there.

His supervisor pulled up as Burke crossed the street. The two officers took measured steps as they entered the city park, cursing the lack of working lights in the public area. The area kids threw so many rocks at the lights the city quit fixing them. The police officers were professionals, first, they were fathers and that took precedence.

The full moon provided enough light they could recognize the two bodies lying in the grass. Burke halted and examined the bodies.

A strange flash of color blinded him for a second. "It's them!" he called out to his supervisor, realizing the other boy was the supervisor's son.

The fathers knelt over the bodies of their dead sons, searching for a pulse or any sign of life.

"How. . . ?" Burke's supervisor moaned. He didn't attempt to hold back the anger in his voice.

Burke knelt beside Shawn and felt more than heard the squish of liquid beneath his knee. He turned his flashlight to the ground and discovered a large pool of blood. He shined the light on Shawn's face. The eyes of his son were wide and his mouth open, the absolute paleness of his dark-brown skin shocked Burke most.

He dialed 911 and called in the crime of the two boys' deaths.

The ambulance returned after delivering Cory to the emergency room. The EMTs ran toward them and started to work on the bodies. It was too late. They loaded the bodies into body bags to deliver them to the county morgue where autopsies would be required.

Burke clenched his fist as he stood. "What happened to my boy?"

His supervisor removed his glasses and wiped his eyes and face as he whimpered with the pain of loss of a family member.

Again, the flash of colored light passed in front of Burke's eyes.

"Did you see that?" the supervisor asked. "What was it?

"I saw it earlier," Burk asked. "It looks like a reflection of something."

"Yeah, of what?"

Burke's father's heart gave way to the investigative mode of a crime-scene police officer, even though he was not technically on the case, he would use all his skills as a detective to find out why. The heart of a parent is to protect their children. Why was Burke unable to protect his son? He would spend the rest of his life looking for that answer. They spent the rest of the night looking for evidence that could lead them to answers. Neither wanted to go home and tell the mother of their sons that they couldn't save them.

"I hope Cory makes it. Maybe he can tell us what happened," Burke said. His supervisor nodded.

The vampire dragon of death, Asmodeous, roared with laughter as it took the arms of the two boys' eternal spirits, "Come, let me escort you to the throne room of my master."

Shawn and Derrick cried like small children as the darkness of evil surrounded their spirits. They raised their voices and shouted, "I'm scared."

The dragon of death roared, "You should be." Then the horrid beast laughed with the satisfaction of a double kill. Belial will be proud.

The morning arrived much too early for Daniel. The years were catching up to him. Retirement from medical practice loomed in his near future. He and Barbara wanted to organize medical mission trips, right now another hour's sleep would be most welcome.

Barbara entered the bedroom, drying her hair with a towel. "Time to move," she chided Daniel.

"Whatever is going on, it's wearing me out." Daniel rose from the bed with a groan.

"I just got a call from the hospital."

Daniel moaned, "Another day like yesterday?"

"No, it was Sally, the head nurse. She said two boys died in the park last night and a third was admitted."

"How?"

"That's the question of the day, I'm going to the autopsy. I'll tell you more this afternoon."

Daniel nodded and stumbled to the shower.

Barbara watched him, "Lord, give us physical strength." She whispered in prayer.

Merilee and Buster waited in Barbara and Daniel's den for them to arrive home after a hard and stressful day at the hospital.

The stress of a citywide epidemic brought exhaustion to all medical staff especially to the only doctor in town. Barbara stood beside him as the interim director of nurses, so they were both dragged out. On top of this, their constant search for a new doctor or doctors to come to their town, along with their excessive workload, brought them to a point of total surrender to their energy-drained bodies.

Merilee had gone to their home and prepared dinner for them. She told Buster her love language was food. Buster laughed and agreed.

"They're almost too tired to eat when they get here." Buster said.

"At least they'll have some color in their face when we leave. The door opened as she spoke.

Barbara and Daniel sat their coats on the bench at the door and greeted their parents in the den.

"Mm. Smells good in here," Barbara said as she gave her parents each a hug. "Mom, you don't know how much this means."

"How was the count today?"

"Down a little bit. There weren't as many accidents, however, we did lose two . . . possibly three . . . teens last night."

"Who?" Buster spread his napkin over his chest and tucked it into the neck of his shirt.

"Cory Frye, Shawn Burke, and Derrick Mayfield."

Buster's jaw dropped. "They were just kids. How?"

"It looked to be pretty brutal, they were definitely murdered, and Shawn and Derrick lost all their blood before the ambulance arrived," Barbara said. "Cory was brought in while there was still enough lifeblood in him to be rescued. He's not out of the woods yet. Still we were able to get a couple of pints in him.

The family ate their meal in relative silence and disbelief. None of them had much appetite.

Merilee broke the silence. "I'll take some food to the families."

On the way home, Daniel took a deep breath. "Your mom is a good cook. I think her cooking is all that's keeping us going these days."

118

Barbara smiled and chuckled lightly. She rubbed her tummy and nodded. "You want to hear about the autopsy report?"

Daniel grimaced and looked her in the face. "I need to; I just don't want to."

"Do you believe in vampires?" Barbara asked him.

Daniel laughed. "I've found a malformed dragon by your apartment in college, remember. I'm not surprised at anything."

"Do you think a dragon could be a vampire?"

"They are mentioned in the Bible," Daniel said as he winked at Barbara.

"Get outta here!" She shoved the palm of her hand against his shoulder.

"No, really, it's in Proverbs 30," Daniel assured her.

"I bet you can quote it too." She chuckled.

"Not exactly, you may be more surprised that the context talks about cursing one's father and not blessing one's mother."

Barbara sighed. "What was the reference again?"

"It's in Proverbs 30 somewhere around verse 11 through 17."

"What does it say about vampires?"

"Well, it doesn't call them vampires, it does say they have teeth like swords, and their jaw teeth are like knives. They cry for blood and are never satisfied, always wanting more."

"It sounds like our victims met them," Barbara responded with a melancholy tone.

"You know; some say it is referring to Sheol; it's always wanting more people.

"Could be, three young boys were found in the park completely drained of blood."

"So, they bled out?"

"Not exactly. One of them came to Officer Burke's home, probably to ask for help, when Burke answered the door, he saw a small cut, and the boy's blood draining from him at a rapid speed."

"Weird," Daniel said. "Especially for a small cut . . . must have cut an artery."

"No, there weren't even any veins severed."

"What did the Medical Examiner say after the autopsy?"

"Shook his head and said, if this were a movie, I would say they died by vampire bites."

"I can't imagine Steve 'by the book' Hassel saying that," Daniel said.

"That's why I ask him if I could examine the bodies."

"And. . ."

"I agreed, there was no reason for those boys to have died, and there were no exit wounds large enough for them to bleed out."

"Did you find any blood?"

"Officer Burke said a small pool of blood was under each of the bodies, however, it wasn't enough to account for the body's complete lack of blood."

Barbara shook her head. "We know it had to be a dragon."

Daniel nodded. "Why those boys?"

"I think it was a simple matter of availability." Barbara mused before falling into a pondering silence. Once they arrived home she opened her Bible. Daniel laughed at her. "Are you checking me out?"

"You bet, I am, you said that was Proverbs 30: 11-17."

"Yes, read it aloud." Daniel said as he sat on the couch to listen to his wife read from the scripture.

> *"There is a generation that curses their father and does not bless their mother, there is a generation that are pure in their own eyes and yet is not washed from their filthiness, there is a generation, O' how lofty are their eyes and their eyelids are lifted up. There is a generation, whose teeth are as swords, and their jaw teeth as knives, to devour the poor from off the earth, and the needy from among men. The horseleech hath two daughters, crying, "Give, give." There are three things that are never satisfied, yet four things say not, it is enough: the grave; and the barren womb; the earth that is not filled with water, and the fire that will not say it is enough. The eye that mocks at his father, and despises to obey his mother, the ravens of the valley shall pick it out and the young eagles shall eat it."*

Barbara turned toward Daniel. "What does it mean the eye that mocks the father and despises to obey his mother?"

Daniel took her hand and gently squeezed it. "Don't look for things that aren't there."

A tear crept down Barbara's face. "I don't look; it hits me every blasted moment of the day. My daughter hates me, and I have no idea why. I asked if Stacy and Henry could come over tonight, you know what she said?"

Daniel shook his head. "Is Hannah talking to you?"

"No, when I speak to her, she nods her head. No smile and only the faint recognition that I spoke. If she says anything, she screams at me. If I don't speak, she walks past me as if I am invisible."

"What do you mean?" Daniel asked and put his arm around his trembling wife.

"If I say anything to her, it offends her, and then she starts screaming at me, usually pointing out some fault of mine. Like the last time she spoke to me when I asked if Stacy and Henry could come over, she kept saying, 'It's not about you.' She repeated the phrase, and each time got louder until she was screaming at me. Then she said, she had to protect her children from me."

"What's not about you?" Daniel took Barbara's hand in his.

"I don't know. I gave a book to the kids, and I don't think she liked it."

"What was the book? The Vampire Bible?" Daniel sneered.

Barbara snickered at his joke. "No, it was a children's book about the orphan train."

"I still don't get the connection."

Barbara patted Daniel on the hand. "Join the club. When she talks to me, it makes no sense. It may make sense in her head. Her screaming doesn't help me understand. It feels like she wants to lash out at me with a bullwhip. She's different."

Barbara and Daniel settled into their recliners with a glass of tea. They both sighed and leaned their heads back to relax in spite of the tenseness of the conversation.

Then the phone rang.

15
The Cemetery

NATHAN ENJOYED EMILY'S company. He didn't want the ride to end. "Anywhere special you want to go?" he asked her.

"Have you heard about the glowing tombstone?" he asked.

Nathan laughed. "Everyone in town has heard about it."

"Is it real?" Emily's eyes lit up.

"After what we've just seen, a glowing tombstone would seem pretty tame, don't you think?"

"Maybe that's why I want to see it. Something I can touch that's weird."

The young couple drove up to the cemetery about a mile south of town. When Nathan turned the car to enter, Emily gasped.

"What?" Nathan responded.

She pointed to the gate entrance, fear showing on her face and in her eyes.

When he turned toward the place where she pointing, he knew why. A group of dragons tossed a young woman from one to the other.

Nathan looked at Emily. "Do we leave or rescue her?"

"We'll go get her. I'll pray; you grab her." Emily said and leaned forward in the car seat.

Nathan rolled his eyes and cocked his head, "Yeah, I'll fight three dragons by myself."

"No, I'll be praying," she insisted. Nathan winked at her, patted her hand and stepped out of the car. He heard the screams of pain with each slap of force against her body. As he approached, the three dragons turned into three dirty muscular men. They tossed the woman around like a rag doll with torn clothes Nathan could see her body covered in blood and bruises.

"Hey!" Nathan screamed and ran toward the woman. One of the men stood. He towered over Nathan, and with one swipe, he backhanded him across the face.

Nathan fell to the ground. After a few seconds, he rose and stood in front of the men and growled in his deepest voice, "Let her go!"

"Or what?" Another man snarled at Nathan.

"Or I'll have to make you." Nathan was a sturdy, young man at six feet, three inches tall with the body of a football guard. He'd taken beatings by opposing guards at many football games and wasn't afraid of pain. However, facing dragons did stir up some dread in him.

Nathan saw the evil in the eyes of the men. Suddenly, they morphed into horrendous dragons with wickedness dripping from their huge snouts. Their open maws revealed rows of spear-like teeth.

The very sight of a huge dragon caused his skin to crawl, and his bravery left him. His legs felt as if they were made of wax, and his blood stopped flowing. His feet refused to move, and his mind turned off. Only his eyes focused on the horror before him.

"Can't we do something?" Peggy asked Mrs. Waithe as they watched the dragon attack Nathan. "That's Rance and Jennifer's son."

Mrs. Waithe grabbed Peggy's hand; Michael and Paps followed. They came to the endless gold door. Mrs. Waithe knocked, and it swung open. She entered the temple and approached the throne with a bowed head.

"Master, we plead for our son. Three dragons stand before him. Nathan is seeking to rescue a young woman."

The Master seemed to be listening to something else. Mrs. Waithe took a step closer and repeated herself. The Master reached out to her with a scarred hand and squeezed it. "We are listening to the prayers of his companion," he said. "We have sent a warrior angel to attend. You call him Davis on earth."

Michael couldn't help himself he shouted. "Yea, Davis my man!"

"You know him?" Peggy asked at the sudden outburst.

"Sure do. He fought a demon and a dragon for me. He also fought for Rance, Zay and Barbara."

The Master pulled the curtain back that separated heaven from earth and let his children watch the drama of their earthly family.

Emily prayed with her eyes shut, then with them open. Then she sat on the edge of the passenger-side seat of the truck and she raised her hands and shouted to the roof. In all these positions, she never quit praying, even while she loaded Nathan's hunting gun he kept in his truck.

Two of the men pulled Nathan's arms behind him, and the other one pulled his fist back and landed a hard blow in Nathan's solar plexus. Then came the lighter blows to his jaw and his shoulder, after the fifth blow, the man stopped, holding his bloody, clenched fist in the air. He groaned and strained to deliver another punch, his hand wouldn't move.

Emily kept praying while she slid out of the truck ready to defend her friend . . . with her life if need be. She raised the rifle with assurance. Coming from a poor family, she learned to hunt for dinner at the age of four.

She could easily hit one of those guys square between the eyes. She wasn't sure she'd be able to fire fast enough to get the other two. Stepping in front of the truck, she saw the three dragons in the men. She aimed and fired, hitting the one holding on to Nathan.

Nathan slumped to the ground and moaned. The young woman raised to her feet. Emily fired another shot that struck the man beating Nathan from behind. He turned toward her before he fell at her feet.

The third dragon raged and started toward her. Emily shouted, "Greater is He that is in Me, than He who is in the world!"

Davis landed between Emily and the Dragon.

He gave her a thumbs-up, even though he knew her earthly eyes wouldn't see him, her spiritual eyes would. With an iron fist, Davis landed a blow square on the snout of a dragon and the hard jaw of a hardened man.

Emily ran to Nathan and the young woman. Both were bloodied and badly wounded. Emily managed to get them into the truck and took them to the hospital.

"Why did you let it get so bad before you stepped in?" Peggy asked Davis when he returned to the realm of heaven.

"I follow the instructions of the Master," Davis answered and then departed from them.

Mrs. Waithe stepped up to Peggy and hugged her. "Did you know the whole time you were being abused Davis stood beside you?"

"Then why didn't he. . ."

"It's not ours to question, it's ours to trust," Mrs. Waite said.

Peggy pondered a question for a while before she finally asked it, afraid of the question, yet she was more afraid of the answer. "Do you think the dragons are as strong as the Master?"

"The Master is all-powerful," Mrs. Waithe assured her student.

16
Fury of Hell

RANCE AND JENNY GALE met Barbara and Daniel at the Emergency room.

"What happened?" Daniel asked.

"We don't know yet. That's why we called you." Rance paced as he spoke, his eyes misty and his face twisted in pain. "Daniel, you've got to help him," he pleaded.

Barbara stayed with her brother and sister-in-law while Daniel went to the room where they were working on Nathan. When he arrived, he was shocked at the bloody mass of flesh lying on the gurney and another horrific scene.

A dragon was sitting on his chest with both claws dug into his body—one on his head and the other in Nathan's chest.

The trauma staff worked furiously on Nathan, with every action they took, the dragon countered it. They would never get anywhere with that monster choking the life out of Nathan.

Daniel pulled on a surgical robe and entered the room. "Let me help," he said to his newly acquired partner fresh out of medical school, Dr. Sid Long.

"What have you found so far?"

"A puzzle. His insides seem to be turning to mush, and we can't stop it. We've given him coagulates and blood, he keeps getting worse."

"I'm going to do something, please do not be alarmed, just trust me," Daniel pleaded, knowing the dragon would soon squeeze any life and hope out of Nathan.

Daniel pulled up a stool and looked the dragon in the face. Those in the emergency room saw him staring at the lamp distending from the ceiling. Daniel began to pray, loud and forceful. Some of the hospital staff backed away in fear, while others pleaded with Dr. Long to remove Daniel.

Dr. Long had worked with Daniel before through many strange events, and he knew there was supernatural healing power in Daniel's prayers. He stood back and watched and told the staff to do the same.

"Lord Jesus, I ask you to come and fight this monster sucking the life from one of your precious children," Daniel started his prayer, and the dragon Asmodeous, filled with wrath, roared in anger.

The hospital staff felt the wind in the room and looked around. No one spoke, their eyes widened, and they put their hands over their mouths to stifle any noise.

Again, Daniel hit the dragon with another spear known as the Word of God, even though Daniel couldn't quote it exactly, the dragon would hear God's Word not Daniel's. "You wicked dragon who works in deceit, release your grip on this one who lives in righteousness. His reward will be in Christ."

The monster's grip on Nathan's chest began to loosen. Asmodeous breathed a plume of fire over Daniel. The fire stank of death and sulfur. Daniel gagged and then caught his breath. He spoke the words he had read only a few hours earlier, "Every Word of God is pure. He is a shield unto them that put their trust in Him."

Asmodeous growled and answered, "So, this one isn't righteous or pure."

Daniel searched his memory for another blow to the dragon with his sword—the Word of God. "Rather, blessed is he who hears the Word of God and keeps it."

Asmodeous knew Nathan studied his Bible, and this was the reason he so desperately wanted to kill him. It would also give him revenge for losing Rance, his father. Asmodeous opened his huge maw to envelope Daniel. In the monster's own horror he couldn't move. His jaws clamped shut. The claw on the torso of Nathan ripped away.

Daniel smiled and went for the deathblow. "And the Word of God increased, and the number of disciples multiplied in Jerusalem greatly, and a great company of priests was obedient to the faith!" Daniel shouted.

Asmodeous knew the incident with Paul. The monsters pushed Saul into doing their work in the name of God, then the Supreme One entered and told Saul the truth, changing his name to Paul. The mere mention of that name made Asmodeous spit with anger, and the bloody mouth of a dragon filled with a bitter taste.

The Supreme One determined Nathan would not die at the hand of a dragon, and these sword blows moved past stinging to outright burning. Asmodeous decided it wasn't worth the hassle of fighting with this one.

Daniel kept his sword sharp, and he practiced welding it. Asmodeous released his other claw from Nathan's head and flew away.

Nathan coughed and opened his eyes. "Boy, am I going to be sore in the morning." He smiled at his uncle.

The staff shouted.

Dr. Long smiled at Daniel and shook his head. "I'll never understand you."

Daniel rejoined Rance, Jenny, and Barbara. "He's going to be alright."

Jenny sighed with relief and then grabbed Daniel's hand. "It was a dragon, wasn't it?"

Daniel nodded. "I know you were praying because the beast gave up too easy."

Emily listened and watched. She rose and slipped out of the waiting room to see Nathan.

Shawn and Derrick opened their eyes; or rather they thought they commanded their eyes to open. Still, the darkness surrounded them.

Shawn called out, "Derrick?"

No answer came.

He stood and walked around with his hands in front of him feeling nothing. Then his foot fell into nothingness, pulling his body behind him. He tumbled in space for several minutes. He put his hands out to stop his fall, his grasp found nothing. Then the darkness lifted like the light of dusk on a cloudy day.

With red filtering light dancing around him, he could see walls as he passed them. In those walls were faces and hands. They all seem to be falling beside him yet not seeing him.

Suddenly, he hit bottom with a thud. Shawn got to his feet and looked around. He heard a crash and turned toward the sound. "Derrick!"

He reached out to his friend and ran to him. He could get no closer.

Derrick ran toward Shawn, yet the more the two of them attempted to get close, the further away they were from each other.

"What's happening?" Derrick yelled in a high-pitched panicked voice.

Shawn opened his mouth and tried to answer. No sound emerged even when he yelled. He stopped and so did Derrick. They heard the laughter of many rough voices. Then one sound rose above the cacophony of discordant noise.

"Hello, boys!" The gravelly voice surrounded them with tentacles of dread. The two boys spun around, looking for the source. They both yelped like wounded pups when they saw the monster sitting on a chair or throne made of bones and blood.

Shawn clamped his hand over his mouth, and Derrick squealed.

"Come." The voice pulled them toward the monster sitting on the horror throne. The laughter rose as the voice scooted them closer to the horrible chair and the awful stench of death.

"Welcome."

Shawn mustered up his courage and spoke with a frail voice, "Who. . . who. . . are you?"

Again, the laughter rose, and the Monster stood and glared down at the two boys with his yellow eyes poised with a horizontal black pupil like the eyes of a goat, only huge.

"I am your master," the monster said without moving the spikey mouth in front of them. Shawn realized the beast spoke directly to their minds.

"I've been in there a long time; you are just now seeing me." The claw foot of the monster tapped a sharp talon at their heads.

"What? No!" Shawn argued.

The beast raised a clawed foot and scratched across Shawn's face—deeply. Shawn reached up to catch the blood. He found none. He looked at his hand and felt his face. The deep gash healed. "What?" Shawn said and looked at Derrick, whom he could barely see through the dense night with barely any light.

Derrick formed words with his mouth. No sounds came forth. His eyes were wide, and he pointed his finger at Shawn's face. At that moment, the beast used the huge claw to rip through Derrick's face.

"Let me show you." The beast roared with laughter and a crowd of laughter joined the ruckus.

Shawn watched as the beast tore Derrick's face off.

Derrick screamed in agony. The beast licked the claw and blew a puff of smoke. When the smoke cleared, Shawn could see Derrick's face had returned.

"You see, in my kingdom, we love pain, especially causing it. This will be your fate."

"For how long?" Derrick whimpered.

The crowd laughed, "Forever!"

Cory felt the thick darkness on his skin. He squinted his eyes, hoping to adjust to the dark. Still no light came, only heat. A dry heat creating a thirst that reached to the bottom of his feet. He brushed his hand over his arm. It felt like sandpaper. He tried to take a deep breath. He labored as if he were cloaked under a thick cloth. His body couldn't suck in any air.

He called his friends names, Shawn and Derrick. Only the echo of his voice returned. "Where am I?" he shouted.

He heard a gruff, low-pitched sound, so he repeated his question, and the sound became more audible with a gruff edge. Cory trembled and pulled his knees up to his chin, wrapping his arms around them. He ducked his head into his knees.

"Momma, Daddy, help me, please!" He sobbed. With so little air, he couldn't wail as he wanted. His mind searched for answers. He wanted to hear his mother's soothing voice. Instead, he heard his voice mocking her for the Bible stories she told him.

Then he stood and shouted, "Help me!"

Cory's mom saw sweat beads forming on her son's forehead. His hand and body felt cold. He writhed in the bed.

She went to the door and called down the hall for a nurse.

"Help me!" he screamed.

She stopped and looked back at her son. His eyes were wide and bouncing from side to side.

She grabbed her husband's hand and screamed, "Oh no! He's in hell!"

17
Brokenness

HANNAH PUSHED HER food around on her plate. She took a sip of water and then faced Trey.

"We need to move," she told him.

He set his glass down and glared at her. "What are you talking about?"

"I want to leave this place."

"This is where our jobs and family are."

"We can get jobs elsewhere."

"You want me to pick up and leave the farming to your dad? Trey growled.

"No, you can sell the farm and buy another one somewhere else," she moaned.

Trey shook his head and rose from the table. "You're getting crazier and crazier. That's the dumbest thing you've said." He left the room, leaving Hannah with the two children.

"Where would we go, Mom?" Stacey asked her mother.

"South Dakota," Hannah answered without pausing.

Trey heard her as he left the room. He stopped and glared at her. "What's in South Dakota?" he snarled.

"It's what's *not* there."

Henry spoke up, "You mean Mimi Barb, don't you?" He grimaced as tears welled up in the corner of his eyes.

Hannah stared at her young son. His trial loomed in the near future.

"Yes, away from Mimi because you failed to get her out of my life." Hannah's eyes narrowed and her voice raised in a fury.

Henry sniffled while tears crept from the corner of his eye. He made no effort to wipe them away. "Then maybe you need to go and leave us here."

"Look at what you're doing to your family," Trey said. "If you want to go to South Dakota, just go. The kids stay here with me."

"Seriously?" Hannah asked.

"Seriously. I don't like you much anymore, and it'll be nice to have some peace from your constant whining." Trey picked up his coat; Stacy and Henry followed his example. "Come on, kids, we're going to see Mimi while mom packs."

Hannah was left sitting alone at an empty dinner table with a half-eaten meal.

The dragon of the Philistines, Dagon, wrapped a spiky, scaly fishtail around her and whispered in her ear, "At least you'll be free."

With a set jaw, Hannah packed a bag, grabbed her car keys, and headed north.

Rahab fed Hannah visions of cruelty inflicted on her by her mother and the unfairness of her husband and the nuisance of her children. She would finally be free to discover real life. Not the one her mother planned for her or the one in which her husband and children trapped her.

Belial pointed the council of dragons to Rahab. "Now that one knows how to destroy a family!"

The council roared at their victory.

Nisroch noticed Trey, Stacey, and Henry spent the night at Merilee and Buster's house with Daniel and Barbara. The family knelt in prayer for their beloved Hannah.

Nisroch gazed at Belial and the council celebrating their victory, not realizing the action set ablaze a fire of prayer to the Holy One. Jorkphat stood beside Nisroch and watched the lightning bolts of prayer in the distance deliver the sweet smell of faith and trust to the Holy One calling for the Dragon Warrior to come to fight the battle.

"We're doomed, aren't we?" Jorkphat asked.

Nisroch nodded.

After two months of getting acclimated to her new job, Hannah finally had time to unpack her meager belongings and place them in the tiny furnished apartment she found— one room with a small kitchen and a bath. The living room contained a couch on one side and a twin bed on the other side of the room with a narrow walkway between them. In three days she found a suitable place to live. She smiled and sighed. "Thank you Lord for watching over me."

Rahab hovered over Hannah. "I hate it when they give the Holy One credit for my work."

She took a deep breath and settled on the well-worn couch. Looking around her new home, she realized the reality of being alone was a lot different than the fantasy. She looked at her watch. Normally, if she were still back in Church Creek Falls, she would be hustling to prepare an evening meal for Trey and the kids. Now she munched on the left over chicken from her lunch.

She had found a federal job as a Chief Nurse Executive in a hospital for Native Americans and Alaska Natives the first week. In addition to that job, she snagged a part-time teaching gig at Ogalla Lakota Nursing School. She didn't need a husband, although she did miss his teasing. And she really missed Stacy. Even though she worried about Henry there was little she could do to help him. The cost of not being with her kids was high. She deemed it acceptable to be away from Barbara, her mother. The last two months had been peaceful without her mother's constant presence nagging her.

Hannah put her suitcase away in the closet. This would be a good spot while she did some house hunting because as soon as she found the perfect house, she'd bring her kids to join her in Pine Ridge, South Dakota.

The last two months with Hannah gone had been hard on Barbara and Daniel as they gave all they had to help Trey with meals and the kids.

Trey helped clean up after dinner. Barbara told them they could stay another night. Trey insisted on getting back to a normal routine as quickly as possible. With Hannah gone, the three of them needed to become self-sufficient.

Henry ducked his head and shuffled his feet on the floor while Stacy sobbed.

Barbara loved having the children, however, these circumstances were painful for all of them. Barbara felt the tears forming in her eyes as she watched Stacy lean into her dad and held him tightly as if she were afraid he'd leave them too.

"I'm so sorry," Barbara said as she hugged Stacy and Henry. "I don't know why she hates me so much that she'll give up her own family to get away from me."

The confusion of the situation gave way to a note of gratitude. At least Hannah didn't drag Stacy to a foreign place away from family. Henry still had legal issues to resolve, he couldn't leave the county.

Barbara stared at the ceiling. *Lord, I love her so much, but I don't know what's wrong with her or why she's doing these cruel things to the people who love her the most. I give her over to You, and I beg you to turn her eyes back to You.*

Tonight, they left soon after dinner instead of spending the evening. Barbara turned out the kitchen light and stumbled into the living room.

Daniel followed. "I think we're getting too old for this." He smirked as he rubbed his shoulder.

Barbara nodded. "You know what Henry said to me today?" she asked Daniel. "He said, 'You treated my mother bad.'" Barbara's voice choked on the sentence.

"What happened for him to say that?" Daniel asked.

Barbara shrugged her shoulders. "I've noticed Trey doesn't stick around and visit with us anymore. He comes and gets the kids and barely says hello and goodbye."

"I've noticed that too. I can almost feel the ice cycles growing on me."

Nisroch laughed. "You ain't seen nothing yet," The dragon snarled.

Hannah decided to stop and eat something from the hospital cafeteria, even though she'd just bought a cart full of groceries for her little place. She looked around at the other tables, and for the first time noticed her pale skin in contrast to the others. *I guess I don't fit in.*

A young woman carrying an infant car seat with a newborn and a young child about three years old holding on to the woman's dress stopped at Hannah's table. "If you're alone, may we join you? There are no other tables."

"Sure," Hannah answered and moved her purse from the chair next to her. "I will enjoy the company."

"My name is Mary Running Wolf," the young woman said as she sat the car seat on the floor and helped the three-year-old into a chair.

"Hannah Mitchell." She extended her hand to Mary who didn't notice as she settled her little ones Hannah let her hand fall on the table.

"Are you visiting?" Mary asked as she settled in the chair opposite Hannah.

"No, I just moved here."

"Why?" Mary asked. "I've lived here all my life and can't imagine anyone coming here on purpose." Mary winked at Hannah.

"I'm working at the hospital and teaching at the school."

Mary nodded. "Welcome to the community; I hope you stay awhile. I'm actually here to enroll in the nursing school. I guess I'll be seeing you."

Hannah nodded and took a bite of her sandwich in silence. Her mind and heart shouted in response, *I want to go home.*

18
Reality

"NO, HE'S NOT in hell. He's right here," Cory's dad said while attempting to calm his wife's hysterical claim that their son was in hell.

She took Cory's hot hand. He squeezed back. "We gotta pray," she said. Cory's dad took his other hand, and the couple prayed over their son. His father prayed for healing from his wounds. Cory's mother prayed for his release from hell.

Sitting in the corner, a beast sat unseen by human eyes yet visible to Cory as he writhed on his bed, begging for his mother. The beast laughed at the boy as he raked a sharp claw over his neck, causing a little bleed. The beast raised the claw to the huge split tongue flicking from his mouth and licked the blood.

When Cory's mom opened her eyes, she screamed, "He's bleeding!" She grabbed a tissue, pressed it to his neck, and pushed the nurse call button.

Barbara came running into the room because the screams coming from Cory's room were louder than the obnoxious buzzer at the nurse's station. When she entered the room, she saw "it" hovering over Cory.

Mrs. Frye saw Barbara and started shouting, "Help him!" She removed the tissue to show the streak of blood flowing from the cut of the dragon's claw.

Barbara walked over to Mrs. Frye, took the used tissues, and tossed them into the waste can. She looked at Mr. Frye as he stared at his son's neck with blank eyes. "What's happening?" she asked.

Barbara looked at the Fryes and with the softest voice she could manage in the presence of the beast blowing hot air on Cory, she said, "I know you're a praying family. That's what he needs the most."

Mr. Frye took his wife in his arms, and they bowed their heads and started praying.

Barbara looked the beast in the eyes and snarled. She whispered to the brute, "Back off."

The dragon laughed. "You know it's the leech dragon with two daughters who are never satisfied, they call out, 'More, more. I will never be satisfied!'" The dragon spoke to Barbara's mind. "I'm not leaving. This is too much fun mocking you stupid, intolerant Christians."

Barbara took a deep breath. As long as the leeches had their vile blood-sucking mouths on him, there would be no recovery. *How do you kill a vampire?* She recognized the verse the dragon used from Proverbs 30:11 -17. The answer had to be there.

Barbara opened the nightstand drawer and pulled out a package. She opened it and placed the cold compress against

Cory's neck. "Mrs. Frye, hold this on his neck. I'll return shortly." Barbara headed out of the room.

"I hope he doesn't fight me," Mrs. Frye said through tears.

Barbara stopped and returned to the bedside. "What do you mean?"

"He usually yells at me and pushes me away." Mrs. Frye groaned.

Mr. Frye shook his head. "He yells ugly curse words at me."

"How long has this been going on?"

"I think his disrespect for us came in his early teen years," Mrs. Frye said as she kissed the back of his hand. "He always was a rebellious kid. I did my best to teach him. It felt as if he had some sort of barrier in his mind that rejected my teaching."

Mr. Frye nodded in agreement, "You know, Maggie, it may be better to let him go. He seemed to hate us, so maybe he'll be better off without us."

Cory lay writhing on the bed, he could hear his parents and the nurse talking. His body was present with them, while his spirit stretched between earth and hell.

He raised his arms to his parents and screamed, "Please don't leave me!"

Barbara looked at the Fryes. She could tell by the tender look of a mother attempting to rescue her child that the words pierced her ears too.

Mrs. Frye looked at Barbara. "How do I rescue my son?"

Barbara pulled the Bible out of the drawer. The passage she'd be giving these parents wouldn't be comforting, it would sharpen their sword to do battle with a vile serpentine entity—the one called Asaubosam or sometimes called Ishtar. *What is holding it back from taking Cory?*

She opened the Bible to Ephesians 2:1 and read, "And you hath He quickened who were dead in trespasses and sin."

Mrs. Frye took the Bible and read the next verse to herself. She looked up at Barbara. "How?"

Barbara wrinkled her brow.

"How can he repent in this state?"

Barbara looked at the face of horror on Cory's face. "I think he's trying. Sit here and read the Scripture to him. She turned to Colossians and told Mrs. Frye, "Read this book to him."

"All of it?" Mr. Frye asked.

"Yes, and if he is still in this state, start over, and read it again. He needs the understanding of what it means to be 'in Christ.'"

Mr. Frye pulled up a chair next to his wife and said, "We'll read it together."

Barbara left the room and headed for Daniel's office. She sat down hard in the patient chair across from his desk. "We've got to do something about Hannah." She slumped and held her head between the palms of her hands.

"What?"

"I don't know . . . Cory is suffering, and he may be seeing monsters in their natural habitat because the look of his face is hardcore fear."

"What does this have to do with Hannah?"

"I just learned that he was disrespectful to his parents," Barbara moaned.

Daniel raised his eyebrows. He didn't say anything.

"Matthew 15:4 says, 'God commanded honor father and mother and he who curses father and mother let him die the death.'"

Daniel nodded. He put his steepled fingers against his lips as he said, "And even worse is Exodus 21:17, 'He that speaks evil of father and mother shall be put to death.'"

"What should I tell the Fryes? There's one of those horrible beasts hovering over Cory. I left them reading Colossians as protection."

Cory could feel the weight of the darkness lifting a little. He could hear his mother droning on in the distance. He never thought he would be so glad to hear her voice.

"You liked being mean to your mother, didn't you?" An owl-like creature said to him.

Cory couldn't see the creature with clear eyes, and for that, he was grateful for what he could see was repulsive.

"Yeah, I did."

"Why?" The creature cooed in discordant sound waves.

"I don't know; I just did. She was always nagging me."

The owl-like creature became plainer, and his mother's voice dimmer.

"How did she nag you?"

"She wanted me to go to church."

"Did you?'

"Did I what?"

"Go to church?"

"Yes, until I had my twelfth birthday, and then I refused to go. That's when I realized my mom and dad were. . . well monsters to me."

The creature smiled as much as a hideous demon could smile. Asaubosam raised a crow-like foot and scrapped Cory across the chest. The blood transfusions replaced his missing blood in a slow methodical drop. His body welcomed the life-giving fluid. The horrid vampire goddess of death wanted to drain every drop from him. Not until then could Hades consume Cory.

"How were your parent's monsters?" The creature urged Cory on even as she fed him images of his mother's distorted face yelling at him.

Then Cory heard his father's voice. He turned toward the sound and listened. His father was reading something about Christ. Cory repeated the phrase, "In Christ." The creature faded into the darkness with a screech.

19

Hanging by a Thread

"IT'S NO USE," Cory's dad sobbed. "He's gone."

"We can't give up," his mom responded.

Cory heard the comments fading in the distance as he found himself clinging desperately to a thin string. Flames of heat lapped at his feet as he pulled himself higher to escape the pain of the burning. His hands felt clammy. He kept raising one hand over the other to get higher away from the burning flames. The string faded into a black nothingness above him. The more he tried to climb the more he stayed in the same place.

He heard a familiar voice call his name. He gasped and lost his grip on the fragile string for a moment.

Shawn's vacant eye orbs and saggy gray skin came into view.

"What?" He screamed at the horrific sight of his friend.

"Don't let go! Don't ever let go!"

Just as Shawn made the statement, Cory saw the claws of a huge dragon cut Shawn in half, spreading body goo all over Cory. He yelped and clung tighter to the string. The string appeared to be unraveling. Shawn screamed in agony as the two parts of his body came back together. He held his mid-section and came close to Cory's face.

"It never stops," Shawn whispered just before the claw pulled Shawn back into the smoky gloom of despair.

"Nooo!" Cory yelled. "Help me!"

"We can't let go," Cory's mother's voice passed by his ear like a gentle breeze. Then it faded again. Cory's arms began to tremble with the effort of holding his weight.

The deep resonant laughter of many dragons filled the dark chamber with vibrating tones of doom. Cory looked around in the darkness and could see nothing. He could feel the hot breath of something. It stank so bad, he vomited. He wanted to hear his mother's voice again.

"Who ya talkin to?' Jason asked as he grabbed a cookie from the cabinet and walked to the living room where Naomi reclined on the sofa, her phone in her hand.

"Your sister," she answered with a broad smile and a quick goodbye to the person on the phone.

"Which one?" Jason plopped next to Naomi.

"Barbara."

"That's odd for her to call. Must be medical."

"Yeah, it is. She said Mrs. Frye requested to see me."

"Sure, go on." He smiled and patted her on the leg.

"I don't need your permission." She smirked at him.

With a wink, he rose. "Okay, I get the message, I'm leaving."

Twenty minutes later, Naomi entered the hospital with trepidation. Mrs. Frye, was her mother's best friend.

Naomi wondered if she would accuse her of stabbing her mother the same way her dad had done.

She spotted Barbara walking down the hall and motioned to her.

Barbara smiled and headed toward Naomi. "I'm so glad you could come. I think you can be a comfort to Mrs. Frye."

Naomi nodded, not knowing what to say.

"I understand your family is friends with Cory Frye's family," Barbara said as she led Naomi down the hall.

"Yeah, maybe. Cory's mom is my mother's friend.

"Anything I should know?" Naomi asked Barbara.

"No just be a friend, I think she needs the comfort of someone who understands strange things."

Barbara went to Cory's room with Naomi.

However, Naomi stopped at the threshold, refusing to move further into the room.

Barbara recognized the obvious distress of the boy and didn't hesitate. She called for a cardiac team. In seconds they whooshed into the room and took command.

Naomi, Barbara, and Mrs. Frye moved as far back as they could as the team worked on Cory.

Cory's grip on the thread slipped. The flames leaped higher, in spite of the fear of the flames they were not the source of his greatest fear. It was the huge serpent head breathing on him. . . and the flimsy string.

He tried praying.

The dragon laughed. "Don't you know your God isn't here? He can't hear you."

Cory groaned. *Why didn't I listen better in Sunday School?*

Again, the dragon laughed. "You think Sunday School had the answer? I was with you all day every day, and you think a measly little hour sitting in a room with a bunch of other kids and a boring lesson from the Bible would give you answers to your current dilemma?"

The dragon roared, and the others joined him in a jarring sound of raucous and evil laughter.

Cory trembled and climbed up his string as far as he could. It seemed to be getting stronger.

"They're pulling him back!" the owl-like vampire dragon, Asaubosam, screeched.

Again, Cory heard a moaning of pain coming toward him. He searched the darkness for something. He was certain he wouldn't see it until it came face-to-face, and it would scare him. Maybe, he could prepare. The sound of pain grew louder and closer. Cory could feel a drip of sweat inching its way down his face.

Boom! His friend Derrick's face was only inches from him. His eye sockets, blackened and hollow, surrounded by his pale-grey face leaning to one side.

Then Cory saw the scaly claw clinging to Derrick's neck and squeezing. It let go, and Derrick turned his black eye sockets toward Cory. "Don't let them get you; the pain never stops."

Cory turned his gaze toward the upper regions of the string and started climbing with all his might. The dragon grew small, and the noise grew less as a small stream of light penetrated his addled mind.

The crisis ended when Cory's heart began a normal sinus rhythm. The crash team left almost as quickly as they'd entered. A follow-up crew came and cleaned the mess left by the team.

Mrs. Frye turned to Naomi as they waited for the cleanup crew to finish. "Thank you for coming," she said between sobs of both agony and relief.

"It's okay, why did you call for me?"

"I want to talk about your mother."

"What about her?" Naomi asked while staring at her hands.

"What did you see the night she was . . ."

"Stabbed?"

"Yes."

"She was cooking dinner. I had a date with Jason Troye. I came in to show her my finished look before he arrived. She was chopping vegetables and had a knife in her hand. She didn't put it down. She exclaimed how pretty I looked.

"We both saw a flash and heard a pop like a lightbulb burning out. We looked toward the noise and the flash. Then all went dark, and I heard my mother scream. When my eyes adjusted to the darkness, I saw my mother lying on the floor with the knife plunged into her stomach . . ." Naomi choked at the memory and had to stop.

"The strangest part." She stopped again and stared at the floor as if she were trying to recreate the scene. "What?" Mrs. Frye asked.

"My mother still gripped the knife. She must have tried to kill herself . . ."

Naomi nodded and finished her account of the evening with a sigh.

As an afterthought, she asked Mrs. Frye, "Why did you want to know?"

"Because something strange is happening to Cory and . . . that flash of light you saw. . . "

"Yeah?"

"I've been seeing in Cory's eyes. She stopped and sniffed, took a deep breath, and said, "It's a reflection in his eyes."

Naomi didn't know what to say. She took Mrs. Frye's hand and patted it. "You might talk to Jason. He saw something strange at the Honey Tree."

"The Honey Tree?"

"A woman tried to stab her friend. Jason said it was a dragon."

Mrs. Frye smirked. "A dragon?"

Naomi nodded. "I didn't see it, he talked nonsense about it."

"What kind of nonsense?"

"He called it a monster. He said it caused the woman to attack her friend."

"I don't understand?"

"He said the dragon was causing people to get mad at one another, especially family members."

She let out a loud wail and cried, "Is Cory in hell?"

Naomi didn't know what to say or what to do. She simply shrugged. "I've got to leave."

She left the hospital and went straight to Jason's apartment. She practically pounded on his door. When he opened it, she rushed past him into the room.

"Tell me. . ." she gasped. Her heart pounded hard in her chest, and she was covered in perspiration despite the cool, fall weather. She didn't care.

"Tell you what?" he asked.

"I think it's from hell."

20
Message of Hope

NATHAN'S WOUNDS HEALED with little scaring. The beating damaged some deep inner tissue and was taking longer to heal. His movements often resembled an old man. He stepped into the living room of Emily's foster family.

"Still hurt?" her foster dad, Burt asked.

Nathan nodded. "Getting better, though."

"Where do you plan to take Emily tonight? I hope it's a lot safer." He chuckled.

"In our family, I don't think there is a safe place."

"Maybe we shouldn't let her go." Burt offered Nathan a candy from the dish on the coffee table.

"It's not anything physical, it's just that—" He stopped, not knowing how to explain the spiritual battle his family found themselves fighting.

"I've noticed a lot of scuttlebutt about the family."

"I guess that's it." Jason took the exit strategy and focused on community gossip, rather than spiritual battles.

"Especially my grandfather." Nathan moaned. "Yet, there isn't a better man anywhere."

"I can agree to that. He saved my bacon a couple of times. He's getting on up there in years, isn't he?"

Nathan smiled. "Only chronologically. He's still got the same fighting spirit he had when I was a kid."

Burt smiled.

"Do you know much about him?" Nathan asked.

"Only that I don't want to cross him. That's why it surprises me there is so much chatter about his family. Probably comes from his granddaughter, Hannah. She's become known in the community as a well-spring of gossip, especially about her mother. I think it's a good thing she's gone."

Nathan shook his head and pursed his lips. "We can't figure out what's wrong with her. Her attacks on my aunt Barbara hurt us all."

Buster moaned as he moved around in his chair. The dragon wound on his shoulder grew worse with each day.

Merilee watched him with sorrow. "Can I get you one of those pills Daniel brought for you?"

Buster stared at her and shook his head.

She knew he'd refuse. He always did.

He explained to her how the pain served him as a measurement of his family's need for prayer.

"What about you?" Merilee argued.

Buster smiled again. The unspoken language that passed between them came as the result of nearly sixty years of marriage. Life dealt them some difficulties, but their love for each other and their reliance upon the Lord brought them through it all.

"Our kids will get through their journeys on earth like we did," Buster reminded her.

Merilee dropped the subject. She pulled the chocolate cake from the oven and set it near the fan on the counter to cool.

Buster moaned a happy sound and rubbed his tongue across his lips.

Merilee laughed at him. "I wonder why this makes you feel better?"

Buster continued smiling and rubbed his shoulder.

"Hurting?" Merilee asked while she whipped up a batch of frosting.

"Don't worry; I'll be okay. You know it's worse when—" He stopped mid-sentence with a groan of pain.

"I know, the dragon's evil deeds must be multiplying." Merilee faced the window, putting Buster's pain behind her. The sky filled with wisps of clouds passing by. Black clouds shaped like dragons.

"I wonder if they are really out there or if I'm imagining them," she said.

Buster followed her gaze. He rose from his chair with great difficulty.

Merilee knew to let him do it on his own . . . if he could.

He came over to her and placed his arms on her shoulders.

She could feel him resting his weight on her and patted his hand.

He kissed her on the top of the head. "No, my dear, they're real."

"It looks as though they're surrounding our house."

"I think they are."

"What do we do?" Merilee squeezed his hand hard.

"What we always do—pray."

"I know. I do. I bring Barbara's pain to Him every day."

"What about Hannah?" Merilee frosted the cake, though it was still warm because that's the way Buster liked it. Then she cut a slice, put it on a dish, and set it in front of her husband. She sat in her usual beside his.

Buster adjusted his body with a string of groans and moans. He accidentally knocked his dish off the table. It crashed to the floor with his half-eaten cake laying amid the shards of broken glass.

"You okay old man?"

Buster slumped over in his chair. The pain caused him to take on many different positions to find relief.

Merilee stood to help him get adjusted and clean up the mess before replacing his cake on a paper plate.

Walking beside Merilee is the family guardian angel, Davis. His sword is drawn his compassionate arms hold Merilee.

The dragons gather outside the house.

Davis will not allow them entrance.

While Merilee cut Buster a new slice of cake, she prays, *Lord, give him some relief.*

The dragons whistled, yelled, and mocked Merilee. "Yes, holy one, give him some relief from the damage we caused him." The dragon raised its ugly head to the heart and ears of Adonai, The Most High God, and roared in boisterous laughter.

Davis looked to the face of the Father for instructions.

When Merilee hands a new piece of cake to Buster, he continues the conversation regarding Hannah. "I just leave her in the Lord's hands. He has to deal with her unreasonableness."

"She won't even talk to me or her mother anymore."

Buster let Merilee moan about their daughter and granddaughter. He knows Hannah's actions are as painful to his wife and daughter as his dragon bite. Even worse than the heart pain of her family is that her disobedience to the Lord's commands makes Hannah vulnerable to the life destruction by evil dragons.

"Trey is taking all the blame," Merilee continued. "He shouldn't do that. Hannah has some . . . I don't know, something in her heart that is separating her from the Lord."

Buster sighed and nodded. "Unforgiveness."

"I think you're right?"

"Remember the job Trey had before he came to take over the farm?"

"Yeah, he was working for that coop farm."

"I think his boss was pretty hard on him. Hannah got really mad at his boss, remember?"

"Yeah, I do, and she couldn't stop talking about how bad he was. She'd talk to anybody who'd listen."

"Then she switched from the boss to Barbara."

"Why Barbara?"

"Barbara was her boss for a while," Buster reminded Merilee.

"Yes, I forgot. Are you saying she got mad at Barbara because she was her boss?"

"Not exactly. something must've happened in their jobs. Before that they were close."

"So, what can Barbara do?"

Buster picked up his well-worn Bible and opened it to Jeremiah 4:4 and read, "'Circumcise yourselves to the Lord and remove the foreskins of your heart . . . or else My wrath will go forth like fire and burn with none to quench it, because of the evil of your deed.'"

"That sounds harsh," Merilee said as if apologizing.

"It is. Hannah's breaking several of God's laws, starting with the fifth commandment, then John reminds us in his letter, 'If someone says, 'I love God,' and hates his brother, he is a liar, for the one who does not love his brother whom he has seen, cannot love God whom he has not seen. This commandment we have from Him, that the one who loves God should love his brother also.'"

Merilee gave a little laugh under her breath, "Barbara's not her brother."

Buster smiled. "You know brother is a generic term for other Christians."

"Yeah, I know, it makes our Hannah a liar."

"And separated from God."

"Do you think she hates Barbara?"

"I do."

"I don't understand how she could."

"The dragons are liars and murderers. Their main weapon against us is deceit. They plant lies in our thinking when we allow them to get into our minds."

Davis puts his hand on Buster's dragon wound and draws healing to the wound.

Buster straightens up and laughs.

"What are you laughing at?"

"My pain is gone! Completely gone! Must be that second piece of cake." He took a deep breath for the first time since his son Zay's wedding, twenty-five years ago, when the dragon bit him.

Merilee removed the bandage from his shoulder. "Buster! It's healed . . . completely!" Merilee laughed and cried at the same time.

Buster stood and walked around with his shoulders held high.

The dragons watched closely. They weren't allowed to enter the home. Still, a burst of energy erupted, and the small group of slit-eyed reptiles writhed around each other as if they were dancing. But they weren't dancing they were mourning.

Buster grabbed his bride and danced around the room with her. "I don't know why or how, it's so nice to feel good."

Davis watched as the patriarchs of the Troye family enjoyed a dance of youth granted them by the Most High.

Buster squeezed his bride of sixty years. "Soon, we'll be in the presence of the bridegroom. Won't it be glorious?"

"And pain-free," Merilee added with a smile.

Davis took Buster's hand from around Merilee's waist. As he did Buster's vision transferred from his bride to his angelic escort.

"It's time you met the Master. Your battle is over."

21
Day of Rejoicing

SHARON SAT ON one side of Merilee and Barbara on the front pew with Daniel on the other side. The beautiful smell of fresh-cut flowers wafted over the audience and surrounded the casket.

Buster looked so handsome in his suit and tie, his aged farmer hands crossed over his chest.

The new pastor didn't know Buster well. However, seeing a church full of mourners for a ninety-something-year-old man spoke volumes about the man's character. All ages sniffled, even some young toddlers displayed sadness.

The family smiled through tears of loss.

After the service, the family gathered at Barbara and Daniel's home in town. The table was covered in food and flowers.

Buster joined his nephew, Michael; his army buddy, Paps; his friend and supporter, Mrs. Waithe; and the cute little girl he knew from church, Peggy Strand.

When Davis escorted Buster to the throne of grace, Buster bowed. He was home.

The Master welcomed Buster. "Well done, my good and faithful servant."

Buster asked Davis about some of the giants of the faith who guided him through his journey on earth, Charles Spurgeon, D.L. Moody, and many others including the apostles Paul and Peter.

Davis introduced him to all he requested. Then Buster asked Davis if he could inquire about someone from his time on earth.

"Who?" Davis asked.

"Jason and Alyssa's father. We never found him after the blast.

Davis nodded and took Buster to a small house, simple in design and magnificent in its appearance, and knocked on the door.

When the young man answered, Buster introduced himself. The young man grabbed Buster and gave him a big bear hug. "

"Thank you for taking care of our kids," he said then called to a beautiful red-headed woman. She came and stood next to him. "We've been waiting to thank you for all you did. The Master let us watch you rescue them and then adopt them. How are they?"

Buster entered their home. They served tea and cookies while Buster told them of Jason's service in the military. He helped stop a human trafficking operation. Buster started to tell him about Alyssa's experience in the cabin, but the young man stopped him.

"We were allowed to visit her in the cabin. Her faithfulness allowed for our visit to her."

Buster felt so overwhelmed with the beauty and serenity of the place, he forgot about Merilee. He turned to Davis and asked him.

"She is being comforted by Sharon and many others in the town," Davis answered.

Michael and Paps arrived, and Davis departed. "Where's he going?" Buster asked.

"We never know, but we know he's working," Michael answered.

Paps jumped into the conversation and took Buster by the shoulder, "Come on buddy, there is so much to see here, and it will take all eternity for you to see it."

Buster hesitated. "I saw the damned today."

Paps pursed his lips and nodded. "What think ye?"

"I deserve that same misery."

"It allows us to see the sovereign grace of the Holy One that rescued us from the same torment," Paps said.

"Everyone saw that same grace and each one was given an opportunity to receive it," Michael said. "Those in damnation rejected it."

A sturdy man appeared before the three men. Michael and Paps greeted him with a firm handshake.

"I see we have a new resident," the man said.

Michael turned to Buster and said, "Buster, I would like for you to meet—"

"Paul of Tarsus," Buster stated in awe.

"That's right. I heard you guys talking about my letter to the Romans."

Buster squinted his eyes. "Paul said, those who've heard the gospel have a greater opportunity to respond to Christ, but every unbeliever, through sin, has rejected God. I think you call it estrangement and your daughter is experiencing it."

Buster nodded. Another man joined the crowd and continued the conversation, "Everyone deserves hell and damnation; no one deserves Heaven. The Most-High desires that no one be sent into torment, but many will perish because of unbelief."

"Buster meet the apostle John," Paul said as he patted him on the back.

"I hope our God will be patient with my granddaughter, Hannah Mitchell."

The group laughed.

"Don't worry: I'm willing to stop and say He's already solved the problem of her strong-willed heart." Paul said. "Remember what He did to me on the road to Damascus?"

"The Most High will bring her out of the lies of the dragons if she sees and accepts His grace." The Apostle John remarked.

"And if she doesn't?" Buster asked in a whisper.

Michael pointed to the sea of damned souls.

Barbara and Sharon rummaged through Buster's closet. Merilee didn't have the physical or the emotional strength. Since his death, she ate little, spoke less, and spent a lot of time in his room. Occasionally she would make a chocolate cake and then give it away. She called it Buster's pain relief. She gave them to people that were ill or suffering from some emotional trauma.

166

Sharon pulled a piece of paper from one of Buster's jackets. "Look, here's a prayer list." Sharon handed the paper to Barbara.

She opened it. "It's a short one." She turned the paper toward Sharon to see the names on the list, 'Hannah, Trey, Henry and Stacy."

"I remember my grandmother saying, you pray hardest for the kid that needs it the most. Guess daddy felt the same way." Barbara said.

"Is there any change in Hannah?" Sharon asked.

"Yes, but not for the better, she's getting angrier and screams at me more. I don't engage her anymore. I can't handle it." Barbara answered.

"Her thinking is so twisted. Sounds like the mind of a dragon." Sharon said as she pulled another shirt from the closet.

"How did the dragons get into Hannah's mind?"

"Who knows how it started," Barbara said. "Remember how I acted when the mask scrapped my shoulder?"

"Boy, do I." Sharon threw a shirt at Barbara. "You changed into a monster yourself. You're lucky I stayed your friend."

"Well, if you hadn't, you would've never met Michael."

Sharon smiled at the memory of their college days. "I wonder what he and Buster are doing now?"

"Probably talking to Paul," Barbara answered as she folded the shirt and packed it in a box.

"Or the Apostle John," Sharon added.

The two women laughed at the idea. They finished loading the boxes. "Let's get some of that cake I've been smelling all morning."

"We better hurry before mother gives it away," Barbara said and jumped in front of Sharon.

Barbara took a sip of coffee. "I think a seed of discontent grew when her friendship with Shannon Wright fed it fertilizer and water."

"I didn't know that girl. What happened to her?" Sharon asked.

"She was fired for gossiping and divulging patient information."

Sharon raised her eyebrows. "Not soon enough if she fed Hannah. Wouldn't you think Hannah would be stronger than that?"

"You've dealt with the dragons; what do you think?"

Lilith, the goddess of seduction and stealing of children found great satisfaction when emotional pain caused by damaged relationships occurred in the believers in Christ. God's plan to have a family could be thwarted and scared by the estrangement of an adult child from a believing family. Lilith led the destruction of families when she seduced fathers with pornography and mothers with fantasy heroes and lovers. Then the goddess took the children and raised dragon worshippers. The horned winged female creature couldn't help itself and shrieked loudly in triumphant victory over Hannah.

Merilee jumped at the horrid screech. "I hate that sound." She joined Daniel in the kitchen while Sharon and Barbara completed the task of cleaning the closet.

Daniel flinched a bit. He didn't feel alarm. "The wimp can't do anything except scream."

"Hannah has to examine herself, then humble herself and forgive. You know the Bible says that Jesus didn't regard Himself God but humbled Himself even to the point of the cross." Barbara said while staring in Buster's chair.

Lilith squawked, "No she doesn't, I won't let her."

"Hannah is hardheaded and strong-willed. That's not going to be an easy task for her to humble and forgive," Barbara added.

Daniel sighed. "Especially with the dragons painting a picture of her life without us."

"The dragon of old told Eve she could be like God, and now he's telling our Hannah the same lie."

22

The Holy One

MICHAEL TOOK A DEEP sigh and leaned back. "That's my uncle," he said with humility as Davis was dispatched to bring Buster home. The Holy One smiled at Michael and nodded.

"Right now, Davis needs to be on the battlefront." The Holy One stated.

"What about us?" Peggy asked.

"You'll be here listening to the prayers of the saints as the battle is fought, and you will be taking your prayers to the throne room of the Supreme Father," the Holy One answered.

"Will you be with us?" Mrs. Waithe asked the Holy One with her head tipped toward the ground in reverence for the Savior.

"I am preparing for judgment of the dragons." The Savior answered.

"The Dragon Warrior," Paps whispered.

The smile of the Holy One filled the residents of heaven with a peace that could not be understood. A peace that told them, their loved ones on earth would trust in the Holy One and overcome the dragons.

"Yes, many of My good and faithful servants will come home with me after the battle," The Holy One said as He closed the curtain between His family with Him and His family on earth.

The band of servants bowed, then followed Him. The flames of holy fire sparked in the altar of incense.

Michael pointed it out to the rest of the group. "I see Sharon and Barbara are fasting and praying for Hanna."

The Holy One answered Michael, "As the prayers are received, so is their armor made. Those with the sincere humble prayers have the greatest armor."

"It's hard to understand," Peggy said with reverence. "I prayed so hard during my journey on earth. Did I not pray rightly? I was often punished and beaten."

The Holy One stopped and sat down. He motioned for Peggy to approach.

With fear, she took a step toward Him and found herself immediately on His lap.

He wrapped His scarred hands around her and pulled her close to His chest.

She rubbed her fingers over His scars.

"My sweet daughter, you understand My suffering more than most because you shared it with Me."

Peggy smiled a big, toothy grin. "It was my honor to do so." Her question felt so silly in the light of His love. She felt as if she and her Savior sat in a big bubble of warmth and love. She could feel His beating heart in her chest. She understood suffering on earth, which brought her glory in

Christ in His suffering. As she bowed her head, He stroked her hair. She wept with the joy of His presence.

"You will see your reward is great, my child, for many who were suffering saw your faith in my provision in the worse of their circumstances. Many of them called out to Me, and they will be part of My family because of your faithfulness in suffering. Your reward from My Father will be great.

Peggy noticed Mrs. Waithe watching the exchange. She too had spent time in the Master's lap being consoled, and she knew the joy of His presence. The Master saw her watching and gave her a compassionate smile and a gentle wink. She never tired of Him.

Peggy joined her, and they clasped hands in a common understanding of their deep love for their Savior.

Paps smiled at the joy in Peggy as the Savior comforted her. Looking past Peggy, Paps noticed one of the angels making an armor. "For whom is this piece made?" he asked the angel.

"That piece is for Barbara."

"Why so thick and heavy?"

"Because she will need it."

"Then I better get to the altar of incense and add my prayers." Paps took off.

The spiritual warrior standing next to Paps muttered, "Offer up a prayer for me too for I will be standing next to her fighting one of the more fierce dragons."

"Which one?" Paps asked.

"Belial."

Paps' mouth flew open, "But . . ."

The angel smiled. "Michael, the archangel, will be with me. I have fought the beast before, when he was known as the Prince of Persia. I fought him for twenty-one days until Michael came and helped me when we were trying to get to the prophet Daniel with an answer to give him understanding."

Paps stared wide-eyed at the angel. "You fought for Daniel?" he asked with the wonderment of a child.

The angel nodded. "I will tell you what is inscribed in the writing of truth. Yet no one stands firmly with me against these forces except Michael the warrior."

Paps remembered the incident from the tenth chapter of Daniel. This angel explained the seventy weeks of the end times to Daniel, now spoke to him and said he would tell the truth. If the battle required both this angel and Michael, the archangel to fight the dragon on Barbara . . . why? Paps shuddered.

The angel smiled and pointed to a section of the intermediate heaven where the family of God waited for the final judgment of the world. He saw millions of laughing children.

"She fought for them," the angel said.

Paps knew these were the aborted babies, the ones lost to the deception of the evil one. Then the angel pointed to another corner of teens listening with rapt attention to a teacher. "Those were the ones captured by the deception of a better life through attempts to change the will of the Father when He created them. They thought they knew better what gender they should be. Instead, their lives were cut short, and they didn't reach their potential. The Master revealed the truth to them through Barbara's Bible classes. These are the young ones who accepted the truth of the Master, and He became their Savior."

The angel pointed to another group, "Over there is a place of honor for the innocent young men who fought in wars prepared by wicked men for gain."

Paps nodded. He understood that statement. He observed the many different people there with him. "They all have a story, don't they?"

The angel nodded and put his huge hand on Pap's shoulder.

"So, is this why Belial is after Barbara?"

"Normally, Belial sends the common dragons, also known as the other gods of the nations to do the dirty work. However, many battles over the years have been lost to Buster Troye's prayers. Belial wants to inflict as much pain as possible on the Troyes. He thinks using Barbara as the scapegoat will bring the family to their knees to worship the beast.

Paps laughed. "He doesn't know . . ."

The Angel put his hand in front of Paps. "All are capable of falling. The dragons are strong, and they are cold-blooded murderers. If they get their claws into the mind of one, they can wreak havoc on the person and all who are around them."

Paps closed his mouth. In his thoughts he knew that person the dragons would most likely use, *Hannah!*

The angel nodded. "The only defense of the family is the Word of God, and their only protection is the prayers of the saints both on the earth and here."

Paps nodded. "My prayers will be for Barbara." He started toward the altar of incense then stopped and turned toward the angel. "And you."

A chorus of voices from a teen Bible Study singing praises entered the ears of the Master. He closed His eyes and drank in the beauty of His Bride singing to Him. He sat on the right-hand side of His Father and remarked, "She is beautiful isn't she?"

23
Making Preparations

NATHAN AND EMILY entered his home where his parents, Rance and Jenny Gale entertained the other guests with food and drink. Nathan and Emily joined in the small feast and greeted the members of their Bible Study group. This was indeed a happy place for all of them. It had good food, good company, good teachers, and good messages.

Tonight, it felt different.

"I keep waiting for a crash," Emily whispered to Nathan as they sat down on the couch. The rest of the group gathered in the den where the study and worship would take place.

"I feel it too."

"It's Cory Frye," Kendall said to Nathan and Emily as he sat in the chair next to the couch.

"What?"

"Jason will tell us." Kendall pointed to the fireplace where Jason Troye, their group leader stood.

"Today, Mrs. Frye asked Naomi to come to see her," Jason said. "She wanted to know about the attack on Naomi's mother. She believes the attack on Cory, Shawn, and Derek is the same . . ." Jason stopped and ducked his head. He took a deep breath and then looked over the crowd. He pondered what word to use. "The same thing that attacked so many that night."

The group groaned, nodded, and whispered among themselves.

Kendall spoke up. "What do we do with this information?"

"Cory's mom thinks he's in hell," Jason said with no inflection in his voice.

"C'mon, that can't be," Ethan moaned. "He's been in church all his life. He has to go to heaven."

Nathan pushed to the edge of the couch and gazed at Ethan, "How do you know? Being in church doesn't make you a Christian any more than swimming in the ocean makes you a boat."

The group groaned in agreement.

"I don't understand," Ethan said, frowning. "If Cory is in hell, then I could be there too."

"You're not there now like Cory," Jason comforted Ethan. "And you have a choice."

"Does Cory have a choice?" Ethan sat up and asked Jason.

"He's still alive, so yes, I think he does."

"Even though he's in a coma?" Ethan probed further.

Jason pursed his lips and nodded. "Let's talk about you; do you know what it means to be a Christian?"

"I thought I did. But now, I'm not so sure." Ethan leaned back and crossed his arms.

Jason glanced around at the group and started his lesson. "This is known as the security of the believer. It means you know you are saved from the wrath of God."

"What?" Isabelle shouted. "The wrath of God? You got it all wrong," she said with great indignation.

"Yes, Isabelle, your salvation is from the wrath of God. You see, we all deserve hell. We deserve to be food for the dragons."

Isabelle stood up. "I don't have to listen to this garbage."

Dragons nested in the four corners of the room. They kept throwing their type of justice into the minds of these high-school students. All of them good churchgoers, few of them knew that Jason spoke the truth. The dragons hid the truth from the teens so the truth wouldn't be accepted.

One of the dragons rose a little too high in the pride of their suggestions, and Jason saw the ghoul.

"Sit down, Isabelle, and shut up and listen," Camille, her best friend and ride home, said as she pulled on Isabelle's arm. "You're not going anywhere without me, and I want to hear this."

Isabelle sat down and crossed her arms. Her lips held tight.

Jason ignored the outburst and continued. "When Adam and the woman disobeyed God's orders and ate of the tree of the knowledge of good and evil, they were doing so because of the lie of the serpent."

A hiss filled the room. Jason ignored it. The class looked around. Jason knew they'd heard it, he continued.

"They revealed their lack of trust in their God who gave them life and prosperity and each other and sought to be a god themselves. That's idolatry."

Isabelle relaxed a bit as Jason explained.

"When the Bible speaks of their nakedness, it meant they lost their protection from evil. When they knew nothing of evil, it couldn't hurt them, it couldn't deceive them. Now, they know, and they feel nothing except intense fear. They know they are not gods; they are pawns in the hand of a clever serpent. The Bible calls him a dragon in Revelation 12:7.

"So, get to the wrath of God, I thought He was love."

"You're right, Isabelle, He *is* love. Imagine your little brother is outside playing on a mound of sand. His laughter shows his delight in the sand pile your parents provided. He shovels and digs.

"Then you notice something strange in the sand pile. It's growing and coming closer to your brother. You recognize it as a rattlesnake. You holler at your mother, who comes running. When she sees the serpent coming after your little brother, she runs toward the snake and snatches your brother up in her arms only seconds before the snake strikes at him, the venom doesn't miss.

"Instead, it hits your mother's leg. She deposits your brother in safety, grabs an ax, and returns to the snake to chop him into pieces—even though her leg is swelling, and she's dizzy. She falls to the ground. Was her action love, or wrath?"

Isabelle's eyes grow wide before she answered, "Both!"

"Yes, love toward the child, wrath toward the serpent."

"God's wrath is at the sin that destroys His children, and His wrath will fall upon those who follow the serpent."

"That's what Jesus did on the cross," Camille said. "He took the sting of the serpent."

"Yes, and when we look to Him and recognize what He's done for us, then the wrath of God has turned away from us because it's already been poured out on Christ for our sakes."

"I still don't understand. What do you mean by being saved from the wrath of God? Isn't that already done?"

"Yes, Isabelle, it's already done, and all we have to do is look to the cross and believe it's already done. Jeremiah calls it the New Covenant."

"Don't we do that when we come to church?"

Jason sat down in the center of the group. "Church is where we come to worship our Savior for His sacrifice of taking God's wrath at our sins. God is Holy and pure and cannot tolerate sin, when He looks at those who believe in faith, then He sees the purity of Jesus, not the sin of man."

"So how do we know if we are truly saved?"

Jason smiled, leaned back in his chair, and looked up at the ceiling where the dragons' breath melted into a small stream of smoke and their presence grew small and almost invisible. "We have a desire to know Him, and that means we want to study His Word, and we want to talk to Him in prayer. How do you know if you like a certain boy?"

Isabelle blushed, Emily took Nathan's hand and answered, "You want to be with him, and you want his approval."

The group nodded. Jason thought of Naomi and wished he could share this with her. He grew fond of her but unless she could find her peace with Christ, they would only be friends.

The group chatted among themselves. The ones with a solid faith continued the explanation to those with questions.

Jason let them go, this was a group meeting that didn't need a program, it needed prayer. He took a quick glimpse at the ceiling. The dragons were all gone. They could no longer interfere for the Savior had entered the room. Kendall stood and led the group in singing, "He Will Hold Me Fast."

The Angel of the Lord sat quietly by as he listened to the teens discussing their relationship with Him and then singing of His love for them. He put His arm around Jason. He knew Jason's thoughts. Jason's spiritual army days were just beginning. In today's group meeting, he trained for God's army.

24

Naomi and Cory

NAOMI SLIPPED INTO Cory's hospital room. She sat beside him and looked at his drawn face. She touched his cheek; it was hot.

"Can you hear me?" she muttered.

Cory's body started jerking, and it appeared he was trying to speak.

"Are you in hell?" she asked almost as a joke. She didn't believe hell or heaven existed. Nonetheless, she did know there had been something in her home that injured her mother.

Suddenly, Cory mustered up all his strength, and with a loud stutter he shouted, "Yes, Help m …. me!"

Naomi gasped and stood so fast her chair fell behind her. A nurse came running into the room followed by Mrs. Frye.

"What happened?" The nurse started checking his vitals and his IVs.

"I . . . I . . . don't know," Naomi said.

Distraught, Mrs. Frye took Cory's hand. "He's trembling. What happened?" she demanded from Naomi.

"I asked him if he was in hell and . . . and . . ."

"And what?" Mrs. Frye fought to keep from screaming at Naomi.

"He said, 'Yes, help me.'"

Mrs. Frye squeezed her son's hand and tenderly looked into his terrified face. "Call on Jesus, just call on Jesus."

Asaubosam stomped back and forth blowing smoke, growling, and hissing. "When do I get him?" the angry monster asked Belial, the head beast over this operation.

"I can't say."

"He keeps calling for God."

Belial laughed at the comment. "Which god?" Asaubosam stopped in his tracks and laughed. "Buddha, Shiva, or that ugly mutt in the back?" Asaubosam pointed to the created god known as Ganesh, nothing but a four-armed decorated elephant.

Ganesh ducked his head, letting his heavy jewel-laden truck fall to the floor along with his four arms. He was nothing more than an apparition with no power, no substance. It didn't matter that his name struck fear in the hearts of his followers, an apparition could do nothing. They bought high-quality food when they couldn't feed their families and laid it in front of a wooden image. What did they expect a chunk of wood to do for them?

The elephant god hated them. If only those foolish people would not worship him, he would not be an object of horror. He yearned to be the tree that stood tall and clapped his hands in praise to the one and only true God. Instead, those silly people cut him down, covered the trunk of the tree with silly jewels, and expected the tree to grant their wishes. Ganesh couldn't even grant the one wish that consumed his imaginary heart—to be a tree in the honor of God.

Asaubosam, the vile vampire dragon with a black heart filled with hate—bitter, vengeful hate. The only delight a dragon receives is to see stupid humans fall for the lies and then end up killing themselves with deceptive promises of fun and relationships and feeling good.

Asaubosam saw the hurt inflicted on Ganesh and continued to berate the other 300,000 man-made gods. The only good from these trinket gods was to provide a hiding place for the real menace—the demons! When a poor man laid down a week's wages for one sacrifice to the wimpy little trinkets, the demons shouted with glee. Soon, the poor man's children would die from starvation. The demons consumed their life, and their father gave it to them.

Paul tried to warn them in the Supreme One's Holy Book, few listened.

Cory screamed out, "Help!"

"What's he doing?" Asaubosam asked Belial.

"He's begging for help." Belial laughed. "And he's begging one that belongs to us, the woman called Naomi."

The noise in the blackened den of nothingness raised to a fever pitch as the dragons shouted the name, "Naomi, Naomi, our servant forever!"

They all stopped shouting and stared at Cory in silence. They could see that small stream of light around him. Someone was praying for him.

"No!" Asaubosam shouted. "He's mine!"

Naomi went home as quickly as she could. Her palms were clammy and her heart racing. She went past her parents to her room. She huddled in a corner and wept.

Jorkphat, the orange demon of Nisroch joined her.

She felt a grueling thirst.

25
South Dakota

HANNA SIPPED ON a soda at a table near the window of the hospital cafeteria.

"May I join you?" a baritone voice asked her.

She looked up into the most handsome male face she'd ever seen. "Of course." She motioned to the empty seat across from her at the small table.

"I guess you are alone?" he asked.

"On break. What about you?"

"I'm here for an interview in about twenty minutes."

"With whom?"

"Not sure. I only know it's a member of the hospital board and one or two doctors."

"Are you a doctor?" Hanna asked.

"Somewhat, I am a doctor of research."

"This is a strange place to do research."

"Not if you are researching Native American illnesses."

Hannah smiled. "You got that right, and I'm the only Irish cracker in this joint," he said with a chuckle.

"That bad?"

"Not really, people are nice to me. They just already have their social circles, and I'm new enough that I haven't made one yet."

"I guess we may have to be each other's social circle," he said with a wink.

"I think I would like that."

Nisroch smirked and almost lost his cover. He regained it before Hannah saw the real face of a dragon instead of the handsome man presented to her lonely heart. This would be a piece of cake to seduce this particular 'Troye.'

Barbara felt a lurch in her stomach that grew into a gnawing discomfort. It wasn't physical rather it was spiritual. *Hannah!* She didn't know what or why, she only knew Hannah is in trouble.

She immediately went to Sharon's home.

"I don't know what's happening, my gut says Hannah needs help," she blurted out the moment Sharon opened the door.

"I think you inherited your dad's dragon wound."

"I think so too. Only it makes my stomach heart."

"I understand," Sharon said. She bowed her head and prayed, "Dear Father, Creator of the universe and author of all that is created. I adore thee for making man capable of communion with you, that we may ask 'Where is God, my Maker, who gives me songs in the midst of darkness?' But my Lord, evil has spread over the human race and captured the heart of one of our family, Hannah. I know not what she is facing, you have all knowledge and power, and by that power, you can touch her, draw the wandering child back to a sense of divine things, and render it lasting and effective in living in the joy of the Lord.

"You alone, Lord, know her soul's secrets, and You are aware of her desires. Make me an intercessor for this one I love, and comfort her in her mental illness which comes because of her sin-diseased thinking. Restore her to a hope found in the love of a prodigal daughter. Blow away the ashes of futility and ignite a spiritual fire in her that is gentle, peaceful, mild, refreshing, one that will melt her into lowliness before You.

"Let her mother rest in You with relief from the pain of evil infecting her loved one. Keep her mind and heart stayed on You as You fill the garden of Hannah's heart with Your love and allow her to smell the scent of Your love through her family. Let us see the fulfillment of You in her being to glorify you and be a blessing to others.

"And Lord, Tell Michael I love him and miss him. Amen."

Similar prayers went up from Zay and Marcy, Rance and Jenny Gail, and Nathan and Emily. Jason's prayer was a little different for it wasn't Hannah alone in his heart he prayer for Naomi. He wanted to love her and take her as his bride. This wouldn't be possible until she became a part of the bride of Christ. He loved Hannah, he needed Naomi.

After the handsome man left Hannah's table, thoughts of Trey and her children came to her. She remembered when she met Trey. He was the most handsome man she'd ever seen even more than her recent acquaintance. She smiled with the memory of his touch, and she felt her heart race a little.

She slugged the last of her drink and gathered her things to return to work. As she did, she saw the handsome man standing at the counter paying out. She frowned when she noticed his dirty clothing, his mussed hair, and weathered skin.

Why did I think he was handsome?

Nisroch marched into the chamber of doom and darkness with his snout up in the air and deep guttural breaths that poured the smoke of pride into the air.

"Imbecile!" Belial roared the moment Nisroch stepped into his sight.

Nisroch, taken by surprise, yanked his large tail into the air, ready to go to battle with Belial. That purple monster may be the head of this operation, but in the amount of brute strength, the two dragons were equally matched.

"How dare you discredit my achievement?" Nisroch roared back. The rest of the dragons slinked back into the shadows.

Poor Cory hung on for dear life as he watched his captors hissing and blowing plumes of smoke at each other. His tender skin caught some of those blowhard insults with blisters. Still, he wouldn't let go of the thin string that bound him to life on earth.

"Look!" Belial pointed at the lighting streaks over their heads and the puffs of sweet-smelling clouds coming from below them.

"Ahh!" Nisroch yelped, "They're praying."

Belial stood tall over Nisroch with Ishtar, crouched on fish fins beside the purple dragon.

She smirked and tilted her head with eyes boring through Nisroch. "You're weak," she drowned in the sultry voice that caused many young men to fall to their doom when

Ishtar put the lens of lust in their heads. Then they saw young girls as objects of pleasure rather than the valued souls of the Almighty—her mortal enemy.

"It's not over, you vile ugly owl!" Nisroch roared at Ishtar.

She screeched, spread her wings, and flew off into the darkness.

Nisroch harrumphed, lifted his head, and marched to his domain in the darkness.

Cory screamed, "You evil snakes!"

All the dragons turned toward him. Shawn's emaciated, gray body appeared in front of Cory. "Quiet, they're mean."

"I know, and I'm getting stronger."

"Cory, don't let go. There is a way out of this place."

Cory saw Derrek enter. He nodded in agreement with Shawn. "There's a way of escape."

"How?" Cory begged to know.

"Think about our Sunday School lessons."

"That's been a fruitless endeavor," Cory groaned.

"Think about church; think about it, Cory."

Shawn and Derrek disappeared when dragon claws came out of the darkness and clasped their mouth shut and pulled them back into the darkness.

Cory could hear them screaming. *If there's a way out, why aren't they taking it?*

Nisroch formulated a new plan before he returned to South Dakota, and he instructed Jorkphat to build a plan of deception for Stacy.

Belial crept in on them. After listening to their banter for a while, the purple beast said, "I want to destroy Zay and Marcy. You have any vile plans I can use for them?"

"Always. Vile plans are what I do," Nisroch answered.

Zay and Marcy spent the next few weeks preparing their testimony for the city council. Their work slipped under the rug while they poured over financials for the lab. They both knew they were in danger of losing the lab. They both knew they did nothing wrong. They needed to prove it. Rance and Alyssa spent time with them searching for that proof.

Alyssa spotted it first. One little obscure line revealed something strange but not enough to account for the thousands of missing dollars.

After weeks, they were able to present a crooked little scheme of two of the council members to put funds into some unapproved projects by inflating the lab's expenses. Most of the council members didn't understand the terms on their purchase orders anyway, so adding a few strange objects hid the filtering of thousands of dollars from the city coffers.

Zay and Macy were able to return to their work. That's when they discovered the unapproved projects were the very ones causing the soil's deterioration, the city's disease rate, and the loss of crops.

26
Trey's Dilemma

TEN-YEAR-OLD STACY MITCHELL grew fast when her mother left. She didn't understand what happened, and her dad, Trey, couldn't explain it. She could hear her dad talking and sobbing each night after she went to bed alone in her room.

She missed her mother's nightly visits to her room, where they would have girl talk about hair, clothes, and school.

Her dad barely spoke at all. He half-smiled a lot and nodded his head.

Henry walked around like a zombie, saying nothing. He went through the motions of life with no expression, always muttering, "Why did I do it?"

Jorkphat watched the little girl attempting to make a meal for herself, her brother, and her dad. It was clumsy and probably tasteless. However, it didn't matter; the family sat in silence at the table playing with their food, taking a few bites here and there.

Last night their grandmother, Barbara Holloway, brought them a lasagna. Stacy spent the day with her grandparents, and they visited Grammy Lee at the farm.

When they came home, Mimi Barbara let her help cook the lasagna. Stacey wrote the directions on a piece of paper so she could make it for the family. The family ate the healthy food and enjoyed every bite.

Stacy watched her dad and noticed he didn't seem as sad as usual. Maybe a good meal made things better?

Maybe tonight would be a good time to share the news she held in her heart for the last two weeks... After dinner, when they would read together as a family, she would show her dad and Henry the fascinating bracelet she found at her grandparents' home. It had to be worth a lot of money. Stacy felt afraid her dad would make her give it back to her Grammy Lee.

Two dark-green, emerald eyes of an animal that wrapped around her wrist perfectly as if the bracelet were made for her highlighted the rows of chocolate-brown diamonds encircled by amber topaz gems. It was beautiful, and she wanted to wear it to church.

Jorkphat laughed at the little girl falling for his idol. Girls are so easy. Nevertheless, the gift Jorkphat gave his intended must remain their secret. This time, he would succeed where he failed with her grandmother, Barbara. The plan to blind the eyes of the child's dad, Trey Mitchell, formed in the mind of an evil creature intent on devouring this little girl along with the rest of her family.

After all, a broken heart that can't be mended is an easy target for a demon to habituate.

Trey bent over and kissed Stacy on the forehead. "Tomorrow, we'll talk to your mother." He pursed his lips and attempted to make his disgust look like a smile.

Stacy rose to a sitting position in her bed, put her arms around her dad's neck, and kissed him on the cheek. When she did, the bracelet scratched the back of his neck.

"Whoa, what's that?" He pulled Stacy's arm in front of him.

"Isn't it pretty?" Stacy giggled.

"Where did you get it?"

"At Grammy Lee's house."

"Does Grammy Lee know you have it?"

Stacy shrugged her shoulders. "I guess so. I found it in the trash."

"Okay, sleep tight." Trey kissed his girl again. As he rose from the edge of Stacy's bed, he caught a glimpse of something orange. *Must be some clothing.* He didn't check it out.

He stopped at Henry's room. "You okay son?" Trey called to his son.

"Yeah dad, I'm just . . . just wondering . . . "

"What?"

"Do you think mom will come back if I have to go to trial?"

"Son, your Mimi Barb didn't file a complaint, and the District Attorney is not going to pursue it. Why are you worried about a trial that isn't going to take place?" Trey could feel his anger rising at the continual discussion.

He could only imagine the guilt Henry must feel. The continual questions about a trial and prison wore Trey out. Especially now during planting season when irrigation wells needed to be serviced and repaired, planters needed greasing, seed to be purchased, and so on and so on.

"I'm sorry, Dad, I know, but there is something that keeps—" Henry stopped.

"Keeps what?"

"I'm not crazy, Dad, really."

"I know that. Why do you keep repeating it?"

"Because I hear the voice."

"What voice?" Trey's fatigue vanished, and his parental concern took precedence. He pulled up a chair beside Henry's bed.

"It tells me they'll find out."

"Who will find out what?"

"I don't know, it comes all the time."

"What does it sound like?"

"Like the same voice that told me to shoot Mimi Barb."

Trey slumped back in the chair and steepled his fingers over his lips. He looked at his son for the first time in a long time. Henry looked drawn and thin . . . so thin. Trey hadn't noticed. He knew their meals may be nutritious with little flavor. He also knew all of them were eating it.

"Have you lost weight?" Trey asked.

Henry nodded. "About forty pounds."

"How come? You didn't have that much weight to lose."

"I don't know. I eat, and I still keep losing weight . . . and that's not all."

"What do you mean?"

"I'm losing my mind, Dad." Henry burst out in tears. "I see things I shouldn't see, and I hear things that aren't there. The only relief I get is when I'm playing video games."

Trey sat on the edge of Henry's bed and put his strong, muscular arm around his son, and gasped at the feel of Henry's bones. He let his son cry until he was spent. Trey choked back the sobs, still joining his son in a silent release of pain. Then he kissed his teenage son on the forehead and tucked the covers over him.

"Dad, I'm scared."

Trey encouraged his son before he left the room, wiping a tear from his face.

He shut Henry's door, poured himself a glass of water, and walked to the patio. He strolled through Henry's laptop to discover the games he played. To his shock, they weren't innocent games occupying Henry's thoughts. They were pornographic violent games. However, the game with the highest score revealed Henry's obsession with guns.

He immediately called the only person he knew who would understand, Hannah's Uncle Rance.

❧❧❧

Rance clicked the disconnect button and turned to Jenny Gale. "The dragons are busy tonight."

Jenny nodded and pursed her lips at his remark. "What's going on?"

"That was Trey. He's worried about Henry."

"I'm worried about Stacy."

"Barbara is worried about Hannah."

"You know the Bible says worry is a sin. We need to be praying not worrying."

"I know. It still feels like we should be doing something."

"Prayer *is* something."

"What about Hannah? Why would she leave Trey and the fact she left Stacy shows she isn't in her right mind." Rance paced as he ranted about his niece. He stopped and looked at his wife. "You know what is causing all this?"

"The dragons?"

Rance nodded.

"Why?"

"The war is getting more intense."

"Did you know Alyssa and I found some gross errors in the city budget? It looks like someone is embezzling from the city."

Rance stopped his pacing and sat down in front of Jenny Gale.

"What are you going to do?"

"I don't want to do anything because all the evidence points to Zay and Marcy."

"What? How?"

"It's the lab. Some expenses don't make sense."

"You know Zay and Marcy are looking for a virus or organism to be causing all the illness, don't you?"

"Yes, it's not that kind of expense. It is a general expense with no tags, and it's a large amount."

"Can you correct it and keep it quiet?"

"We've talked about it. I think I need to confront Zay first."

"I agree," Jenny said.

Alyssa and I have decided we cannot accuse Zay with the evidence we have besides I don't believe it. I think the sneaky snakes that hound us day and night are blinding us to the truth."

"That's possible. You can ask him, can't you?"

Rance nodded. "Right now, I've got to make a date with Henry. Trey said he thinks he's getting into pornography."

Jenny gasped and put her hand over her mouth. "Be careful!"

"I am not a snake!" Mammon roars over Rance's head. "I'll destroy you yet."

Belial laughed at Mammon. "That boy's already beat you once; you couldn't even capture him with sex."

Nisroch joins Belial in laughter. "You gonna' get that boy Henry, I bet."

Mammon scowled at Nisroch. "He'll never make his sixteenth birthday. He's got a little suicide party to attend."

Trey felt better after talking to Rance. At least, he felt confident Henry hadn't been overtaken by pornography. Still, something seethed under Henry's skin. Trey knew the potential for something bad would happen to his son or by his son's hand.

Late in the evening Trey was exhausted and was ready to get his shower and get in bed.

"Eeeee!" He heard a scream. He stopped and listened. The scream faded a bit. It came from Stacy's room.

He bolted down the hall to her room and entered without knocking. He saw the angelic face of his daughter sleeping, and to his horror, he saw an orange man sitting on the headboard over her. The sight of the small man with a teal-colored bowler hat and a teal tie with matching suede shoes startled him so much, he couldn't speak.

The orange man raised his head and stared into Trey's eyes. "She's beautiful, and soon she will be mine." The man licked his lips with a tongue that appeared to be split in half.

Trey's muscles froze, and he could not speak or move. His mind wanted to sock the man in his arrogant face. He screamed in his mind.

"See?" Orange man pointed with his teal blue cane to Stacy's wrist with his bracelet idol wrapped around her arm.

"That's me. She put it on herself, and nobody can take it off. She has given herself to me." Orange man laughed. Then he disappeared.

Trey fell to the ground. He took a deep breath and moved his arms. With great effort, he was able to move his limbs and then his body. He crawled to Stacy's bed, pulled her arm out from the covers, and studied the hideous thing wrapped around her arm.

It may be made of fine jewels, but it was an ugly, scaly dragon. That must be why Stacy found it in the trash. Why would Grammy Lee have it? He reached for the bracelet to remove it, the dragon bracelet snapped at him and took a big chunk of his skin.

With continued attempts, he reached for the bracelet, and each time the dragon image bit him.

"Dear Jesus, please help me get this thing off my girl."

At that moment, the dragon turned back to the array of precious gemstones.

Trey took it off. Stacy remained asleep

He ran out of the house with the bracelet, to the garage. With a sledgehammer, he beat it to pieces.

Then he took the pieces and mixed them in with several shovelfuls of dirt. He put that in a plastic bag, took it to the alleyway, and dropped it in the garbage.

He looked up at the sky and saw the many stars. "Thank you," he said and returned to his house.

"Don't you relish in it?" Nisroch asked Belial as the two of them watched the trials the dragons were giving the Troye family.

"Maybe, it will kill them," Belial roared with satisfaction. "Then. . ."

"You better be careful," Nisroch warned.

"What are you saying?"

"Ask Mammon."

"Who is the green beast working on?"

"Jason Troye."

"Oh," Belial groaned. "The Supreme One is equipping another Troye."

Jorkphat stepped next to Nisroch and whispered, "Is Belial aware of Trey?"

Belial heard the question and roared with a burst of gaseous fire. "Anything else I should know?"

With his snout almost touching the ground Mammon added, "The Holy warrior is watching Cory."

27
Heaven's Tears

THE ALTAR OF incense burned with the slow steadiness of a dying fire. The sweet-smelling aroma that normally filled paradise didn't have enough vitality to spread to the residents. Only the Master and the Father. The population looked at their beloved King and noticed the sadness in His eyes.

"He's missing His children," Paps said to Michael.

"Where are they?"

"Busy."

"Too busy to pray?" Michael said with indignation.

"Yes, too busy fighting the dragons in their own strength."

"But—"

"I know, prayer is a weapon."

"My Sharon prayed all the time."

"She still is, her body grows weak and her spirit grows stronger."

"See the Master?"

Michael nodded.

"He's watching the young boy, Cory Frye, waiting for him to call on him."

"He's still hanging on that thread," Michael replied. "I thought I heard him call on God."

"He did. But not the name above every name—the only name which leads one to the Father, the name of Jesus."

Michael slumped onto a nearby garden bench. "I wonder why?"

Mrs. Frye held Cory's hand and prayed. She fell asleep for a few minutes, and when she awoke, she started praying again. It seemed so futile. She couldn't understand why Cory remained the same. A nurse entered the room.

"Is there any news?" Mrs. Frye.

The nurse shook her head. "Dr. Holloway is in the hospital, and he's looking over the lab tests with Dr. Troye. He'll be in soon to talk to you."

Mrs. Frye smiled slightly and nodded. She knew if she spoke, she'd either go into a rage or a pool of tears. Neither option pleased her.

When the nurse left, Mrs. Frye sat on the edge of Cory's bed. "Son," she whispered. "If you can hear me, open your eyes."

Cory didn't know why the thin string grew thicker. This had to be a good sign. He turned his eyes toward the inky blackness above him and away from the leaping flames at his feet. He did this more often.

The sight of his friends and the horrible scaly beasts caused a panic attack. Looking up kept him calm.

Then he heard a sweet voice. A familiar voice. *Mother!*

He opened his eyes, and through a grey, fuzzy haze, he could see his mother's face. She was crying and smiling at him. He listened with his whole heart.

"Cory, can you pray?"

Praying is all he did. What else does one do while clinging to a string that goes nowhere to keep from falling into a fire pit?

"Cory, baby, call on Jesus. He is the only way to the Father."

Cory opened his mouth? He wanted to know more. Belial took his voice, so no sound came forth except a few gurgles, to a broken-hearted mother, it was enough. She continued.

"God tells us, He is patient because He doesn't want anyone to perish," she said.

Cory felt hope, real hope. It may have been a small shred of hope, but in this place of total hopelessness, it felt like a banquet. God really did want to save him. "Oh, God, please save me."

He waited to be rescued. Nothing happened. Was it all a lie? The hopelessness overwhelmed him once again.

"Good catch," Belial said to Nisroch. If he speaks that name, we will lose him. Keep his mind clouded. Make him angry at God for not answering.

Nisroch nodded his spiky head and got in Cory's face. "He doesn't care," the giant dragon roared.

Cory began to cry. He looked for his mother's face. It was gone. It was hopeless. *I might as well let go of this string.*

Cory's mother seldom left his side and as long as she had strength, she read scripture to him. Tonight her tired body offered up a prayer for herself as she read from Psalm 42:3, "My tears have been my meat day and night, while the beast continually roars at me and asks, "Where is my God?"

"I don't know!" Cory screamed. "Help Me, God!"

Then strange words entered his mind, and he shouted them. *"You have taken account of my wanderings; 'Put my tears in Your bottle. Are they not in Your book?'"*

When the words filled the air, the dragons stepped back. They winced and they grew smaller.

Cory turned his focus back on the upper blackness, and there he sees his mother's face. She is saying these words. He pulls himself a little higher on the string and listens with his whole heart.

"More," Cory mutters.

His mother continues reading Psalm 56. *"In God, whose word I praise, In the Lord, whose word I praise."*

Cory knows he read his Bible as words, never considering the meaning. He wished now he had a teacher to explain to him. What did it mean? He could see the dragons didn't like it and even appeared to be fearful when he would repeat the words his mother read. He reasoned in his blackened mind. The Word must be the Bible. Yes, she was reading from the Bible. That is why the words hurt the dragons.

"Stop him!" Belial roared.

Ishtar, the queen of evil creatures in the desert landed on Belials' long, scaly, spikey neck. She screeched in her loud banshee voice.

Cory stopped listening to his mother. He felt the scrape of her scream crawl up his back. He shivered. He looked into the flames. They were mesmerizing; they danced around like a waterfall. He wanted to let go and jump into them. It would be so much easier than hanging on.

Belial and the dragons heard Cory's thoughts. Belial turned back to Ishtar. "Do it again," he smirked.

Ishtar screamed in her worse night-terror voice. The voice she used to steal children from their mother at the altar of Molech, the voice she used to put fear into the heart of sinners seeking redemption. The screech of evil that invaded a human's mind and thinking.

"Momma!" Cory cried like a little child. He listened. He heard the banshee screech and screamed.

Mrs. Frye felt the scream coming from her son. His fear was palatable. Her heart banged against her chest, sweat dripped down the side of her face, her hand shook, and her mouth opened in silent horror. She wanted to let go of Cory. The horrible feeling flowed from him.

If she let go, it would stop. If she let go, her feet could run away. The scream she felt coming from Cory reached her vocal cords and exited her voice in an unholy scream. She held on to her son. She could feel the clamminess in her hands slipping on his arms.

Still, she clung tighter, even though she felt herself being plunged into the blackness of hell. She kept screaming and holding. She would go with her son before she let go of him, no matter how horrific the terrors. Only a mother rescuing her child would endure such horrific terrors.

Dr. Holloway and several nurses, including Barbara came running to the room. Daniel and Barbara saw the horrific screech owl with claws digging into Cory and Mrs. Frye.

It's a new apparition. More horrible than any dragon they faced. The chalky white face was surrounded by a full set of shell-layered horns. The arms raised in the shape of goat horns with scorpion stingers on the ends.

The black eyes bore through Daniel and Barbara, causing them to stop in fear. The sharpened beak of the monster covered in blood opened. Daniel and Barbara put their hands over their ears. The screams were like a hard metal band with each instrument playing in a different key.

Mrs. Frye fainted.

Cory closed his eyes.

One of the nurses stabbed Cory's arm with a syringe filled with a sedative.

"Stop!" Daniel shouted. He knew he couldn't explain why to the nurse. Cory had to keep his full mind in this battle. If only he would call upon Jesus. It could all end.

The Master shouted, "Yes!"

Paps and Michael saw the Master dressed in the armor of a soldier. Paps turned to the Angel near them. "Why does the Master need armor?"

The angel smiled. "He doesn't. He has already defeated them. The armor is for the human He desires to protect. If His child calls upon Him, He can put the armor upon Him to protect him. The belt of truth will protect the child from the lies of the dragons. Then he will be able to reason and hear the Word of God."

"Doesn't he need the helmet of salvation?" Michael asked the angel.

The angel nodded and pointed, "Just watch. The Master goes to great lengths to save His children."

"Why doesn't He go get the boy?"

"Without faith, it is impossible to please the Father."

Barbara fell into the chair in the corner of Cory's room. She pulled her cell phone from her pocket and dialed the lab. Marcy answered.

"Come quick. Cory's room," Barbara said and hung up. She then called Rance and Jenny Gale. "Prayers for Cory. Serious battle time. The demoness Ishtar is here."

Rance felt his muscles freeze at the name of the female demon that sucks people into pornography. He knew the strength of that demon and the fearsomeness her appearance caused.

Dr. Holloway approached Mrs. Frye. "Keep praying." He told the nurses he would stay.

Zay and Marcy entered the room short of breath. "What is—" Before Zay could complete the question he saw the image of Belial and froze. "No, I can't do this again!" he shouted and backed out of the room.

Marcy took him by the hand and brought him back. "Yes, we can for the boy's sake."

Marcy noticed the open Bible on Cory's bed. She picked it up and started reading with a loud and firm voice.

"For You have delivered my soul from death, indeed my feet from stumbling, so that I may walk before God, in the light of the living."

Cory heard the words. He straightened up and held tighter. Then he shouted, "Jesus, deliver me from death so that I may walk before God in the light of the living!"

28
Battle Begins

EVERYONE IN PARADISE faced the Master as his tears fell on a smiling bright face. "It's time."

The warrior angels drew their swords and stood in massive numbers around the Master.

Michael and Paps watched in amazement at the army leaving paradise to fight the dragons for one young man.

Mrs. Waithe and Peggy stepped beside them. When the army was no longer in sight, Mrs. Waithe admonished the group, "We need to get to the throne room and start praying."

Cory felt his body float away from the string. At first, he fought to keep it, and then he realized the strong arms around him pulled him away from the flames. He felt his head and discovered a strange helmet. He gazed into the face of the one holding him. It was covered with a soft comforting light showing through the faceplate of the soldier's helmet.

The horde of dragons surrounded the man carrying Cory.

The man took the armor from His body and placed it on Cory. "This shield of faith will protect you as long as you believe in Me. The breastplate is My righteousness. If you wear this armor, you can stand firm against the dragons. Remember truth, which is the belt you wear. Do not fall for their lying schemes always speak the truth. My Word, your Bible is Truth."

"I don't know it."

"Yes, you do. Your mother poured My truth into your mind as a young child. I will bring it to your mind."

"Are you Jesus?" Cory asked the beautiful man.

"No, I'm the Holy Spirit. I'm showing you, Jesus."

Cory smiled at the man as his body turned to a stream of smoke and entered into Cory's body. Cory felt His presence encompass his body. He felt strong and capable of getting out of hell.

Belial stepped up to Cory and towered over him. "I see you have the armor of God now." He paced, letting his tree-like tail swish from side to side around Cory. "Do you think that's going to get you out of hell?"

Cory trembled and dropped his shield. His free arm landed on the hilt of a sword. He pulled it out and saw that the transparent blade swirled with letters.

"What do I do with this?" Cory muttered.

"You fight," the Holy Spirit spoke to his soul.

"What do I do, sing the alphabet song?"

Mrs. Frye removed her hands from her ears and noticed the silence from the screams. In place of the screams, she heard Cory calling her, "Momma."

He sat up, and she saw his blue eyes as clear as a fresh mountain stream. She grabbed him and hugged him. She saw he was looking through her, not at her. His mind was not present with his body.

Daniel and Barbara, and Zay and Marcy continued to pray with thanksgiving as they evaluated the young man. "It's not over," Daniel said.

"It was Jesus," Cory kept repeating. "I needed to call Jesus."

Mrs. Frye smiled with happiness until she heard her son say, "Why? What can Jesus do?"

The dragons roared and thrashed and cursed. The beasts threw curses at the others.

Belial called them to attention. "This is not the time to battle among ourselves. He pointed up toward the earth's crust. The dragons saw the growing light and the horde of angels with drawn swords approaching them.

"The battle is on!"

"Are we doomed?" Jorkphat asked Nisroch.

"Not yet, our battle plan to destroy the Troyes won't be easy. It's time to push Hannah and her kids. They are the keys to destruction."

"Which one do I go to?" Jorkphat asked.

"Get the bracelet back on Stacy. I'll handle Hannah."

Jorkphat was disappointed. Still the vile demon would follow his father's orders. Time to put the image of a dragon idol back together and put it back on the arm of his next victim, little Miss Stacy Mitchell.

Mammon knew his victim, Henry Mitchell. It would almost be too easy. He just needed to make sure the gun used to shoot his Mimi Barbara was loaded and easily available.

Belial wanted to pay his old nemeses, Zay and Marcy, a visit.

Marcy's memories of her stay in a mental hospital would serve him well.

Zay concentrated so heavily on his work, he neglected his prayer and Bible study. He would be easy pickings for a few deceptions.

They would be so busy defending themselves against money laundering; the monster could divert their attention away from the Holy One.

Belial stood and made an announcement. "It's time for Jason Troye to die."

"Can he do that?" Jorkphat asked Nisroch.

"Yes."

"Didn't the Holy One take that ability away?"

"Yeah, the power of eternal death he took from us, not the power of physical death."

"Does that mean Buster Troye no longer has the protection of the Supreme One?"

"No, it means the Supreme One may allow Belial the privilege of taking Jason's earthly life. Seriously, I doubt it will happen. Belial is boasting."

29
Pain Runs Deep

TREY WANDERED INTO the kitchen with a big yawn. He poured his cup of coffee and sat down at the table where Stacy sat eating an oversized bowl of cereal.

"You gonna' eat all that, Pup?" He asked his young daughter with a wink.

She smiled and nodded. "I miss mommy's cooking."

Trey took a slug of coffee and swallowed with a big gulp. He felt his throat tighten. He couldn't respond to his young daughter, so he patted her on the head as he rose from the table.

Henry entered the kitchen at the same time.

Trey smiled at his son. "Good morning." He tried to sound cheerful, although he could see his once-robust son was melting into a skeleton. He pulled some ham from the refrigerator and put two slices of bread in the toaster. He knew if he didn't fix something for Henry to eat, he wouldn't.

Henry poured himself a glass of milk. Trey sat the chocolate syrup on the table, hoping Henry would add it along with some more calories. He did.

Trey smiled. Maybe some food would help him face the day. Trey worried about Henry giving up on life. *Hannah, why do you hate your mother so much, you can't stay with us?* The thought made Trey grit his teeth. An action that occurred more often than he desired.

He heated his coffee, placed the ham, and buttered toast on plates for the three of them. Stacy pushed her bowl of soggy cereal away.

Trey saw a spark of light. The sun streaming through the window caught the jewels bound around Stacy's wrist. The same jewels Trey had smashed into small pieces. At least he thought he had. It never occurred to him the jewels were real diamonds that couldn't be smashed. He stared at the bracelet, hoping to find some broken or missing stones. Instead, he saw the green emeralds wink at him. He shook his head and rubbed his eyes.

"Stacy, where did you get that?" He stammered.

"I told you, I found it near the chicken house at Grammy Lee's house."

Trey opened his mouth a crack while striving to understand why an expensive piece of jewelry would be in a chicken house. It didn't make sense.

"Stacy, I don't want you to wear it anymore. I think Grammy Lee must have lost it."

"I don't want to wear it, Daddy, but I can't get it off." Stacy's bottom lip quivered.

Trey tried to remove the bracelet, and as he did, he could see gashes appearing in Stacy's arm.

"Come on. Let's go to Grammy Lee's and see if she knows how to get it off."

Stacy nodded and rubbed her arm. "It hurts me, Daddy."

"I know."

With the family fed and dressed, Trey headed out to his pickup, and the kids followed. Like little robots, the family climbed into the truck, took their usual places, and stared out the window.

Stacy kept rubbing her arm.

Trey pulled her soft, little arm toward him and held it.

"That makes it feel better." Stacy leaned into her dad's side.

Trey headed toward the farm.

"Aren't we going to school?" Henry asked.

"No, I think you two need to spend the day with Grammy Lee."

Henry turned and looked out the window. "Ok."

If sorrow had a face, it would be the Mitchell family, all shadowed in colorless faces.

When Trey and the kids drove into the gravel drive of the farmhouse, Merilee came running out with her mouth wide open and her arms flaying in the air.

"Stay here, kids, until I figure out what's wrong with Grammy Lee."

Henry took Stacy's arm from his dad and held it while their dad met Merilee. They couldn't hear what she was saying, they both knew she was scared.

"Henry, what's wrong with Grammy Lee?" Stacy asked him.

"I don't know, sis."

Trey followed Merilee into the house, even though she was talking to him, he couldn't make sense of her words. It was as if she were speaking another language. She pulled Trey into the house. When the door opened, Trey heard screams of torture. He had heard it once before, never as bad as this.

He saw Barbara writhing on the floor, her face purple, and her body contorting in ways the human body—especially an elderly body—should not be able to move.

"Call Zay or Rance. No, call Daniel." Trey shouted. He knows.

"I already have. I don't think they understood how bad it is." Merilee answered.

Trey picked Barbara up as if she were a child. He felt amazed at how light she felt.

"Have you given her anything?" he asked.

"I tried, she refused." Merilee answered.

Barbara opened her eyes and looked directly into Trey's eyes. With a voice none of them had heard before, she spoke. "The bracelet! Save Stacy and Hannah!"

The word struck terror in Trey. His beloved wife was causing this to the woman who gave her life. Hannah once loved and respected her mother, and now she caused a misery so deep, the human body couldn't endure it.

Merilee wiped the sweat from Barbara's brow and gave her some water.

The door opened, and Henry and Stacy entered in time to hear Barbara's word.

"Is mommy coming home?" Stacy asked with a smile.

Henry waited for the answer.

"We don't know," Merilee answered them as she caressed Stacy and held Henry's hand. She saw the bracelet on Stacy's arm and squealed, putting her hand on her mouth.

"Stacy, where?" Merilee touched the bracelet.

"In the chicken house."

Merilee took Stacy by the hand and pulled her over toward Barbara. "Look!" She pointed to the bracelet. Barbara took Stacy's hand. When she did, she grimaced and jerked her body over in pain.

"That's it!" Merilee shouted.

Stacy remained quiet, a stream of tears fell down her face as she watched her beloved grandmother's body jerk and twist and her face contort.

"Mimi," she moaned, "I'm sorry." She started tugging at the bracelet, trying to get it off. The more she tugged, the scratches turned into bleeding wounds. Stacy screamed with the pain.

Trey grabbed Stacy's hand away from the bracelet. He looked at Merilee. "What do we do? that dragon has her in its grip."

Barbara took a deep breath and pulled all her remaining strength into the word, "Jorkphat."

Trey and Merilee looked at each other, "What does she mean?"

"Jorkphat was the demon that. . ." Merilee shrugged her shoulders and tried to explain, the words wouldn't come. The screams of pain coming from Barbara drowned out the few words Merilee could say.

Henry sat beside Barbara and put his arm around his grandmother. He held her tight. It seemed to help.

Trey noticed the action and felt a warmth for his son. *Maybe the memory of the shooting passed.*

Barbara's screams lessened to moans.

Then Trey saw a grin creep onto Henry's face. It distorted his face. The tongue that licked Henry's lips sent a cold chill down Trey's spine. *What is happening?*

Barbara's whole body shook as she yelled out at Trey, "The dragon . . . get the blasted monster off of her!"

30
Fury of Hell

BELIAL STOOD FROM his bloody throne and looked over the horde of dragons and demons. He pulled Ishtar close to him and whispered in her ear.

Then she spread her wings, raised her horned head, squealed with the high pitch scream of a desert owl, and flew into the dark chamber where no light could enter.

Belial smiled as the female dragon, Ishtar, disappeared into that horrific unknown desert. Even the dragons wouldn't enter there. They called it Tartarus, and the very mention of the place struck fear in them. They all feared Belial; they felt deep fearful respect for Lucifer; but for Ishtar, they each trembled. Her evil even surpassed the blackened heart of Lucifer, the archangel who once conducted the choirs of praise to the Supreme Yahweh, the Creator of all things.

With a satisfying belch of smoke, Belial sat on his throne.

Nisroch took his place on the higher level next to Belial.

"It is going well, isn't it?" Belial huffed to Nisroch.

"I must warn you—"

"You have nothing to warn me about!" Belial roared.

Nisroch continued, "Remember Lucifer's temptation in the garden to the woman? He was so sure the war was won when he gained the keys to the dominion of the earth from his deception."

Belial belched a cloud of smoke.

"Remember the temptations of the son of God, Jesus in the desert?" Nisroch murmured to Belial and stepped a bit closer to the dragon commander.

"Remember the cross!"

The blackness of the dragon's domain presented a visual of silence in awe at the mention of the cross of Christ. The dragons slumped to the emptiness below them and let their spiky snouts rest on their claws. There was no roaring, no smoke, and no belching — only silence. Not even a sound of breathing could be heard, except for the sound of one young boy . . . singing!

The sweet melody of a young boy's praise penetrated the dragon's lair with a sword so sharp, not even Belial could respond.

The yellow orbs in the head of hate squinted at the boy. A split tongue flicked around the boy, and still, he sang. "Jesus, Jesus, Jesus, let all heaven and earth proclaim."

The others crept closer to the boy and joined Belial in the flicking of evil tongues loaded with lies and deceit over, under, and around the boy.

Still, he sang. No dragon touched him.

Mrs. Frye heard the muffled sound and rose with a start to stand near her son's hospital bed.

Her husband saw her movement and opened his mouth. Before he spoke, he too heard the sounds coming from Cory. The sound grew stronger, and each breath released a perfect note of praise.

The sweet strains sang words of worship, "Kings and kingdoms will all pass away but there's something about that name."

Mrs. Frye couldn't believe her ears. His melody grew stronger and sweeter. She grasped the hand of her son and felt warmth increasing. A tear fell down her cheek and she joined him in singing the familiar song, Jesus, Master, Savior. In that moment mother and son praised the Lord in spite of their circumstances. Cory sitting in the midst of vile dragons and Mrs. Frye holding the hand of her comatose son.

Jorkphat buried his claws into the delicate tissue of young Stacy's arm. The feeble efforts of her father, Trey, and her grandmother Barbara gave him great delight. It allowed him to dig deeper. Soon Stacy would be his completely.

Stacy moaned. Barbara recovered from her seizure focusing on removing the vile bracelet from Stacy's arm.

"She's burning up!" Barbara screamed. "Leave her alone."

Jorkphat allowed Barbara to see him. "I won't." The orange demon taunted Barbara with the vision of his torture of her granddaughter.

Henry cowered in a corner, watching and weeping and repeating the phrase, "I'm sorry."

Michael, Paps, Mrs. Waithe, and Peggy watched the Master staring into the altar of prayer. As they approached He waved and them and said, "Come."

They approached with bowed heads.

"The time is near."

The four new residents in Paradise remained quiet. When the Master spoke, the audience of Paradise listened with rapt attention to His Words.

He pointed to the low flames. "Why don't My people pray? They fight when they should pray."

Michael looked into the flames and saw his beloved Sharon arriving at the Troye farm with a hot apple pie. He smiled at her gesture.

The Master saw his smile and patted Michael on the back. "Keep watching."

The group watched Sharon enter the home on her own when no one came to the door. She placed the pie on a table and joined the group.

Her friend Barbara was holding her granddaughter Stacy, crying and shouting to an invisible entity.

Stacy's dad, Trey, pulled on the child's arm, and Merilee helped him. The child cried with great wails of pain and blood dripped on all of them. The wounds growing as a puddle in a rainstorm.

Sharon stepped closer and saw blood dripping from Stacy's arm. Her hand went over her mouth when she saw the vile instrument clawing into the child's arm.

"How?" was all she could say. She dropped to her knees and said, "Oh Lord, help them get that evil off the child."

The Master smiled. "That's why I called her to bake an apple pie."

With Sharon's words, Merilee let go of Stacy and knelt beside Sharon.

Barbara pulled Stacy close to her chest.

Trey wrapped his arms around both of them. Prayers begin to ascend to heaven and fuel the altar of incense.

"Forgive us, Lord, for forgetting this is your battle," Merilee prayed.

"My child! Dear God, save my child," Trey groaned while still holding Stacy's bloodied arm.

Barbara held her and wept, "My child, dear God, please bring my child back to us."

Buster watched, pain-free and strong, with his family, friends, and Savior. He saw Jorkphat clinging to Stacy and digging his nasty claws deep into her arm.

"Master, help them, please," Buster groaned along with his family and friends.

Paps could see Nisroch beside Jorkphat telling him to push harder.

Michael saw Belial sitting above it all and pouring supernatural strength into Jorkphat.

The prayers threw weapons at Jorkphat, which caused weakness in his arms to lessen the demon's grip on Stacy.

Belial called for a few more dragons to join Jorkphat to infuse more strength into him.

During the entire battle, Cory clung to the string and sang louder. When he finished one song, he started another, giving praise.

The dragons could feel his song pulling their strength away.

They heard Belial call for backup to help Jorkphat with the girl.

Only one responded, the rest of the dragon's domain remained there.

The song of the boy grew irritating and dangerous. "This horrible ruckus must stop." Belial screamed.

The dragons regained a belly grumble, and soon their jarring noises rose to drown out Cory's song.

Belial returned to the throng of dragons. The evil of the dragon commandant sought to do some major damages to the dragons for ignoring the orders. Belial roared and sent a huge plume of fire across the emptiness of the dragons' lair. The flames lit the area with a smoky light that revealed the human Cory sitting among the dragons . . . smiling.

"It could be another trap," Nisroch warned.

"Where's your demon, Jorkphat?" Belial asked Nisroch.

"Still with the young girl, Stacy. The grip of the bracelet lessens. Jorkphat is weak but still fighting."

The Troye family breeched the threshold of heaven with their prayers. They gave praise to the high and Holy One and they sought an audience with Him. They ask for His forgiveness when they attempted to remove a dragon without Him. They gave thanks for the work He would do and even now was doing.

"Let's get her to the hospital," Barbara said, wiping the tears from her face and looking for a tissue to blow her nose.

Once Stacy entered the safety of the hospital staff, Barbara's memory of the horrible pain marched through her mind. It had to come because of Barbara's connection to Jorkphat. Jorkphat sparked the pain in Barbara when the beast took hold of her granddaughter.

She gave thanks that the pain inflicted by the dragon transferred to her rather than spilling it all on Stacy. Barbara had forgotten the pain of Jorkphat's attempt to inhabit her so many years ago in a "marriage" ceremony conducted by witches.

The ceremony used ribbons to connect her to the demon. It happened because she too put that vile bracelet on her arm. The family threw it in the incinerator along with the mask so they would not harm anyone else.

"Trey, do you know how Stacy found that bracelet?"

"She said she found it in the chicken house at Grammy Lee's house."

Barbara pondered the incident and shared the story of her encounter with the same demon that attacked Stacy to Trey. "Merilee recently had the incinerator dug out and deepened. The sound of the mask and bracelet grew more pronounced, and she was fearful someone would find them. When the backhoe dug the hole, he must have pulled the bracelet from its burial site, and it fell on the ground. Stacy found it."

"Do you think the demon could've pulled it out of the hole?" Trey asked Barbara.

"Possibly. I'm not sure how much they can intervene in the physical realm of man, but I do know they can cause things to happen."

Henry sat in the corner of the den at the Troye farm. His eyes roamed around the room where his great grandfather spent much of his time. The clatter and noise surrounding Stacy now gone, Henry opened drawers, studied pictures, perused book titles, and stroked the pages of an open, well-worn Bible.

He sat in his grandfather's chair and pulled the lap blanket around his shoulders. He rocked back and forth and through his own muffled sounds, he kept repeating, "I'm sorry."

The empty house creaked and popped as old houses do, not one voice comforted a lonely, forgotten sixteen-year-old boy. Nonetheless, Henry was not alone, for sitting in the room with him was Nisroch, the dragon of agriculture from Nineveh.

31

Hannah

ISHTAR LANDED ON Hannah's head and dug her claws deep into her, reaching for her soul. The vile screech owl came to carry out the orders of the horde commander, Belial. Once the claws found Hannah's shrinking spirit, she nestled down to do battle with the Spirit of Christ that still resided in Hannah. Even a calloused heart where the Holy Spirit resides in a dormant state is a formidable battle for Ishtar.

Ishtar couldn't invade the body. Her wicked deceptions caused human bodies to be twisted beyond recognition. The individual who allowed Ishtar admittance to their mind would never be seen as a follower of the Holy One. Hannah had the right Sunday School words. Those empty words did not draw her the Father near. The thoughts of a rebellious heart separated her from Him.

Hannah inspected the clock again. Only five minutes passed since she last checked the clock. Her head pounded with the rhythm of a drum on a slave ship. The image increased as she saw her hands chained to the keyboard. She continued to work or at least give the appearance of working. She pulled away from the keyboard. The chains clung to her wrist and when she stood, she saw chains on her ankles as well.

She approached the Director of Nurses' office. "I know I haven't been here very long, but do I have any sick leave? I have a terrible headache."

The Director Of Nursing, referred to as the DON, raised her eyes and took a deep breath. "It doesn't matter, I can tell you don't feel good."

"Do you see the chains around me too?" Hannah mocked as she raised her arms with great effort.

The DON raised the corner of her mouth, "It's okay. You might go see one of the docs before you leave."

Hannah knew she must look bad. She went to the restroom and splashed some cold water on her face. She caught a glimpse of herself in the mirror. She squealed at her reflection.

"I look like a horned owl!"

She rubbed her hands over her face, and her hair stood on end. It appeared a dull gray.

Ishtar sighed over Hannah. "Don't worry, you'll get used to me."

The doc gave Hannah some powerful pain meds and instructed her to take them after she arrived home. She complied and headed to her apartment, where she took the pills and lay down on her bed to wait for some relief. Ishtar remained connected to her spirit and whispered vile things into her drugged mind.

"Your mother is a cruel person. She's just a narcissist. Everything has to be her way. She's toxic. You have to stay away from her. Trey will see, and he will come join you soon. If he doesn't, you don't have to be alone."

Throughout the next six hours, Ishtar fed many delicious evil thoughts into Hannah. She gave her a dream of a wonderful man rescuing her from certain doom. Hannah never saw his face in the dream. Ishtar couldn't reveal the face of evil, even in a dream. The malicious fiend knew the drugs allowed her unlimited access to the mind of her victim. She would put everything she had into her.

Once she awoke, Hannah wouldn't be able to call on Him.

Trey sat beside the bed of his precious daughter, praying over her. The fever in her body grew.

Daniel stepped beside him. "Where's Henry?" he asked Trey.

"Oh my! We left him at the farm." Trey let go of Stacy and grabbed his jacket. "I've got to get him."

"Let's call first," Daniel said. He returned a moment later. "Good news, Henry is fine. Barbara's on her way to get him. Frankly, that's probably the best place for him to be right now. He needs to mend his relationship with his grandmother."

Trey fell back into the chair beside Stacy's bed. He kissed the back of her hand. "What's wrong with her, doc?" he asked his father-in-law.

"She has sepsis which means she has an infection in her whole body. We're giving her antibiotics—pretty strong ones. And that's why they keep taking blood tests."

"Thank goodness that vile bracelet finally came off," Trey said.

Daniel shoved his hands into his pants pocket and turned his face toward the window. "It's back in the incinerator now."

"Where did it come from?" Trey asked. "Stacy said, she got it from Grammy Lee."

Daniel put his hand on Trey's shoulder. "I'll talk to you about it outside. Right now, Stacy needs to rest."

Trey knew this was code for 'I'm not talking in front of Stacy.' He nodded, "Okay, I'll catch you later."

Trey's phone rang. He pulled it from his pocket and looked at the number. He turned toward Daniel and said, "It's Hannah."

32
Cory

"HE IS WEARING the armor of the High and Holy One. Why is he still here?" Asmodeous asked feeling the sting of losing Cory. "We can't touch him."

"I don't think he has a choice," Nisroch said, staring at the young man now humming. The dragons knew if he broke out in song again, they would all feel the blast of his praise. Even his presence weakened them.

"Many of the Holy One's followers try to live in our world thinking they will cause some people to follow Him."

"And sometimes they do," Belial groaned.

"We . . ."

"Have no hope. I know."

"So why?"

"Don't fool yourself. If the Holy One is leaving him here, even in an apparition, it's not for our good," Nisroch muttered through spear-like teeth.

Cory watched the dragons pace around him. He instinctively knew they couldn't come close to him or harm him.

Shawn and Derrick were no longer present; their essence was no longer in Cory's sight.

He could see and hear his parents and everything else that went on in the hospital room where his comatose body lay. He listened closely and heard a prayer. Surprised he realized it wasn't for him.

His hearing followed the muffled sounds. The sound of a father praying for his child and his wife. A woman praying for her child and grandchildren. The names were Hannah, Stacy, and Henry. Henry, his friend and classmate.

Cody didn't know the people. He liked Henry even if he was a loner. Cody knew these people were the reason he still resided in the damp darkness of the dragon's lair. Even though he no longer had to cling to a string, something mightier than string held him secure in a place that had no ceiling, no floor, no walls, no light, only dragons and demons. They walked on fire and breathed smoke.

"Master, what would you have me do?" Cory cried out in a loud voice. The dragons whimpered at the word *Master*.

A bright light illuminated the area, and Cory saw the true nastiness of the place. Hidden in the darkness lay trampled and crushed bones covered in maggots. The dragons walked or semi-walked and mostly slithered around the stone ruins of man-made idols, each one clothed with the bodies of those they had slain with deception and lies.

The glory of the Master brought air with a fresh aroma. The dragons hissed and lashed out at Him as He walked toward Cory. He swept an arm around the room and with a thunderous voice cried, "No! You will not arise and take possession of the earth. You will not build cities. You will not be united with Babylon. I will sweep you away into the swamp of destruction."

At the announcement, the dragons clung to the bones. They made no noise except to say, "Yes, Holy One."

Cory stood and felt the warmth and love of the Master.

"You will remain here for a little while longer," the Master told him. "You have a task that must be done."

Cory bowed his head. "Yes. What must I do?"

"You are to do battle with the demon, Jorkphat."

Nisroch heard the commission and groaned. The monster knew Jorkphat wouldn't win. Even a dragon heart feels pain. A tear crept down his snout knowing he would never see his offspring again.

The Master turned toward Nisroch. *"You should have obeyed when the Most High gave you the inheritance of Nineveh and separated you from the sons of man. He set boundaries, which you were not to cross, and gave each son of God a territory over which to watch. Instead, you judged unjustly and showed favor to the wicked. You made the sons of man weak and fatherless, you afflicted the orphan and destitute. They didn't know or understand, but you did, and now you gods will walk in darkness, and you will die like men."*

Nisroch roared, it was a noise of grief and regret for the days he took a human woman and conceived Jorkphat with her. The dragons pulled their demon children under their bellies and pulled their snouts into their crossed legs. They had no defense.

The Master placed a sword in Cory's hand. Letters moved across its silver blade like waves of water. The letters formed words.

Cory read the first words, "Blessed are the poor in spirit for theirs is the kingdom of God."

Cory took the sword and knelt on one knee. "As you wish, Master."

"Go!"

Immediately, Cory found himself in a hospital room, not his own. In the room of a small child—the one called Stacy. He saw the demon Jorkphat wrapped around her tiny body.

"Stand up, you coward!" Cory shouted. Only the demon heard.

"Well, if it isn't the scared little boy hanging by a thread." Jorkphat mocked and dug his claws deeper into Stacy. The prayers of the family removed the bracelet idol but not the demon.

Cory stood tall over the demon and raised the sword. The Words of God poured from the sword with each jab into the demon's body.

"You shall not have any gods before The Holy One of Israel!"

Jorkphat laughed to hide the slight sting he felt from the sword. He rose from Stacy's body and slammed himself into Cory.

He landed on a hard surface and broke his knife-like claw.

The sword began to sing.

Cory repeated the words it gave him as he plunged it into Jorkphat's body. *"For He rescued us from the domain of darkness and transferred us to the kingdom of His beloved Son, in whom we have redemption, the forgiveness of sins!"*

Jorkphat fell to the ground and groaned. "How?"

"God gave me truth; His word is truth." Cory took two jabs at the demon who now lay bleeding on the floor.

"What do you want?"

"Remove your curse from the child."

"I can't"

"Why not?" Cory demanded.

"I lost her grandmother; I won't lose her, and she must fall into the depths of hell."

"Her grandmother?"

"Our marriage was arranged. We would have been one," Jorkphat snarled at Cory.

Cory backed off a bit. "Barbara Holloway?"

Jorkphat nodded. "She's a Troye." He said the name as if he was spitting it out.

"What do you mean *one*?" Cory kept his sword aimed at Jorkphat, keeping him a prisoner of the truth.

"I would have inhabited her body."

"Why?"

"I'm a demon." Jorkphat said, "It's what we do . . . look for a body to inhabit, one whose mind is focused on themselves."

"I don't understand."

"I'm half-human and half-spirit."

"What does that mean?"

"It means when my human part dies, I am a spirit without a body."

"I don't believe you," Cory snorted.

"Look at you standing there with the supernatural armor of God wrapped around you and waving that sword. And you say you don't believe me," Jorkphat mocked Cory.

Cory lowered his sword as he looked down at the armor the Master had put upon him. "It is amazing," Cory said.

At the moment of realization, Jorkphat pulled the sword from Cory's hand and threw it in the air. His father, Nisroch pushed it into the air with his snout.

"Now you are unarmed." Jorkphat sneered at Cory.

"I still have my armor." Cory stood tall, even though Jorkphat grew taller. Another ugly dragon joined the demon.

"That protects you! Not the child."

Cory moaned, "I have failed." He fell to his knees and wept as he watched Jorkphat return to the little girl and claw at her tender body. She writhed with pain and grew hot with fever.

"I'll have my revenge on Barbara."

Trey prayed, "Lord I have walked in You, and You have never failed me. Please, if it can be Your will restore my child to health, please do so."

"You know that's His will," Cory said, even though Trey couldn't hear.

Jorkphat wouldn't give up until the death blow. "I won't give her up!" he shouted.

Trey pulled his phone and dialed a number he'd avoided for months—the number of the child's mother, Hannah.

Barbara entered the room. She gasped when she saw Jorkphat hovering over her granddaughter.

"Get out, you ugly beast!" she screamed.

Trey thought she was calling to him. "I'm sorry, Barbara, you can't talk to me that way. You have to leave." He took her by the arm and forcefully pushed her out of the room and closed the door behind her.

"What's going on?" Daniel asked as he ran up to Barbara.

"It's that ugly orange monster. It's on Stacy," she bellowed

Daniel peeked into the room window and saw him gnawing and clawing at Stacy, while Trey desperately tried to get the bracelet off. There was someone else in the room. He appeared to be looking for something.

"Cory's in there, and he's clothed in armor," Daniel said to Barbara.

She stepped up to the little window and saw Cory. "Praise God, He sent a warrior for her."

"He's not fighting the demon."

"What is he doing?"

"Looking for something."

Barbara ran to Daniel's office and shut the door. She slumped in a chair and prayed as she had never prayed before.

"Lord, send the boy help. I know you sent him to battle Jorkphat, he's in trouble." She continued to pray for hours.

Daniel joined her.

Michael saw the battle and asked the Master for help. Prayer in Paradise in the presence of the Master differed from prayer on earth. It came directly to the Master.

Michael asked to join Cory in the battle. "I've done battle with that nasty demon before," he pleaded.

At that time Davis stepped up and smiled at Michael. "Yes, we have."

The Master told Michael, "This is no longer your battle. Davis will help Cory."

Davis raised the sword of the Word in the air. "The beasts think they can throw it away, and it is no more." Davis chuckled and then joined Cory in a twinkling of an eye.

Cory didn't see Davis, he saw the sword. He grabbed it in his hand and shouted the cry of a warrior. He ran toward Jorkphat and raised the sword to land the deathblow.

"You are finished!"

The sword fell on the head of Jorkphat. The demon screamed.

The doorway to Tartarus opened.

Jorkphat glared at Cory. Then a cloud in the shape of a huge hand reached out from the doorway and pulled Jorkphat into the abyss.

Cory watched the child.

She opened her eyes, "Daddy," she said with a weak voice.

Trey smiled with tears rolling down his cheeks. "My baby."

"I'm hungry," she said.

Cory knew his task was complete. He let the sword fall to his side as he wandered over to the next hospital room. There his physical body lay, and his mother hovered over him praying. His father stood beside her, also praying.

He put his spirit arm around her, kissed her, and patted his dad's hand. "Thank you, Mom and Dad, for never giving up on me."

Mr. Frye wiped a tear away. "I love that boy," he said.

"I know you do. You taught him so many things."

"I had so many more things to teach him. I didn't talk to him enough."

"He knew you loved him." Mrs. Frye patted her husband's hand resting on her shoulder. She felt two hands.

"It's okay, son. I know you will be with our Lord. I can give you up to Him."

"Mr. Frye nodded and wailed, "Yes." He moaned and leaned over the bed and hugged the comatose body of his beloved son.

An angel stepped beside Cory. "Are you ready to go home?"

Cory nodded. The angel lifted him, and they flew to Paradise where Cory met his heavenly Father face to face.

Michael, Paps, Mrs. Waithe, and Peggy stood at heaven's portal waiting for his entrance and the celebration of his homecoming.

33
Temptation

HANNAH SAW THE number on her phone. She didn't want to talk to Trey; she had other people, or rather, a person on her mind. The new doc had asked her to join him for dinner. She hummed as she put on a little extra makeup and a dress that would make Trey blush. She fluffed her hair, and the doorbell rang.

Ishtar didn't like the fluffy hair. It made the demon owl sneeze. Still, she didn't lift her talons from the emotions of Hannah's mind.

She had prevented her from answering the phone call from Trey with a promise of attention from one of Lucifer's best servants. In return, Lucifer poured wealth, good looks, and smooth charm on the man. Ishtar felt the man could be Lucifer himself.

Hannah felt herself blush when she opened the door. She had admired her shapely figure in the mirror in her bedroom, standing before this co-worker, she felt almost naked.

"Wow, you look amazing," Parker said when he saw her.

She smiled and motioned for him to come inside. She bent over to get her wrap and purse. She caught a glimpse of herself in a small mirror. The dress didn't cover much and left little to the imagination. She stood and glanced back at herself. The dress tucked neatly around her backside.

"Excuse me a minute," she choked out while heading to her bedroom to change. She may be challenging all that her mother taught her, she still had some respect for herself.

Patrick followed her.

She stopped at the door, and with a firmer voice said, "Excuse me, I'm going to change clothes."

Patrick smiled and stroked the nape of her neck, causing her to melt at the soft touch and cringe at his audacity to do such a thing. She stood helpless with the physical sensation enveloping her senses.

"Sure you want to change?" he cooed.

Ishtar wiggled her talons into Hannah's emotions. She needed to get to those lust receptors.

At the same time, Hannah's grandfather, Buster stood at the altar of incense in Paradise and offered a prayer for her.

She felt confused. She wanted this romantic adventure with this handsome man, a feeling of dread crept alongside the feeling of pleasure.

She cleared her throat, "Yes, I have to change. I'm chilly." *What a silly excuse.*

Once she changed into a longer-length dress with a higher neck, she surveyed the results and felt the dress remained clingy enough to be interesting but not so much as to reveal everything. She smiled at the results. When she opened the bedroom door, she saw Patrick looking through her book collection.

"Are you a Christian?" He wrinkled his nose when he said *Christian*.

"Are you ready to go?" she asked, avoiding the question.

"Go? I didn't plan on going anywhere." Parker winked and gave her a silly grin.

"We're going to have dinner, aren't we?" Hannah insisted and headed toward the front door.

"Of course, we have to keep our strength up," Parker smirked.

Her shoulders slumped at the statement. "I really wanted to try the new restaurant."

"Okay, we'll go there, and then we can go to my apartment." He smiled with one side of his mouth.

Hannah excused herself. She hurried back to the bedroom and removed the tight-fitting costume and put on one of her more modest dresses.

"Why did you change again?" Parker asked.

"I feel more comfortable in this," Hannah answered.

Parker smiled. "Probably doesn't matter." He winked at her.

The statement went over Hannah's head because all she could see was Trey. She remembered their first date and smiled. He was so handsome and kind . . . and gentlemanly!

Hannah looked at Parker. He was a handsome devil, and that was exactly what he was—a devil.

Her friend and co-worker, Sylvia, warned her about him. "He uses his charm to win the heart of a woman, uses her up and then never speaks to her again." Sylvia pointed to the crew of women working on the floor. "Every one of us has had our day with him, and every one of us regrets it."

Hannah slammed the door with a loud noise as she shouted, "Don't ever call me again!" For the first time since she lived in this apartment, she locked all five locks on the door. She never wanted to see Parker again. Not even at work. She would ask for a transfer.

She went to her bedroom, closing the door behind her and fell on her bed. She sat opposite the dressing mirror. When she glanced up, she saw her mushed hair, smeared makeup, and . . . those awful purple marks on her neck. The man was an octopus with suction cups and eight arms.

She took a deep breath and went to the shower.

How was she going to hide this at work tomorrow? *I bet he did this on purpose so the whole floor would know he scored with the new nurse.*

She crawled into bed and turned on her side. Ironically, sitting on her nightstand was her favorite Bible. She reached over and touched it.

Ishtar screamed in pain. "No! Don't touch that awful thing!" she screeched, and with the touch, she felt her talons being pushed away from Hannah's emotions.

Hannah sat up on the edge of the bed and took the Bible in her hands. She thumbed through it. Wanting to read and yet afraid of reading. She landed in the middle of the book on Psalm 118.

She read aloud, "Give thanks to the Lord, his lovingkindness is everlasting, From my distress I called upon the Lord. The Lord answered me and set me in a large place. The Lord is for me; I will not fear; What can man do to me?"

She closed the Bible and put it back. She rolled onto her back and lay down. While staring at the ceiling, she asked in a prayerful tone, not really praying. "What can my mother do to me? More than she has already done? Do I give up my kids and husband just so I can be away from her?"

"If Your love is everlasting, then it doesn't matter what I say or do to my mother. You still love me. She isn't worth my love. The devil can have her."

Instead of asking for a transfer, I'll turn in my resignation and go home.

With the last thought, she smiled a bit and flipped the switch on the lamp.

Ishtar regained her grip on Hannah's emotions. She learned a bit more about her victim. Adultery was not the way to her destruction; hatred was the tool Ishtar needed. Hatred of her mother. A fun tactic because it would destroy several members of the Troye family and be especially devastating to Barbara and Daniel. It might even be the death blow to that horrid family.

Ishtar cackled with laughter as she lay a new plot.

Hannah's phone rang. She picked it up and saw that it was Trey. *He's the last person I want to talk to right now.* She silenced the ringing and rolled over to go to sleep. *I'll talk to him when I get home.*

Trey closed his phone and shook his head at Barbara. "Still no answer."

Barbara rose from her seat and walked over to the window. She crossed her arms in front of her and sighed. "What did I do?"

No one answered her, and the silence broke her heart. She didn't know how to get through to her beloved daughter. She turned back toward the living area where Hannah's family sat, sullen and quiet.

"I'm sorry I drove her away," Barbara said as she entered the room. "I don't know what I did. If she doesn't talk to me, how can I make amends?"

The anger of Nisroch seethed in large, black clouds of smoke coming from the grimace on the monster's snout. "You *are* sorry," he roared at Barbara.

His roar brought more hurt and self-pity on Barbara, and she continued in a tirade she knew couldn't be helpful.

"I don't know what I did to make her hate us all so much."

Henry raised his head. "Mom hates us?"

Trey frowned at Barbara. "No son, she has her own problems she needs to resolve."

"Mimi just said Mom hates us."

"Mimi's hurt just like you are; it makes her say things she doesn't mean."

Henry nodded and turned away from his grandmother. They both understood Trey's statement.

The smoke from Nisroch's snout turned from black to white. A sign that his pleasure at the family's pain was greater than his anger and agony. His pleasure came at Barbara's expense.

"You cursed my son, now I will curse your child," Nisroch said in Barbara's ear.

The pain in Barbara's heart at her daughter's accusation caused her to neglect her Bible study, and prayer became a conversation held with the wall while she bemoaned her own pain, and she could no longer see the dragons or the demons.

The evil plots wrapped around her. She didn't have the strength nor the weapons to battle the dragons.

Trey's heart grew cold and colder with each day that Hannah deserted her family. Her children needed her, she was too busy 'finding herself.' Trey's love for Hannah turned into a cold, lumpy gravy of anger mixed with an undying love.

Davis stayed close to Hannah. He watched her sleep and marveled at how much she looked like her mother. He remembered the day he and Michael fought for Barbara before Jorkphat took possession of her body. Hannah's dilemma was worse than Barbara's. Hannah was very close to grieving the Holy Spirit and from that, she would never return. Christ could forgive offenses against Him, He could not forgive an offense against the Holy Spirit.

Davis knelt beside Hannah's bed, "Master, don't let her go," he pleaded.

Michael and Mrs. Waithe were with the Master at the altar of incense. They heard Davis cry out. They both affirmed the angel's plea, "Amen!" They said in unison. The Master's face held no expression, nor were there any Words from Him.

Ishtar didn't want to do battle with Davis, but the need to get into Hannah's unconscious mind with a dream served as her only path to destroy Hannah. It would be delicious to see Hannah's response to her mother's past. The distorted dream could only work with the knowledge Hannah already possessed.

Nonetheless, there were ways to give a nightmare a realistic feel and a glimpse into some horrible things from the realm of man. Tonight, Hannah would gain more hatred of her mother as she learned of her participation in a witch's coven meeting.

The next morning Hannah woke up with a chill. The dream was horrible. She saw her mother killing a baby and offering it up to a horrible beast. And her mother was laughing.

"That's just like her. She's a narcissistic old bitty. She would kill a baby with no regrets."

Ishtar dug her claws deeper into Hannah's emotions and fed hatred into her.

Davis came at Ishtar with his sword drawn. It caused Ishtar to lose balance for a moment, the talons of the beast stayed embedded in Hannah's brain where her will and emotions lay.

Ishtar screeched, thinking about this so-called child of the Holy One rejecting Him and turning away. Just like it said in the Master's book, *It would be better she never tasted the good things of the spirit, for there is no hope.*

That leaves hope for me to kill this human creature."

Davis put his wings around Hannah and poured her mother's love into her. He hoped it would be strong enough to overcome the evil of Ishtar.

Hannah dressed quickly. She had to get her resignation off to the DON. As she passed by the mirror, she saw the awful huge purple bruising on her neck. "He must be some kind of vampire," She mocked, she looked for bite marks even though she knew it was impossible.

She called Trey. He wouldn't have called her so many times if it weren't important.

"I'm coming home," she said as soon as Trey told her about Stacy and Henry.

Davis said, "Flee idolatry." Then he smiled, although he knew her real battle was only beginning. Her sin was separating her from the Lord, but not from His love. The Master would not let go until total rejection of the Master.

However, to bring her into His family, she would have hard lessons to learn.

Hannah's loss and suffering would be great. He knew the Master's plan for Hannah, and it saddened him. Davis knew because he was the messenger the Master commissioned to carry out the plan.

Davis knew it was better to save the spirit than to save the flesh. Knowledge of the outcome didn't make the battle any easier.

34

Death

A SMALL TOWN knows every loss and feels the emptiness of every soul as they depart from earth. Church Creek Falls lost three of its young men.

Cory's funeral brought the town to the church. The crowd overflowed to outside the vestibule.

"Why do these humans do this?" Asmodeous asked Nisroch.

"They're stupid; that's why," Nisroch growled.

"What are we doing here?"

Nisroch raised a scaly leg and pointed to a young boy about midway in the church audience. "For that one."

"Do you know the plan?"

Nisroch whipped his long, spikey snout toward Asmodeous, the vampire dragon, and shouted, "The same as always, we are here to kill him!"

Asmodeous smiled. "Do I get to feed on that bag of blood?"

"That's not how it works." Nisroch extended a sharp claw and reached out to the back of Henry Mitchell's neck. He stroked the boy.

Henry could feel the fly or spider or whatever going across his neck. He tried to swat it away. It came back in a few seconds.

"I like to play with my food," Nisroch chuckled.

Asmodeous smiled and joined Nisroch.

Nisroch pushed his hand aside. "Don't be a fool. We don't want him to know we're here."

"So, then what?" Asmodeous asked.

"Whisper in his ear."

"What?"

"Tell him he's ugly, he doesn't have a future; tell him he's a murderer. It doesn't matter, just tell him all the bad things."

"Do they have to be true?"

Nisroch laughed at Asmodeous. "We're dragons. We never tell the truth."

Hannah smiled to herself, and her heart felt happy. Today, she would see her family again.

The empty house filled Hannah with disappointment. Maybe they gathered at the farm. On the drive to the farm, she saw the large crowd and the hearse at the church.

With a sigh, she turned back to her house in town. They would be home as soon as the funeral ended. Whomever the deceased, they drew a large crowd.

She rummaged through the refrigerator looking for something to eat. After heating the few leftovers she found, she took a bite and spit it out. *I thought Trey was a better cook than this.* "It's probably the vile poison of mother's cooking," she spouted aloud.

Tired from the trip, she thought a nap sounded wonderful.

The cackle of her mother's voice woke her. Hannah rose from the couch and opened the front door. Her mother had her filthy hands on Stacy.

"Leave her alone!" she shouted at her mother.

Barbara gasped. "I wasn't . . ."

Stacy and Henry stared at their mother. Barbara stood beside the children gazing at her.

Hannah squinted her eyes at Barbara, and with a sneer, she said, "If I wanted to see you, I would come to see you."

"Hannah, I love you," Barbara said with a quiet voice.

Hannah turned her face to one side, and for a brief moment, her demeanor softened. "I know you do," she responded.

Then her brow knitted, and a frown covered her lips. "Now, leave me alone and respect my boundaries. This is my house, and I don't want you in it."

Trey finished locking the car and opened the front door to see everyone standing in the doorway of the living room. "What's going on?" he asked as he unburdened his arms. Then he saw her, his wife, Hannah facing his children and mother-in-law.

He walked past everyone to the kitchen. "Anyone hungry? Mimi brought a casserole for us."

"Yes!" Henry exclaimed. "Some good food."

Hannah's anger rose. "If it's not poison. She's evil, you know."

Stacy glared at her mother. "She didn't leave us."

Barbara told Trey she would go outside and wait for Daniel. He had served as a pallbearer and was delayed getting to the family home.

Trey nodded in understanding.

Barbara walked outside and down the road. She managed to keep herself in check until she reached the end of their block. She stood on the corner with a ducked head, a broken heart, and a tear-stained face. Her own daughter, her precious baby, the girl she prayed for had just cast her out of her home and her family. How would she ever recover?

Henry walked past his mother without looking at her. "At least I didn't kill her."

Hannah snorted at Henry's remark. "Too bad."

Trey closed the oven door and glared at Hannah. "You better be careful; you may not have a home either."

Hannah could feel her spirit falling. Trey had never spoken to her in that tone. She noticed his hair graying around the temples, wrinkles around his mouth. He had aged, and it wasn't good.

"Trey, I—"

"I don't want to hear it." He sat down at the table where he placed three plates.

"Don't I get one?" she said with a slight smile.

"You think it's poison, eat at your own risk."

"I don't think—"

"That's right, you don't think and besides it doesn't matter what you think." Trey interrupted her again, making it plain he didn't want to hear any of her excuses.

Before she left, Hannah had shared every thought and activity with him. He was her greatest admirer. This indifference scared her more than anything else. She got herself a plate and sat down at the table. Henry was sitting in her place. She didn't mention it.

Trey and the kids spoke of Cory and his family. They talked about the service. Hannah sat in silence and listened.

Trey and the kids finished eating. They each rose from the table, rinsed their plates, and placed them in the dishwasher.

Hannah started late, and she had to admit the casserole her mother made was delicious. She didn't realize how hungry she was for good food. She wanted to finish, so she stayed at the table while her family left the dining area.

Before he left the room Trey turned back toward her and said, "I made up the guest room for you. You can stay in there."

"For how long?" Hannah gasped.

Stacy swallowed a big bite of the cookie and answered the question. "Until you love us—all of us—again."

35

Home Bitter Home

ISHTAR LOVED BEING in Hannah's home. There was so much love and respect to destroy. The ugly creature pondered what method of suicide to put into Henry's head. It wouldn't be hard with the hatred Hannah spewed for her mother. She taught Henry that grandparents are disposable.

Retirement didn't meet its expectations for Barbara and Daniel. The new doctor called almost every day. He was young and inexperienced. He also lacked confidence in his abilities. The nurses helped him as much as they could. Still they felt frustrated with his many mistakes.

Barbara received calls almost every day from the nurses. The call she received today left her speechless.

Hannah applied for the Director of Nurses job. That wasn't surprising because she was well-qualified and had been considered for the job before she left for South Dakota. A problem arose with the nursing staff. They didn't want her.

"What's wrong?" Barbara inquired of Brenna, the day shift charge nurse.

"Her attitude. She makes everyone miserable around her."

"I don't understand. Is she not doing her job?" Barbara asked.

"Not very well. She's too busy grumbling and sputtering about how bad everything. She especially denigrates you."

"Did I mess things up?" Barbara asked Brenna.

"Hannah wants to completely do away with all our software and purchase a different program. We all like the one you purchased, and we know how to use it. If we get a different program . . . that means entering all the data again."

"In the end, the hospital board has to make that decision, so you need to file your concerns with them."

"We did. Hannah went and met with all the members and apparently convinced them you were not of sound mind, and they couldn't depend on anything you had instigated."

Barbara fell back in her chair. "I'm sorry, Brenna. Is there anything I can do?"

"Can't you talk to her?"

"That's the last thing I can do."

Barbara laid her phone on the table. She rose and went to the bathroom. Her stomach rolled like a tornado. When she came out, she sat down in her chair, bent over, and cried. Through her tears, she prayed. "What can I do?"

A few thoughts went through her head nothing productive. She pulled her Bible from the bottom shelf of the end table. Turned on the reading light behind her chair and opened the Bible. She had no plan, so she read a few passages, they made little sense to her.

Then she turned to Psalms. That was always a place of comfort. She read the eighty-third Psalm.

"O God, do not remain quiet; do not be silent and, O God, do not be still. For behold, your enemies make an uproar. And those who hate You have exalted themselves. They make shrewd plans against Your people and conspire together against Your treasured ones. They have said, 'Come and let us wipe them out as a nation, that the name of Israel be remembered no more.' For they have conspired together with one mind; against You they make a covenant."

Barbara dropped the open Bible into her lap, leaned back in her chair, and sighed. "This is what's happening, isn't it?" she asked the Lord.

She read the rest of the paragraph and in verse eight, she read, "They have become a help to the children of Lot."

The last sentence put her on a quest. Why would the children of Lot be helping the dragons?

Of course, the dragons are the enemies of God and His family! She pulled out her big concordance and looked up Lot. She found the genealogy of Lot in Genesis 19:19. He had two sons by his two daughters: Moab, and Ammon. So why do these people become a help to the dragons? The question still reigned in her mind.

She found Deuteronomy 2:9, and her jaw dropped. The Israelites were not to bother the Moabites because they had destroyed the Emims. The Emims were the giant and evil people who lived in the land before the Moabites. That meant the Emims could have been Nephilim. Why would they be called the help of the children of Lot? What are the children of Lot doing?

Barbara had to ponder this statement. Not because she was curious about what happened. Rather because the passage in Psalm described her current situation so plainly. God remained silent regarding Hannah's hatred. From this passage regarding the enemies of God, she learned the uproar in the dragon's lair was against Israel, and they made shrewd plans against God's people.

"Well, that includes me. I'm one of your people," Barbara said to the ceiling, hoping for some insight.

Daniel entered the room just as she said it. "Whose people?"

"God's," she answered while staring into her Bible.

"What are you looking for?"

Barbara read the passage to Daniel. He sat down in his chair next to Barbara, steepled his fingers over his mouth, and nodded. When she finished he spoke, "Look at Jeremiah 2:5."

As Barbara thumbed through her Bible, the doorbell rang.

Daniel rose to answer it.

Barbara continued to read the passage; she read the verses before and after.

Zay came into the living room with Barbara, and Marcy took a plate of food to the kitchen.

"What's that?" Barbara asked her sister-in-law.

"Your favorite cake."

"A homemade Red Velvet with French Buttercream?" Barbara asked with a big grin.

Marcy nodded and filled the coffee carafe with water to make coffee. "We'll have some as soon as the coffee's done." She smiled and joined Barbara in the living room. She noticed Barbara's Bible in her lap. "Looks like some good reading," she said. Barbara smiled and squeezed Marcy's hand.

"Not only is it good, it's giving me some explanations for Hannah."

"Uh oh!" Zay said, "That's the reason we came."

Daniel nodded. "Tell us. . ."

"The hospital staff wants her to go away. Did you know she went to each of the board members begging for the DON job? Even though it has been filled."

Barbara pursed her lips and ducked her head. "I heard."

"What is the board thinking? Or do you know?"

"Not much, they have questioned me and Marcy about her."

"What did you tell them?" Barbara asked.

"That she has estranged from her family, and we don't know much."

Daniel raised an eyebrow and grunted.

Barbara leaned back and turned her face toward the glass doors looking out on their patio with her chin resting on her fist.

Marcy spoke up. "Tell me what you were reading." She pointed to the Bible.

Barbara read the verses in Jeremiah 2. *"Hear the word of the Lord, O house of Jacob, and all the families of the house of Israel, Thus says the Lord, What injustice did your fathers find in Me, that they went far from Me and walked after emptiness and became empty?"*

"Wow!" Marcy said with wide eyes.

"I know, God knows what I'm going through. He knows my hurt."

"And you know His heart now," Marcy added. She patted her sister-in-law's hand.

After a few moments of silence, the coffee pot beeped. Marcy went into the kitchen, poured the four of them a cup of coffee, and cut the cake. She brought the treats into the living room on a tray then sat down,

The doorbell rang again.

Daniel finished the bite of cake on his fork. "It's a busy place today."

"We called a family gathering," Zay said. "It's probably Rance and Jenny."

"And Jason," Daniel added as he opened the door.

Marcy served as host and prepared plates for the rest of the family.

"Why do I feel like this is an intervention?" Barbara asked.

"Because it is," Rance added. "It's your turn now."

"Actually, we're here to pray for Trey and Hannah." Zay explained.

Barbara and Daniel clasped hands. Barbara leaned her head on Daniel's shoulder. "Thank you."

Ishtar clung to Hannah's emotion by planting more ideas that had a germ of truth. She could turn a simple act of saying hello into a monumental abuse situation. Hannah's black heart received the lies like desert rain.

Hannah came home from her shift, satisfied she would be given the DON job. She was the most qualified. Besides, the lamebrain new doc needed her expertise. He was a lawsuit waiting to happen, and she let the board know it. His little wife filled the DON job, and that was like a high schooler doing a CEO job.

Hannah showered and pulled on a housedress. She went to the kitchen where Trey and the kids were eating dinner. "Humm, Smells good," she said as she walked over to the stove. No one responded except Stacy.

"I made it, Momma. You can have some if you want."

Hannah glanced at Trey. He didn't acknowledge her presence.

Henry glanced at her and smiled. She smiled back as she put a little of the food on her plate. She worked real hard at not grimacing For a ten-year-old, she did a pretty good job for taste. It was the appearance of a conglomerate of refrigerator leftovers.

Hannah sat down at the table. Trey rose, took his plate to the kitchen, washed it, and put it in the dishwasher. He went to his pickup, started the engine, and drove off.

"Where's your dad going?" she asked Henry.

He shrugged his shoulders and kept eating.

Stacy asked her mother, "How do you like it?"

"It's delicious, darling. You did a good job."

"Mimi taught me," Stacy volunteered.

Hannah pursed her lips and bit her tongue to keep from saying anything. However, Stacy's comment stole her appetite. She pushed the casserole under a slice of bread and ate her salad.

After Stacy finished her dinner, Hannah rose and cleaned her plate too. Henry went to his room, and she could hear his video games firing up.

Stacy turned on the television and plopped in front of the cartoon channel. Hannah sat down in a chair and picked up a book. It didn't take long for sleep to overtake her.

Ishtar loosened a tight grip on Hannah and flew back to Sheol and the dragon's lair. The creature flew straight to Belial's throne and landed on the commander's claw.

"Have you been watching?"

Belial didn't like being interrupted, and Ishtar committed that sin. The monster pushed Ishtar off his leg and growled. "What do you want?"

"Reporting in. The Mitchell family is falling apart."

"Why are you here?"

"She's asleep, I wanted to come to make a report," Ishtar added.

"You want some praise?"

She turned her horned head around full circle and cooed.

"Well, it isn't coming. Get back to your post. Don't you know sleep is a prime time to work on her and, if you aren't working on her, then who is?" Belial spat out a flame.

Ishtar screeched and made sure to dig deep into Belial's scaly flesh with long talons before flying back to the post in Hannah's emotions.

Hannah slept with no dark dreams and woke refreshed. She stretched and looked around. Stacy was gone. She wondered to Henry's room where it was eerily quiet.

He was gone too. Trey's pickup was gone. She walked outside. It was so quiet, not even cars passing. *Am I still asleep?*

She decided she would call a friend and invite them to the movies. She called three of her former co-workers. They all declined. She called a couple of her high-school buddies, and they too declined.

"I guess I'm alone."

The one movie theatre in town carried one movie at a time. This wasn't one she'd choose. It was billed as a family movie. She bought some popcorn and a soda then entered the theatre and searched for a seat.

She almost dropped her popcorn when she saw Trey and the kids. She noticed that of the so-called friends she invited, most of them were there with their husbands and kids.

She stood in the middle of the aisle like an idiot deciding whether to sit or leave. At that moment, Ishtar landed on her emotions. Her heart hardened, and she sat down behind Trey and the kids.

"Why didn't you tell me you were coming? I would have come with you," she cooed with a sugar-sweet voice.

"Just leave us alone," Stacy heard her dad say.

Hannah leaned back in the seat and looked around at the families sitting together. Pain pierced her heart at the realization; she no longer belonged to a family, either as a mother and wife or as a daughter. A tear crept down her chin and she felt more alone at home, than she had in South Dakota. She rose and left. With nowhere to go and no one to see, she drove around the countryside reliving memories of her childhood –happy memories.

Ishtar panicked at the smile on Hannah's face. The monster owl was losing her grip on Hannah's emotions.

The next morning, Hannah tried to start a conversation with Trey. He stared at her with a firm lip. She wanted to kiss those lips and hold those broad shoulders. She could feel her body craving his attention and his touch. She truly loved this man.

Ishtar dug around a little deeper. Her love for Trey interfered in the plot of evil against Hannah. Hannah's hatred for her mother should destroy the whole family. Ishtar felt an urgency to conclude the devised plan.

The Troye family including Merilee, Zay, Marcy, Rance, Jenny Gale, Jason, Alyssa, Daniel, and Barbara prayed for Hannah every day. The repetition and mundane prayers continued in spite of seeing little change in Hannah's character.

36

Jason

JASON LEANED BACK in the tractor cab and watched the sun come up. He loved working on the farm in the mornings. Today his emotions took a different route. He had a real weekend date with Naomi. At least he considered it a real date, Naomi may think he's proselytizing. He planned a trip to his favorite Christian campground in the mountains. Naomi would hear solid preaching, beautiful music, play games, eat good food, and sit in classes. Ever since she asked him about hell, he fed her more information about Jesus and heaven.

He knew the beauty of nature at the campground would set the stage for an in-depth weekend into the working of the Lord. The primary speaker was a well-known scholar who could explain the Bible to a non-believer better than anyone he ever heard.

Jason told his brother-in-law Trey he would be leaving around three p.m. He wanted to stop and talk to his brother, Rance before he left.

When Jason walked into his brother's home, he felt sadness at seeing Rance aging. The once-robust man carried Jason on his shoulders for the first year when the Troyes' adopted he and Alyssa.

Jason went to the kitchen where his Jenny Gale was baking a cake. "Smells like mom's cake," he said and picked up the empty bowl to lick it.

"It's her recipe. There was something about the cake that held the family together." Jenny Gale smiled at him and handed him the mixer beaters.

"She always said it was the love." Jason and Jenny Gale smiled.

"Mom, doesn't cook much now that dad is gone," Jason mused.

"No, and my cakes don't have the same effect, or we would be a complete family."

Jason shook his head, "I don't know how we can get through to Hannah. I wish a piece of cake would do it," he said as he washed the bowl and the beaters.

"Have you seen Barbara lately?"

"She comes by often. I want to help her. All I can do is listen, and she doesn't talk much, so we pray."

"She's hurting."

"She fears for Hannah's spirit."

"So do I. There's something different about Hannah. And it's not good."

"Stick around about twenty minutes and have a piece of warm cake."

"I would love to, but I've got to go. I'm picking Naomi up at six tonight."

"You leaving tonight?"

"No, tomorrow morning. We're packing tonight."

Jason heard Rance moving around. "Did you want to see me?" he asked.

Jason followed Rance into his office and sat opposite him. He leaned over his legs and stared at the floor.

"What's on your mind?" Rance asked.

"Naomi."

"That's no surprise. Anyone can see your puppy-dog eyes when you look at her."

Jason laughed and sat up looking Rance in the face. "She's not a believer."

Rance nodded. "I've seen . . . that same demon we dealt with when looking for Jenny Gale."

Rance leaned toward Jason. "That horrid owl?"

Jason nodded. "It's on Hannah."

"I felt it. Did you see it?"

Jason nodded. "Once, when Naomi was with me. I saw it with a claw on Hannah's head and one on Naomi's. Just for a second."

"Do you think you actually saw it or was it a memory?"

"That's why I wanted to talk to you. I'm taking Naomi to Rolling Hills Campground tomorrow."

"That's great!" Rance sat back and rested his arms on the chair.

"How do I—"

"Tell her the joy of Christ?" Rance interrupted.

Jason nodded.

"You know that is the work of the Holy Spirit. It says in Matthew that the Holy Spirit introduces Jesus to the soul. Trust the camp. She'll not hear anything there that will turn her away."

"Even if that vile thing goes with her?"

"It can't. Too much Scripture around. Besides, it'll stay here with Hannah. The bruts can only be in one place at a time. I just pray the experience at the campground brings us another warrior against that owl. It's a fierce one," Rance said.

Jason pursed his lips. "Did you know Hannah lost her job?"

"No, I heard she visited all the board members begging for the DON job. I thought they would keep her as a nurse."

"It appears she schmoozed them all."

"Then why didn't she get the job?"

"Trey is a well-respected man, and Barbara has been in that position longer than Hannah's been alive. I heard she tried to convince them of Barbara's ineptness."

Rance shook his head.

"Trey moved her out of the house," Jason continued.

"What? Where is she?"

"I think Trey is paying rent for her at the Boise House."

Hannah surveyed her new habitat. A camping tent would have been nicer. She dropped her suitcase on the bed and noticed it leaned to one side.

She went into the kitchen to see a rusted sink, an old, fifties-style refrigerator, and a two-burner cooktop. A small toaster oven sat in one corner of the five-foot cabinet area.

She sighed. *Maybe I need to go back to South Dakota. I came here to make up with Trey, but I don't think he loves me anymore.*

Davis followed behind Hannah.

Ishtar clung to her head.

"I'm so alone."

Ishtar laughed. "If you could only see the crowd gathering around you."

Several dragons clung to the ceiling of the small garage apartment. They flicked their tongues in delight. This was their kind of place, and they loved seeing humans wallowing in such disarray. It felt like home.

"Look over there," one dragon said to the other, pointing at Davis.

"What's a messenger of the Holy One doing here?"

"She still belongs to the Holy One and her family prays for her continually."

"You're kidding, and we're all around her?"

The dragon nodded. "We take what we can get. This one is so full of hate and unforgiveness she has a wide-open gate for us."

"Don't kid yourself. Battle with the Holy One for one of His children is never easy."

"She—"

"Don't even say it."

"She's so . . . so . . ."

"Bitter!"

"Do we get to crush her body, even if we can't take her spirit?"

"Don't know yet. We have to wait on Belial. He'll give the orders."

Hannah opened her computer and sat down at the distressed kitchen table. She snickered. Distressed wasn't a decorating term for the table but a description of the reject from a flood. Hannah took a piece of paper, folded it, and placed it under one of the legs.

That helped.

"I don't understand how they could fire me," she moaned to herself.

"I gotta find a job."

Rance grabbed Jason's upper arm. "Watch out for Naomi; she might have a rough road ahead if that old screech owl is looking at her."

Jason nodded. "You know I will."

"You'll have a hard time too. Stay in the Word," Rance warned his brother. "Trey is so hurt he can't make good decisions," he added. "Don't join him."

"I know. I'm taking over more of the farming management. He's still the boss, but a farm is a dangerous place and needs full attention."

Jenny Gale came in with three pieces of warm cake and three glasses of cold milk. Jason could almost see the delight in his brother's eyes.

Rance took a big bite, closed his eyes, and let the warmth of the cake cover his senses. After a big gulp of milk to wash it down, he turned to Jason and said, "Love will always overcome evil."

"You're not kidding about the love," Jason said to Jenny Gale

"No, love will see you through any trial because God is love, and that's the only true cure for anything," Jenny Gale replied and winked. "Believe me, I know. It rescued me." She gave Rance a hug and a peck on the head.

Jason prayed that someday he could bring Naomi out here and that she would understand the things of the Lord that came from his family.

"We'll keep praying for Naomi's salvation from the dragons and her entrance into the kingdom of God," Rance said as Jason left.

"Maybe it's time for a big dose of pain," Belial roared.

Dragons wouldn't give up a human that belonged to them without a battle. Most people would faint before the battle finished. Belial noticed that humans often didn't even draw their swords, God's Bible, when they had one. They certainly didn't spend any time getting it sharpened and prepared for battle. So, devouring them came easy.

It wasn't true with the Troye family. They all had sharp swords. All except Hannah. Ishtar found a compliant adversary against the rest of the family in that human. She planted a seed of hate and nurtured it to take root in the family.

"I think that's about it," Jason said, staring into the back of his SUV loaded with a week's worth of camping gear. They'd be staying in rustic dorm-like cabins for the week. He with the guys and she with the girls on opposite sides of the camp.

Naomi thought that was so old-fashioned.

Jason felt grateful. When he was around Naomi, he lost control of his good sense.

Next to Naomi walked the female dragon, Venus. "We'll help her seduce him," Venus said to Ishtar.

37

In Heaven's Eyes

PEOPLE FROM ALL different races join with their tribes, their family linage to join the nations in praise to the Master. "In Your presence is fullness of joy; at Your right hand are pleasures forevermore." The chorus written by David, the son of Jesse, resounded as the Master entered among the family of God.

Cory felt joy bubbling inside at the mention of the Master. As the center of light walked among the heavenly family, Cory knew he was home, and new adventures waited around every corner.

"You've learned something new today," The Master spoke to Cory.

With a big smile across his face, Cory answered, "Yes, Master."

"What have you learned?"

"On earth, I thought being in heaven would be boring."

"Why did you think that?"

"Because Christians were boring." Cory blushed as the words came out of his mouth. "I'm sorry."

"It's okay; I know what you are saying. Most people think sin is fun and Christianity is boring."

"I can't imagine why, I know I used to think that too." Cory stepped closer to the Master.

"What did you discover?"

"The art section."

The Master smiled and put his arm around Cory's shoulders. "You know I put the heart of an artist in you." The Master led Cory to a private area.

Cory ducked his head and nodded. "I was ashamed. I thought I needed to be a football player."

"I didn't give you the body to play football. I gave you imagination and the ability to see color."

"How come? I never showed any of my work to anyone."

"Your parents found your secret stash of drawings." The Master told him, and he sat down on a bench.

Cory sat next to him. "Oh, no!"

"What's wrong?"

"I drew those before—"

"Before you received the helmet of salvation." The Master finished his sentence.

Cory nodded. "My mother always loved you; she will be disappointed."

"What did you draw?"

"Dragons."

The Master smiled. "They were good representations too."

"They were."

"Yes, and they will be helpful when your hometown sees the dragons."

"I saw them and . . . I—" Cory shuddered.

"There are no dragons here, no need to fear them. I defeated their vile plans for humankind when I died on earth and was resurrected."

"How did you do that?"

"Peter told you in my book, but few people understand it."

"I'm sorry, I didn't read Your book much when I was on earth. My mother read it to me. I didn't pay much attention." Again, Cory blushed in the presence of his Savior.

"You saw the dragons and their pit."

Cory nodded. "Thank you for taking that horrible experience from me."

"When I died, I went there too."

"You did?" Cory looked up at the beautiful face of pure love.

"I did, and I told them they would never escape that place."

Cory's whole body shuddered. "Thank you for removing that curse from me." Cory leaned his head on the Master's chest.

"I did it for all mankind."

"Then why?"

"Why were there people there with the dragons? Is that what you wonder?"

Cory nodded.

"Because they thought I was boring. Few people understand the eternal thrill of constant joy and happiness. People rejected me. All people are born sinners and automatically belong to the dragons."

"Then how did all these people get here?"

"They accepted My free gift of salvation from the evil of the dragons and the wrath of the father at the dragons.

"Once the dragons claim a person at death and they go to the place of the dragons, known as Hades, then they have no way of escape."

"Then how did I escape?"

"You didn't, you were never there."

"What?"

"Remember that string you kept holding on to?"

"Yes, and I was grateful for it."

The Master laughed. "That was Me holding your life. The dragons were drooling over you. I didn't want them to have you. My Father and I are patient; we will wait for one to see us and call upon My name."

"How come the dragon came in the first place?'

"What were you doing when the dragon came to you?"

Cory shook his head. "I can't remember, except it wasn't good."

"That's right. Your actions were the deeds of the dragons. When you follow the dragon's lies and live in those lies, then the dragon has access to your mind. They wander around the earth seeking weak people so they can devour them. You were available to the dragon."

"How did I escape, and the others didn't?"

"You mean your friends Shawn and Derrick?"

"Yeah."

"They rejected Me, when their spirit departed from their physical body, they were instantly in Hades."

Cory frowned. "I saw them with the dragons—"

"Illusions the dragons conjured up to make you scared enough to let go of Me. You were found before your lifeblood was gone. I gave the gift of the knowledge of healing the body to the people who found you. Although you were almost gone, they were able to keep you alive for a little longer. That's when I gave you the string. Because your mother and father were praying for you, I saw you."

"Their prayers saved my life?"

The Master nodded.

"About those pictures I drew; you said they were good. How?"

"The dragons are planning a huge war on Church Creek Falls and the people there. They will not be able to hide as easily because of your pictures."

"How did I draw the beasts so accurately?"

"Because they were always around you. Their image was imprinted upon your mind so you would not see me."

Cory took a deep breath of the crisp, clean air. "Thank you, Master." Cory clung to Him and wept. "I'm so sorry for my sins against you."

The time in Heaven is not like time on earth, and Cory basked in the love of his Savior holding him tight. Then a thought occurred to him.

"If prayer saved me, then can prayer save the Mitchell family?"

The Master nodded. "It can, sometimes the sin is so willful, there has to be discipline."

"What does that mean?"

"I love Hannah, the problem is that she will not forgive those whom she perceives wronged her."

"Was she wronged?"

"Everyone is wronged. The dragons will do whatever they can to cause one to harm another, and they are having a party over Hannah."

"Can't you stop them and tell her the truth?"

The Master didn't give Cory an answer instead He asked him a question. "What did it take for you to believe?"

Cory understood. "You won't make her, will you?"

"No, I give her the gift of being a member of our family, if she cannot forgive, she will not be forgiven."

"I don't understand. She's a Christian."

"One who loves me will keep my commandments and forgiving is one of my commandments. If she doesn't forgive many people in her life, then she never belonged to Me."

A chorus of voices rose to the Master's ears. He raised his head high in the air and took a deep breath. "The sacrifice of praise smells so sweet."

"When you arrive back at your home, you will find many artist materials. I can't wait to see what you create." Then the Master moved.

Cory could see His light moving among the crowd. He would comfort another member of His family. *My family.*

A beautiful, grey-haired, young woman stepped up beside Cory. "It takes God's image-bearers to develop, expand, and enrich the earth, even the new earth."

Cory smiled and greeted his sister in Christ, "Hello Mrs. Waithe. My earthly mother often spoke of you and your faithfulness."

"Your mother and grandmother came to my house for Bible study during one of our wars with the dragons. Your mother was a little girl at the time. I loved holding her. She would always go to sleep in my arms."

"That's what she told me." Cory smiled. "I have a question. How come you still have grey hair, even though you are young?"

Mrs. Waithe laughed at Cory and gave him a gentle pat on his arm. "It's my crown. I served my Master faithfully during my earthly life. In His book, he says the grey hair has wisdom and they earn it. I fought those nasty dragons for years; I think I earned this crown." She snickered.

Cory gave her a toothy grin and said, "It sure is pretty."

"Come, I'll show you around. This is a beautiful place, and there is always a new adventure waiting."

38

When Love Enters

TREY STOOD TALL next to his in-laws. He loved them, but he truly wanted the peace of solitude. They came to his house every night to pray over Hannah. They didn't understand until he explained his heart hardening toward Hannah.

Trey was through with Hannah. He loved her with such a fierce love that the pain of her rejection pierced him to the core of his spirit. He couldn't pray for her anymore. He asked them to keep praying somewhere else. He could no longer host the prayer sessions.

He told them Hannah no longer lived at the house. Henry went to the movies with his friends, and Stacy was at a birthday party. When Barbara and Daniel arrived, they exchanged hugs and tears with few words. Trey asked them to stay and have dinner with him. His mother and father-in-law provided him with the comfort of shared pain and understanding.

Barbara asked, "What did I do?"

Trey pulled Barbara close to him and wrapped his arms around her. "I don't know, I've looked back over the years, and it wasn't one thing. She's been angry at someone most of her life. When it wasn't me, I ignored it." He let go of Barbara and she stepped back.

Daniel nodded in agreement. "We spoiled her."

Trey chuckled a bit. "And I picked up where you left off."

The trio sat at the dinner table and didn't mention Hannah again for the rest of the night. They discussed Nathan and Emily and decided there would be a wedding in their near future. Jason wanted a wedding, with a bride filled with love and obedience to the Lord, and he wanted Naomi to be the bride. The two weren't compatible yet.

Nisroch, Asmodeous, and Belial sat on the roof of the house. "How do we get to them?" Asmodeous asked.

"We don't. We have to wait until they come out of that hedge the Holy One built around them. Our only hope is Henry."

Henry finished another bottle of beer. He didn't much like the taste, he liked the way it made him feel. He stopped so he could have some semblance of sobriety.

When he arrived at his house, he was surprised to see his grandparents there. He popped a breath mint in his mouth and joined them.

After eating a nice serving of dinner, his dad suggested they play some cards. Henry was looking for an excuse to get away from his grandmother. He did love her.

When she started trying to have a conversation with him, he didn't know how to talk to her, and she didn't know how to talk to him. After all, how do you talk to someone who tried to kill you?

The card game was fun: the four of them laughed and teased. It felt good.

Nisroch felt the sting of family love. "We gotta stop it."

"What do you propose, Mr. Agriculture?" Belial snorted.

"We go—"

He stopped. The dragons couldn't get near Henry as long as those prayer warriors and faithful followers clung to him.

"How do we get Henry away?"

"In his sleep. You know what the Holy One wrote in His book about night terrors."

"Yeah, the one who dwells in the shelter of the Most High will abide in the shadow of the Almighty. It is He who delivers from the snare of the trapper and from the deadly pestilence. He will cover you with His pinions and under His wings, you may seek refuge as a shield and not be afraid of the terror by night."

"That's us, you idiot. Dragons are the terrors of the night."

"That says He protects them," Nisroch argued.

"You don't pay any more attention that those stupid human children He created. It says the one who dwells in the shelter of the Most High."

Nisroch roared. "Henry doesn't dwell in His shelter. I get it!"

The group broke up when Stacy came home from her party. She hugged her grandparents and grabbed a piece of chicken from the leftovers on the cabinet. "Looks like you had a party."

"We did," Mimi Barbara said. "We missed you too."

"I had a good time. I felt happy. Haven't felt that in a long time." Stacy finished her chicken, washed her hands, and kissed her grandmother goodnight. Then she gave Daniel a big hug. "I love you bunches," she said.

"I love you more," he answered.

Stacy and Henry left to go to their rooms.

"Are we going to wait until Jason and Naomi get back before we have mom's birthday party?' Trey asked Barbara.

"Jason said we didn't have to. He noted that Mom is getting weak."

"I'll check with the others and see what they want to do," Trey answered. "Let's plan it for Saturday. That's only two days late and Jason will be back."

Stacy rolled into bed, turned her music on, and plugged in her earbuds. She picked up her latest book and started reading.

Henry put on his earphones and plugged them into a video game where he could practice his shooting.

Belial roared with laughter at the game. "Next time he won't miss."

39
Confrontation

HANNAH BANGED ON the door, shouting so loudly the neighbors heard. "Let me in you jerk! This is my house too!"

Trey jumped from his bed and ran downstairs to the door. He knew Hannah's strong-willed personality. She wouldn't stop until she got what she wanted. He opened the door and faced a strange-looking woman. He knew this was his wife. She looked like Hannah but her bitterness made her a stranger. His heart sank. He wanted his wife back, he didn't want this person. This thing standing in front of him was nothing more than a human body full of hate. She pushed past him into the house and headed toward the living room.

Before he could shut the door, she launched into a vicious tirade against his personality, her mother's faults, and even the unruliness of her children. Trey let her go. He had seen her angry, but never this out of control. He sat down in his chair across from Hannah in what had been her chair, and let the fiery darts she threw land on him. He steepled his fingers and held them tightly over his lips so he wouldn't speak. Anything he could say would be like adding fuel to her tirade.

After ten minutes of watching Hannah wave her arms in the air, causing her voice to raise while she rose and paced back and forth in front of him then sitting with a thud, he quit listening.

Occasionally, she would stop in front of him, put her hands on her hips and lean into him, pointing a finger and making awful accusations. She accused him of being in love with another woman. He knew then her accusations were confessions. He didn't want to hear about her "adventure" in South Dakota. He wanted his loving tenderhearted wife back. He knew that truth couldn't be seen or heard through hate.

While she continued in the verbal devastation of her family, Trey prayed. *Dear Lord, please give me my wife back. I still love her, but I don't know how to reach her. If there is a dragon on her please release her from it.*

Ishtar heard Trey praying, with a little help from Ishtar Hannah's vocalization of evil against her rose to a higher pitch. The creature scratched Trey's face and watched his face twitch with the sound of Hannah's voice. Trey faced Hannah. Even though she continued her tirade, Trey interrupted and spoke in a loud voice. "Not this time, you beast. This girl is mine."

Then Trey said something that caused the loathsome monster to lose the grip on Hannah for a moment.

"Lord, if she belongs to You, do whatever it takes to bring her back to You, even if our family doesn't come back together. Please don't let her perish."

Ishtar screamed at the painful prayer, "Let me have her." The owl fled and Hannah fell into her chair exhausted.

40
Birthday Party

MICHAEL HEARD DAVIS calling him. "Come, you're going to want to see this," he said as he whooshed past Michael with Buster following. He followed Davis to a circle of other angels who could see that the curtain between the realm of heaven and earth pulled back.

"What's going on?" Michael asked Davis as he called to others to join them.

"It's a Birthday party."

Michael smiled. He knew this had one of two meanings: either someone was being born into the kingdom of God and the angels loved watching that, or someone born into the kingdom of God would be coming home to the kingdom of God. If he and the others were invited, this meant it was someone he knew.

Paradise filled with joy and praise. The heavenly orchestra played chords of beauty until the Father stepped into the gathering with the Son at His right hand. The Holy Spirit would be ushering the new resident in soon.

The audience watched intently as the Troye family gathered at the farm of Buster and Merilee.

Michael watched for Sharon. She was the first to arrive and helped Alyssa and Barbara prepare the meal. He secretly hoped she would be joining him in Paradise.

The family members began to arrive. First came Zay and Marcy. Rance and Jenny Gale brought in food. Jason brought Naomi and a big smile, and Nathan brought Emily and a big chocolate cake from the new bakery in town.

Trey came with Stacy, Henry, and a boxful of cards from the church.

Barbara scurried around the kitchen giving Daniel orders, which he carried out with a smile.

"Is anyone coming home?" Michael asked Davis.

"I don't know. Only the Holy Spirit knows who He is escorting today."

At that moment, the Master called Davis to Him. Michael could see Davis listening closely to the words the Master spoke, the joy on Davis' face faded as he listened.

Soon Davis came and stood next to Michael. "Sorry, old friend, I'm not going to watch here with you. I'll be there."

Michael didn't know what that meant, he saw another angel join Davis, and the two of them disappeared from Paradise and appeared in the earthly realm.

"Mom, how are you feeling?" Barbara asked Merilee.

"I'm overwhelmed. One hundred years. I never thought I would live that long." She chuckled. "It's been a ride."

Barbara continued to fill containers with food. "It has, hasn't it?" she responded, thinking of her own life.

"I invited Hannah," Merilee said with her head ducked.

"Great. I hope she comes. I promise I'll stay out of her way so she won't cause a scene."

"I think she needs to face you."

"Probably," Barbara replied, "I'm not sure I can face her. Her hatred toward me is so vile, I don't want to be around her. It's more peaceful without her."

"I thought of that, I also know the best present Buster can give me on my one-hundredth birthday is to see his granddaughter reconciled to his daughter."

Barbara kissed her mother on the cheek. "That may be wishful thinking. I do hope your present happens."

Davis put his hand on Barbara. She felt his calming presence. "Thank you, Lord, I can't do this without you."

When the family sat down to dinner, an empty chair sat at the table since Hannah didn't show up. Barbara and the rest of the crew felt thankful and sad. They wanted their family to be together, but they didn't want to listen to her.

Rance sat next to Trey. "I know how you feel, buddy. I lost my woman too."

"And you found her again."

"You will too. God is faithful."

"I don't know how she'll ever overcome the hateful things she's said. And her need for vengeance against her mother is . . . well . . . it's unbelievable."

Daniel stood to say the blessing over the meal. After the closing Amen, the clatter of dishes and utensils mixed with the cacophony of voices rejoicing in a milestone of life.

Then the group fell quiet when Merilee told the story of Buster's dad and granddad. He told how the dragon known as Phillip Donnigan first encountered a Troye when his granddad built the first church in the middle of town.

"Is that the same church as Grace Church?" Stacy asked.

"Sure is. A few additions have been made since then, the original building is now the youth center."

Stacy smiled. "Tell us the story again about our great-grandpa standing up to a dragon." The rest of the family agreed.

The dragons sitting on the roof of the Troye house laughed and pointed at Nisroch.

"This be good!" Belial shouted

"Don't forget, you did battle with Zay—the weakest of the Troy clan—and lost," Nisroch retorted.

"I did some real damage. What did you do?"

"I had an impressionable death count," Nisroch roared.

"Look at *my* death count," Belial bragged.

"Yeah, you have the diseases and abortion brought on by abusing the Holy One's gift of sex."

Belial leaned back on his haunches. "Yeah, you're right. That little gift of sex for marriage between one man and one woman for life turned out to be my greatest tool of destruction among the human race and causes the highest death count." Belial sneered.

The rest of the dragons hushed their bragging because they knew Belial held the record for death count—the unit used to measure a dragon's value and position in Lucifer's kingdom.

The Angels watched with joy as the Troye family gathered to worship the Holy One with the joy of family.

Michael asked the angel next to him, "Why are the dragons allowed to look in?"

The angel smiled at Michael. "It's not ours to question."

Michael felt if the angel didn't question, he couldn't either. He just hated those ugly serpents, and their presence spoiled the joy of the occasion.

Barbara and Jenny Gale passed plates of cake and cups of coffee to the party revelers.

"This cake is good but not as good as my Meri's cake," Nathan said.

"That's because my cake is always warm and made with love."

"This one was purchased with love; does that count?" Nathan responded

The group laughed and nodded.

After they finished their dessert, the family went to the den where Merilee could sit and open her gifts and read the bountiful number of cards she received.

Merilee opened the gift Stacy brought first. A newly released book by Merilee's favorite pastor and author. She rubbed her hand over the cover and kissed Stacy. "Thank you, sweetness, you know what I like."

Stacy gave her a big grin and sat at her feet.

She opened each of the gifts, receiving a new coffee mug, a lap blanket, and a heating pad.

Halfway through the card reading, Hannah arrived. She quietly slipped into the room and sat on an ottoman near the door.

Trey looked at her and smiled.

Hannah smiled back and mouthed the words, "I'm sorry."

Trey went over to her and sat down in the chair next to her. He leaned over her shoulder and whispered in her ear, "I'm glad you came."

Henry saw his mother, smiled, and waved.

Stacy didn't acknowledge her. The rest of the family gave her a nod and a smile.

Barbara was in the kitchen and Merilee called her to come into the living room. She entered the room and stood behind Merilee who whispered something to her.

Barbara smiled and went to the bookcase and pulled out a scrapbook. She handed it to her mother and then stood back away by the bookcase.

"My dear heart, when I started this, I couldn't imagine how fat it would be." Merilee handed the book to Zay.

Zay gazed at the hand-decorated cover that read, "The Miracles of Our Lives."

He opened it and recalled the working of the Lord in their lives over the years. The first miracle was the adoption of Alyssa and Jason. The book contained pictures of them the first day Buster rescued them from the blasted rubble in town. Their dirty faces and the bloodstain of their mother still on their clothing tugged at his heart.

The next several pages told the story of them. Alyssa, Jason, and Naomi listened with rapt attention at their history considered a miracle by their one-hundred-year-old mother, Merilee.

Hannah wished she could have been a miracle to them. She was surprised and jealous when Merilee read the miracle of Barbara's rescue.

Davis stepped up to Ishtar. "It's time for you to go," he said with authority.

Ishtar yelled in his face, "She's mine!"

"No, she belongs to the Master, and He will not let you have her."

Davis raised his sword made from the oracles of God. "Go!"

Ishtar screeched and lifted sharp talons from the emotions of Hannah disappearing into the realm of dragons. Belial and Nisroch watched the wretched owl leaving.

"What are you guys doing here?" the creature screeched.

"We're not sure," Belial answered.

"Think I can stick around?" The multi-horned owl, Ishtar asked.

"No!" A direct command from the Master.

Ishtar vanished into the waterless wilderness with a scream of terror and dread.

Hannah could feel a tear flowing down her cheek as she listened to her grandfather tell about her mother's battle with witchcraft. *I thought she was a witch.*

Shame flooded her as soon as she commented to herself. She remembered calling her mother a narcissistic witch. She didn't realize the implications of the name.

Zay handed the book to Rance, and he continued to read. Hannah rested her elbows on her knees and her face, listening.

Barbara noticed and smiled. The ugliness of Hannah no longer consumed her, instead, Barbara could see the loveliness of her sweet daughter. As Rance told Barbara's story she moved toward Hannah.

Bang! Bang! The loud report of gunshots rang out, and Barbara fell to the ground.

With all eyes on Barbara, Henry aimed the gun in his hand at his temple. Every one's eyes focused on Barbara and no one saw him except Trey who rushed toward Henry in time to pull the gun away from Henry's head and under his own chin.

Henry pulled the trigger.

The dragons raised a ruckus and shot plumes of fire into the air. They danced on the roof of the Troyes and shouted in victory.

Heaven gasped, except the Father. He sat on His throne watching as a Father waits on a child. The Master stood and watched the scene, weeping.

Daniel immediately fell over Barbara's body, not as a doctor but as a husband. He groaned and cried when he lifted her limp body. The hole in her head and the blank stare on her face told him she was gone.

Davis patted Daniel on the shoulder.

"You've fought a good fight," he said to Barbara as he clasped her hand in his.

"Hello, old friend," she said as she saw him come into focus. Davis translated Barbara into the presence of Her Savior.

Zay jumped to Trey. The bullet blew the left side of Trey's face off. Zay pulled off his tee shirt and wrapped Trey's face. The wound bled profusely; the bullet grazed the skull but didn't crack it.

Reacting out of instinct, Marcy pulled their SUV to the door while Sharon wrapped a sheet around Trey.

Stacy lay on the floor where she'd been sitting, covered in blood—the blood of her father, for she had been directly under him when Henry's bullet ripped through his face.

Merilee stood behind Henry and held him. He motioned for her to lean over to him. When she did, he said, "I'm sorry"

Merilee took a final deep breath. Her spirit joined with the angel standing nearby who ushered her to her eternal home with the Father and Buster. Merilee's earthly tent lay crumpled on the couch next to Henry. He closed her eyes and kissed her cheek. Then he rose and left through the back door.

Rance and Jason loaded Trey into the back of the SUV, and Zay and Marcy headed toward the hospital. Nathan and Emily stood on either side of Merilee.

"Grammy, where's Henry?" Nathan asked as he put his hand on her shoulder and realized her soul had departed her body. He gently lay her down on the couch. "Happy Birthday, Grammy," he said and kissed her on the forehead.

Hannah stood watching the scene with her hand over her mouth. Davis returned and hovered over Hannah to protect her. He hovered around her to keep the dragons from attacking her. She rested in the hands of a loving Father, who would discipline her.

Davis knew it's a terrible thing to fall into the hands of an angry God, and God was angry with Hannah. She didn't know at the moment how severe her punishment would be. The Master dismissed the dragons, their task complete. They destroyed Hannah's worldly desires allowing her spirit to be redeemed.

41
Discipline

HANNAH WATCHED AS the police brought her handcuffed sixteen-year-old son through the front door. He'd waited on the front porch swing for the police to come to get him.

He smiled at Hannah and said, "I got rid of her for you, mother. You can be happy again."

Tears streamed down Hannah's face at Henry's declaration of love for his mother. "Oh son, what did I do to you?" she moaned.

The blood-spattered den revealed the consequences of her selfish pride and unforgiveness. Her mother lay dead with her father moaning over her. Her father would be lost without her mother.

Trey's blood covered her, Henry, and Stacy, who lay prone on the floor. Why wasn't she moving?

Hannah couldn't get to Stacy, so she called to her nephew, "Nathan, check Stacy, somethings wrong," she squealed to her nephew while trying to get through the people and equipment brought in by the ambulance.

Nathan bent over Stacy. "Are you okay, honey?"

"I don't know. I can't move."

Hannah finally reached Stacy. She grabbed her arm. Nathan slapped her away. "Don't touch her!"

"She's my daughter," Hannah retorted and touched Stacy's arm.

"I mean, she says she can't move."

Hannah understood. She sat on the floor beside Stacy unaware she sat in a puddle of her husband's blood.

It took hours before the medical examiner allowed the bodies of Barbara and Merilee to be removed from the premises.

Hannah went with Stacy to the hospital.

Nathan and Emily took Jenny Gale home and stayed with her until Rance returned.

Zay and Marcy stayed with Trey at the hospital.

Jason returned to the farm after he took Naomi home and cleaned the den. Between sobbing and praying, he completed the task before morning.

The bullet ricocheting from Trey's skull had hit Stacy in the back. The docs weren't sure if the bullet severed the spine. Time would tell. Since the bullet lost some of its momenta before it struck her, they hoped the damage would be superficial.

Hannah went to Trey's hospital room. He lay so still in the bed with his head half-bandaged. She walked to his bedside, touched his hand, and stroked it, looking at every nuance of the veins and muscles. Her hand traced the muscles in the arms that once held her with tenderness. The arms that built their home, the strength that moved tractors, trailers, and cows. She came to the bandage and pulled her hand away.

She shuddered and said, "What did you do to Henry while I was gone?"

Trey heard the accusation. He hated the tear inching out of the corner of his eye. He hoped Hannah wouldn't see it. She brought a tissue to his closed eye. "I don't know if you can hear me or not, now you see the damage my mother can do. Maybe we can get back together."

Trey felt stunned at the statement. *Did she not even realize her mother was now dead?*

Taking her delusion with her, she left the room. Davis followed her, his sword remained in the scabbard. He didn't need it for this mission. He was her prison guard, not her protector or rescuer. The Father released her to the dragons to do their worse—short of death. It would take the punishment from her Master to heal and redeem her rebellious spirit.

Hannah left the hospital and went home. When she arrived, she took a deep breath and hoped Trey hadn't changed the locks. If he did, she'd break a window. She determined to reclaim her own home. Before she inserted her key, the door came open.

Nathan stood there glaring at her.

"What are you doing here?" she asked him with a wrinkled nose.

"It's good to see you too."

His sarcasm was not lost on her as she shoved past him into the house. Nathan shut the door and returned to the kitchen, where a bevy of women hovered around a banquet of food.

"What's going on here?' Hannah asked. "Why are you all in my home?"

Mrs. Belingrove spoke to Hannah. "We are so sorry for your loss. Your mother was much loved and respected."

Mrs. Allen stepped up and took Hannah in her arms. "I'm so sorry, dear, she was a wonderful woman."

Joan Bates took Hannah's hand, "Our prayers for you and your family. If we can help let us know."

Then she saw Jenny Gale. She walked up to her. "What are we going to do with all this food?"

"Marcy is bringing her family here. Since your home is the largest in town, we're having the family meal and visitation here."

"Who gave you permission?" Hannah barked at her aunt.

"Sweetie, we don't need your permission. You need our help," Marcy said with a smile.

Hannah headed toward her room. She passed the master bedroom stopping at the doorway. She entered. Pacing around the room she designed and decorated she spread her arms and did a twirl.

She shouted aloud, "My house, my room. And no one can take it from me!"

Nisroch held the anxious Lahash back. "That's not an invitation."

Rarely did the dragon legions call upon Lahash to interfere with the will of the Father. The dragons preferred to be unseen by humans and the true God known as Yahweh.

Lahash spent most of his time torturing those who fell into the dragon's lair with no hope of escape. The inability to exercise a natural skill served to make him vicious when he received an assignment.

Even Nisroch and Belial felt a little sorry for Hannah, knowing Lahash was about to be unleashed on her.

"You've already taken her family. What is left for me to do if I can't kill her?" Lahash shouted at Nisroch.

"I guess that's why you have been released from Tartarus; you are to find her source of greatest pain."

Lahash dug into the roof of the Mitchell house with extended sharp claws. "I think I know the way to cause this mortal complete destruction."

Nisroch and Belial nodded their snouts and puffed a dark cloud of approval toward Lahash.

Lahash opened his snout wide and released a full-blown gust of fire. The dragons raised their howls and grunts in approval.

The rest of the Troye family joined in Hannah's home. Hannah crossed her arms and bit her lip. When someone spoke to her, she nodded and said thank you. She didn't want to talk to any of those hypocritical church people. She wanted them out of her house, especially her family. They were fawning on Barbara's accomplishments and reputation. They all had a story to tell Hannah about her.

As people left one by one, Joan Bates sat beside Hannah, took her hand in hers, and spoke in a gruff voice.

Hannah could swear she took on the features of a snake when she spoke.

"Hannah, my dear, you must examine your heart, your accusations, and then forgive or you will not be forgiven," Joan said.

Hannah shook her head and squinted her eyes. When she opened them, she didn't see a human woman She saw an overgrown serpent staring at her and flicking its tongue in her face.

She pulled her hands away from the body of the serpent wrapped around her hands. She stood and screamed.

Daniel raised his head to see his daughter screaming, he made no move toward her. Hannah continued to scream even though several women attempted to calm her.

Daniel rose and went outside. He returned with a filled syringe and injected his daughter with Valium.

She calmed and sat down.

The medication may have made her body calmer, however, more serpents were surrounding her spirit, and she couldn't scream or get away from them. They were crawling over her and flicking their tongues around her. In her drugged state, she found her daddy at the back of the rumba of rattlesnakes coiling around her and wagging their rattlers on the end of their tales.

"Daddy, help me!" She cried in a garbled tongue no one could understand. The snakes consumed her body, and her heart raced. She could feel the sweat of fear crawling down her spine, or was it one of the dreaded serpents.

 She mustered all her strength and screamed, "Help Me! Snakes!"

Marcy took her to her room and helped her get into bed. The snakes came with her. Marcy left and turned off the light.

Hannah lay in her bed paralyzed with fear.

Lahash whistled at the dragons. "Back off, we have more tricks we want to use. Let's drag this out as long as we can," the beast barked. "However, leave a little residue for her own twisted thinking to torment her," he rumbled.

Lahash released the realistic dream on his prey.

Barbara walked into Hannah's room. She saw the snakes. She swiped at them, only to have them bite her one after the other.

Then Hannah stood and heard her voice repeating the charges made against her mother. "You're narcissistic; you're a liar; you're toxic!" With each accusation she watched the serpents bite her mother.

Hannah smiled. Barbara writhed on the ground in pain with swelling breaking out over her whole body, and the serpents kept biting.

Barbara called out to Hannah, "What did I do?"

Hannah answered with a sneer, "You told my husband I exaggerated."

"Why are you so vengeful?"

Hannah answered, "I'm not vengeful. I've forgiven you."

Davis pulled his sword and touched Hannah's heart, "Vengeance is mine, says the Lord." When those words penetrated Hannah's dream she woke and sat up. She looked around her room, on her bed, under the covers. There were no snakes, nor did she see her mother.

It was just a dream. "No, it was a nightmare. I need coffee."

When Hannah stumbled into the kitchen to make coffee, it was empty. She looked around and found no one. Nothing was in the same spot as it was when she left a year ago.

She opened every cabinet looking for coffee and then realized she had no pot. Trey didn't drink coffee.

She closed the last door, opened the refrigerator, and looked at the mountains of dishes filled with all kinds of food. A cake pan sat on the cabinet. She opened it and found some blueberry muffins. She grabbed one and stuffed it in her mouth. *I've got to get rid of the awful taste of that horrible dream.*

After getting dressed, she drove to the gas station a few blocks away to get coffee. When she was there, she saw the donut case. *Why not?*

Once, home, Hannah took a draw on her large coffee with cream and pulled a donut out of the box of a dozen. An hour later, she swiped her hands, brushed off her chest, and threw the paper cup and empty donut box away.

Lahash winked at Asmodeos. "She's ready now. Funny how those human bodies work."

The doorbell rang. Hannah rushed to answer it while trying to cram a swollen foot into her shoe. It wasn't going in.

She opened the door. "I'll be ready in a minute," she said without seeing who stood at the door.

When she changed shoes into some older wider ones instead of the designer heels she planned to wear to her mother's funeral, she came to the vestibule expecting to see Rance waiting for her, but it wasn't Rance.

Sitting on the bench by the front door was a face that spoke of pain, speaking infinite messages without a word.

Trey's lone eye stared deep into Hannah's soul with the light of examination and revelation. The other eye no longer existed in his half face.

With a twisted mouth, he spoke. His words frightening her almost as much as his horrible face. The face she once caressed with love and covered in kisses now repulsed her to the point of gagging.

"How do you like your work?"

His words hit her brain like ice-hard knives. "What?"

"Didn't you hear your son's words when he pulled the trigger?"

Hannah shook her head. "No."

"He said, and I quote; 'Now you can be happy.'" Trey sat silent as the wound on his face seeped blood. "Does this make you happy?" Trey pointed to his face.

Hannah held her hand over her open mouth. She felt her stomach roll. She ran to the bathroom and vomited a dozen cheap, greasy donuts. She wiped her mouth then sat on the toilet doubled over, holding her cramping stomach.

Lahash laughed and pointed a claw at Hannah. "See, I told you those donuts would be fun."

Asmodeous laughed with the dragon using his skill to remove the Holy One's will from a human heart.

Ten or fifteen minutes later, Hannah pulled herself back together. She would never eat another donut. She took a deep breath and prepared to meet the monstrous face on the other side of the door.

When she came out, Rance sat on the bench. "Are you ready now?" He asked her.

"I thought you were Trey." She said to her uncle.

"He's still in the hospital." Rance stated and stood to escort Hannah to the waiting car. Hannah shook her head. *Am I still dreaming?*

Even the overflow room filled at the church. The strong, sweet smell of flowers filled the seven-hundred-seat auditorium.

The family walked in together, with Jason leading the tribe of Troyes and holding on to Hannah and Trey. Rance and Jenny Gale and Zay and Marcy followed them. Nathan led the grandchildren, great-grandchildren, and cousins.

Lahash sat on Hannah's shoulders accusing her during the entire service. After the burial, the family gathered at the farmhouse.

When Hannah entered the farmhouse, she glanced toward the den. There everything changed. For the first time since the tragedy, her mind registered the vision of her mother lying on the floor with her daddy hovering over her.

"Where's daddy?" Hannah asked Jason.

"He didn't come. Said he couldn't take two funerals in one week."

"Who?" Hannah asked.

Jason didn't answer. He glared at his niece for a second. "You really are cold."

"Man, you are good at this," Asmodeous bragged to Lahash.

"You ain't seen nothing yet, little brother." Asmodeous roared at the comment.

When Rance dropped Hannah back home, she slumped into the house with her stomach still roiling from the mornings' indulgence in junk food. The meal at the church added to her discomfort. She threw her clothes over the chair, pulled on her sweats, and fell into bed herself.

Lahash and Asmodeous curled up on each side of

her.

42

Realization

MERILEE AND BARBARA entered the gates of heaven singing, "O, God, you are my God. Earnestly I seek you; my soul thirsts for you; my body longs for you in a dry and weary land where there is no water." Their earthly bodies' longing for God found satisfaction in the heart and soul of Paradise.

They received the greatest desire of their heart, the unthinkable occurred, and they both knew they were wrapped in the holiness of Christ and standing before the holiness of the one true God. They were aware of His beautiful presence, and as He extended His open palm to them to approach, they knew they stood in the presence of the King of Kings.

He stood straight and strong as a warrior with the wisdom of an aged King. His deep, clear eyes appeared as great wells of knowledge and love that held the memories of the ages and the hope of eternity.

Merilee and Barbara accepted the hand of the Most High and Holy One as they entered the throne room of grace.

They bowed at His feet.

"Well done, My good and faithful servants."

His words washed over them as a cleansing, warm shower. His voice reverberated with the melodic sounds of a babbling brook, and they knew the bright smile came from the God of the universe, and they looked upon Him face to face.

They worshiped and sang. Then their angel escorts took them out of the throne room and into a place of beauty. It reminded Barbara of the lobby of a grand hotel with rooms rising above them and the beauty of trees and flowers and clear running water all around them.

People came out of the rooms to greet them, and they called them by name.

Buster took Merilee to meet his great-grandfather who spent his life on his knees in a hidden prison. She met his father, and he met an angel who brought him to a stable where a most beautiful horse lived. Upon the horse's back sat a saddle with burn marks. The decorations held the initials of RT.

The angel spoke. "This is the saddle your father made for you and the one that I placed over your infant body in the fire."

Buster reminded Merilee of the scars. His head turned toward his ankles. The scars were gone.

"You are healed."

Merilee heard the melodic voice of Mrs. Waithe. They hugged and rejoiced.

Barbara listened, spellbound by the stories of her family and their survival from the dragons. She asked the angel, "Why did our family suffer so much destruction from the dragons?"

"Because your family stood for truth, and dragons can't tolerate truth."

"What about my daughter?"

Buster took his daughter's hand, and with a slight twist of his head, he shook his head.

"It's okay." The angel saw Buster try to stop Barbara. "Heaven is aware of Hannah. Be assured the Master is applying discipline to give her opportunity to repent and return."

Barbara didn't ask the questions on her heart because the beauty and love surrounding her dismissed the thoughts of life on sinful earth. Soon, the reunion of family and friends came to full swing. Generations of family and years of friendships on sinful earth renewed in Paradise where they would gather and worship until the day of the new earth.

Michael and Paps greeted Barbara with a firm hug. Paps picked Barbara up and swung her around. "Bet you didn't know we could do these kinds of things," Paps said to his old friend.

She shook her head. "No, I didn't."

"Just wait till you see all the other things up here." Barbara looked over Pap's shoulder and saw Michael. She walked up to him and put her hand on his. "So good to see you again."

Michael no longer saw the weakened body of his entrapped cousin rather he admired the strong warrior body of a victor. "You know there is about to be a battle," he said.

"I guess the war goes on as long as the sinful earth turns," Buster added.

"This time the battle will not be about you," Michael said as he bear-hugged Barbara. "This time the battle will be *for* you. Your prayers for Hannah have been heard."

"Is Davis fighting for her?"

"Not exactly, Davis is with her but not like he was with me and you."

"This battle will be fought with the power of the dragon warrior," Paps said.

"Who's that?" Buster asked.

"The one you've been praying to all these years," Buster's dad answered.

"Jesus?"

"The battle is the Lord's."

43

Jail Time

HENRY ENTERED THE psychiatrist's office with slumped shoulders. This doctor held his future since he alone would determine if Henry was able to stand trial for murder as an adult or as a juvenile, or if he will be committed to a psychiatric facility for the criminally insane.

Henry moved slowly and deliberately. He seldom spoke. The guards watched him since he'd been beaten twice in his short stay in the juvenile facility. Henry wouldn't defend himself. His body was covered in bruises and cuts.

Dr. Overby stood when Henry came into the conference room. "Rough day?" he asked.

Henry nodded then sat in the victim seat. That's what they called it on the floor where he lived with other youth who broke the law. They all knew it was either their condemnation or their redemption.

Henry squinted his eyes and stared straight ahead. He took his weekly beatings without screaming and curling up now. His feelings, emotions and even physical pain beaten out of him. When the gang of mindless thugs gathered around him, he stood still and let his mind drift to other thoughts. He found they became bored much quicker and even beat him less. Today was his usual beating. His scars were fresh and still bleeding. He made no effort to catch the dripping blood from his wounds. There was no reason to clean it off.

Henry's heart and body grew cold, and all that surrounded him grew cold. He couldn't remember love anymore and only a few months had passed. His aunts and uncles visited him with his cousins, and even his dad had been to see him.

His mother never came or called; even though it was for her love that he killed his grandmother. He knew what he was doing when he brought the gun to the birthday party. He'd trained for months with the video games. He dreaded the need to kill her, he saw it as the only way to help his mother. He truly believed his grandmother's death would return his loving mother and restore their family.

Not only did it fail, his dad's appearance forever altered into a gross mass of scar tissue. His voice sounded as if his mouth was filled with gravel. Each step his dad took caused a swing to the left. His left arm hung limp at his side and his face . . . Oh, his face! Henry cringed at the idea.

Love was all he wanted—a love to ground his family together. He wanted that love that protected their family and fought battles to save each other. He wanted the love their family experienced before his grandmother—

He turned his head toward the ceiling. "What did my grandmother do to my mother?" he asked.

Dr. Overby responded, "I'm not sure. What do you remember?"

Before Henry could answer, Dr. Overby's phone buzzed. He looked at the message, closed his notepad, and said, "You have a visitor today."

Henry raised his eyebrows and wondered why Dr. Overby would let any of his family interrupt their meeting. He rose and opened the door, and Hannah, his mother, walked in.

Henry stood up and sprinted toward her. He pushed her hard against the wall. "Look what you've done to me!" he shouted.

Hannah wrinkled her forehead. "What?"

Henry held out his arms. "Look at me. I get this at least once a week. And you put me here."

Hannah's mouth fell open.

"Don't look at me that way," Henry said as his demeanor calmed a bit. He sat back down in the victim chair.

Hannah remained against the wall.

Lahash flew around Hannah. "What are you doing?" Asmodeous asked.

"Building up hate."

"Can you turn a mother against her son?"

"I turned her against her mother, didn't I."

"You never turned Barbara against her."

Lahash stopped spinning around Hannah and sat on his haunches. "You're right. This will be a great victory."

"You haven't been in the field that long. Look over the boy's head," Asmodeous scolded Lahash.

Lahash noticed the prayer cloud hanging over the boys head and growled with a big cloud of black smoke.

Hannah coughed.

Lahash looked over her head. "It's expanding. Who?"

Belial appeared in the room. "Buster and Barbara," The commander answered.

"Can't be. They're dead," Lahash roared back.

"No, they're not. They are in Paradise with the Master, and they bring their petitions face to face now."

"Anyone else praying for these bags of goo?"

"The rest of the family offer casual prayers for Henry. The prayers for Hannah are no longer offered since they no longer believe she will return to the family. That's why we can torture her."

"What's our plan?" Lahash roared.

"Kill Henry."

The Holy One called Davis to the throne room. "It's time to banish the dragons; they are overstepping."

Davis bows to the Holy One and backs out of the throne room.

Michael sees the bright light pass from the throne room to earth. "God has sent a dragon warrior to rescue His own."

With sword blazing, Davis stepped in front of Lahash. "Stop! This one is sheltered in a prayer covering."

Lahash roared at the other dragons.

Ezequeel stepped beside Lahash. "What's this? Is the angel fighting dragons today?" Ezequeel mocked Davis.

Davis held his sword in front of him and remained steady as he spoke with a firm voice. *"Those who indulge the flesh in its corrupt desires, and despise authority, daring, self-willed, they do not tremble when they speak evil of angelic Majestics, even angels who are greater in might and power do not bring slandering judgment against them before the Lord. But creatures of instinct will be captured and killed, insulting where they have no knowledge, and will in the destruction of the humans also be destroyed."*

Lahash balked at the words of Davis. "Ezequeel, what is he saying?"

"He says if we destroy Henry, we will destroy ourselves."

"Is he talking about the dragons?"

"Yes."

"He can't kill us, even if we kill Henry," Lahash said. "We are immortal."

"Have you ever heard of Tartarus?" Ezequeel asked Lahash.

Lahash belched a blast of fire. "I'll never go there again."

"You will if you kill Henry."

Davis stepped directly in front of the dragons and glared at them eye to eye. "Back your thugs off Henry, no more beatings or you will pay the price."

A blast of hot air came from Lahash's maw and surrounded Davis.

The angelic majesty sent from the throne of grace stood firm.

When Lahash's fire died, Davis spoke once again with his final message from the Most High. "Back away from Hannah."

This was too much. Lahash, Ezequeel, and Asmodeous surrounded Davis, knowing they could defeat this one angel. "She was given to us."

"You have done your duty; the Most High no longer needs you."

With the final message delivered to the dragons, Davis joined Hannah. The time had come for his assignment. It would be difficult. He hated discipline assignments, however, he loved the results the Master brought about in these times.

The dragons destroyed Hannah's flesh by ripping all of the Most High's blessing from her. Now she would be able to hear the Master's instruction as she walked through the most difficult trial of her life.

44
Endurance

JASON NO LONGER rang the bell when he arrived at his niece Hannah's home. He used his key. Pulling his small wagon behind him, he headed toward the kitchen where he unloaded a day's worth of meals for Trey. The family noticed Hannah cooked food Trey could not eat and she wouldn't take the time to blend food for him. The family took over providing wholesome food for Trey. Trey insisted he didn't need it and that he could prepare food for himself. The family knew it took all of Trey's strength to do simple tasks.

"When are you going to stop doing this?" Hannah asked Jason as he placed Trey's food before him.

"Until you start doing your duty and taking care of your husband," Jason scolded Hannah.

She pulled some lunchmeat out of the refrigerator and made herself a sandwich then sat down next to Trey. This way she didn't have to look at his scarred face.

Jason left them to go back to the farm. Because of Trey, work doubled for Jason. At least Nathan was helping when he could.

Trey reached over and took Hannah's hand. In his gravelly voice and short sentences, he said, "Napkin."

She retrieved napkins for both of them.

"Read?"

"Okay, what do you want to hear today?" Hannah knew his answer, she asked anyway, hoping for another one.

"Bible."

She nodded.

The Bible reading included a Psalm and a passage. Trey would have her read it four times. Ever since she visited Henry, she knew this was a small price to pay. Hannah recalled Henry saying he killed his grandmother out of love for her . . . so she could be happy.

As Hannah consumed her sandwich, she remembered telling Henry how much she hated her mother and wished her dead. She never thought Henry would take it literally.

Trey must have read her thoughts because he finished his dinner, rose to wash his hands and his glass. He came back and facing her, he asked, "Why hate your mother?"

Hannah knew every word Trey spoke caused him pain. If he asked, he really wanted to know.

Her answer spilled out of her mouth in anger. "She's a liar, or rather was."

"What lie?"

Hannah opened her mouth, and nothing came out. She closed it again then answered, "Well, she told you I exaggerated."

"Not lie. Truth. All do it."

Hannah stammered around for a few minutes, trying to remember why she felt so much anger at her mother.

Davis stood by placing true memories in her mind.

Remember when you were sick, and she nursed you back to health? Remember how she stayed with you and helped care for you when your babies were born? Remember how she made a separate Christmas dinner for you because you were on a special diet? Those were deeds of love.

Davis continued to pull out acts of love and place them in Hannah's mind.

She finished her sandwich and rose from the table. "There were lots of things. She was a selfish woman."

Hannah stopped, and for the first time, she touched the bright red, twisted, ruffled skin on Trey's face. "I'm so sorry for your pain. Thank you for saving our son."

Trey put his hand over hers.

Davis saw a crack in the shell of hate that covered her heart.

Hannah poured herself a cup of coffee and made cold coffee for Trey's mug and straw. For the first time since he arrived home, she truly looked at his face. The one eye remained the same. She felt her heart flutter a bit at the sight of his face untouched by the cruelty of a speeding bullet.

The couple sat in the den, and Hannah took her Bible in hand. It was dusty. She opened it to 1 Thessalonians 5:9 and read to Trey.

"God has not destined us for wrath, but for obtaining salvation through our Lord Jesus Christ, who died for us. Therefore, encourage one another and build up one another. Live in peace with one another."

Hannah paused.

Davis dug his sword into her, performing spiritual surgery.

"I haven't had peace in years," she mused.

Trey watched and prayed.

Hannah went back to the Scripture. *"Admonish the unruly, encourage the fainthearted, help the weak, be patient with everyone."*

Again, she paused.

Davis continued to dig at her heart with his sword. *"Never pay another with evil for evil."*

Hannah gasped. "Even if the things I believe about my mother are true, then—"

"No give evil," Trey finished her thought. "All people sinners . . even mother."

Hannah understood his words. There was no excuse for her attitude and behavior. Worse, it came at a terrible price. "It wasn't worth it," she moaned.

Davis placed the words of the Master into her heart, recalling the words Barbara had quoted to Hannah. *"He who curses his father or his mother shall surely be put to death."*

Davis spoke to Hannah's willing heart. "There are no reasons to curse a parent, even if they do not meet expectations."

Trey heard Hannah repeat Barbara's frequent admonition. He added, "Leviticus 20."

Hannah turned to the passage in Leviticus. It took a while to understand what Trey was trying to tell her until she read verse nine in the book of Law.

"If there is anyone who curses his father or his mother, he shall surely be put to death; he has cursed his father or his mother, his bloodguiltiness is upon him."

Hannah felt a knot in her throat and knew it was her bloodguiltiness. Her unjustified hatred caused her son to kill her mother and disfigure his father. Her son sat in a criminal hospital, and her daughter lay in a Stryker frame in the hospital. A bed for those who could not move.

She rose from her seat and fell at Trey's feet, laying her head on his lap. "What have I done?"

He rubbed her hair as she cried.

Davis removed his sword. There would still be more surgery, but for now, she recognized her hatred against her mother was a sin against the Most High.

Trey took a deep breath, and despite the pain, he spoke in a complete sentence from scripture to his beloved wife. *"Examine everything carefully and hold fast to that which is good."*

Barbara rose from her seat in the theatre of heavenly revelations. She turned to the Master as he closed the curtain. "I pray you will bring her back to You."

The Master smiled and nodded. "She has much to learn."

"So did I." Barbara bowed to the Master as did all others in the theatre. Each one observing their own loved ones battling the dragons on the old earth.

Once the curtain closed, the Master began to teach His family. "I gave my servant Jeremiah the promise of the New Covenant, *Behold, Days are coming when I will make a new covenant with the house of Israel and the house of Judah. This is the covenant, which I will make with the house of Israel after those days. I will put My law within them, and on their heart, I will write it, and I will be their God, and they shall be My people.'"*

The Master pointed to one of the listeners and said, "As the one I called to write the book of Hebrews told you, 'Their sins and lawless deeds I will remember no more. Now where there is forgiveness of these things, there is no longer any offering for sin.'"

Everyone sitting at the Master's feet raised a voice in joy and praise.

Barbara turned to the angel sitting next to her. "There are so many."

The angel replied, "Yes, and all of them have a loved one that has estranged from them."

"Really?" Barbara looked around the crowd of thousands.

"Why?"

"You were all estranged from God when you lived a life filled with selfishness and sin. When you gave your life to the Master and allowed Him to wash you clean, then you were able to see Him as your Savior, and you could also see the evil of the dragons."

"I still don't understand."

"By experiencing the estrangement of your earthly children, you understood the heart of God who made a way for His human family to return to Him."

"God lost his children?"

"Yes. The prophet Jeremiah wrote God's lament in his book in chapter 2 verse 5. *'What injustice did your fathers find in Me, that they went far from Me and walked after emptiness and became empty?'*"

"I saw that in my Hannah."

The angel nodded and let Barbara meditate on the words.

"By Hannah's estrangement, I saw the pain of my Lord?"

"That's right, and all these other people felt it too."

"I don't understand why He didn't bring our children back to us?"

"Remember, He had to leave His children to their own devices. He told them if they wanted the other dragons in their lives, they would have to live under the rules of those dragons. He wept when He told them they brought their calamity upon themselves with their wicked deeds."

"What calamity is my Hannah going to experience?"

"She lost you," the angel said and rose to teach another.

Barbara joined Mrs. Waithe, Michael, and Paps. She told them the lesson the angel shared.

"I don't understand how losing me is going to be a calamity for Hannah."

Paps said, "Did you ever read Ezekiel 10?"

"I guess not." Barbara searched her memory for the passage.

Michael jumped into the conversation. "It tells about God leaving Israel—His children—because they rejected Him."

Mrs. Waithe added, "It was their greatest loss, but they didn't realize it until the Lord departed from them. They spent seventy years in captivity, and God was silent for four hundred years. Can you imagine not hearing Him for four hundred years? "You are now gone from Hannah's life, and she will not hear from you again until she becomes a resident here in Paradise."

The group turned their attention to the throne of grace and the beauty surrounding it. The river flowing from the throne almost sang as it rippled along nourishing the trees beside its banks. The pure white light of love surrounding the Ancient of Days.

Barbara smiled at the beauty of Paradise and responded, "No, I can't imagine being away from Him for even a second."

"Hannah is about to learn life without you. Before, she could ignore you and seek her own way, but she knew you were there. Now you are gone. She will feel the pain of your absence similar to the way Israel felt the pain of God's absence." Mrs. Waithe explained to Barbara.

The angels gathered around. "Remember, He said He would be their God and they would be His people and He loved them with an everlasting love."

Buster listened to the conversation and stepped up behind his daughter. "You had your rebellious days too," he whispered.

"I didn't want my daughter to go through the horrors that I did with those awful dragons."

Buster sat down beside Barbara. "We can't avoid it. God told us the children would repay the iniquity of the fathers in their bosom."

"I didn't think the children had to pay for the sins of the fathers and vice versa."

"Look at it closer; the iniquity of their fathers in their bosom. Could it mean in their heart? In their soul?"

"What does that mean?"

"On earth, it was stated as a cliché."

Michael laughed. "We pay for our raising."

The rest of the group joined Michael's laughter. Buster nodded and hugged his daughter. "Hannah is learning to endure the evil of the dragons by trusting in her God. He's all she has now."

45

Perfection

DANIEL SAT AT the bedside of his granddaughter. Her appearance glowed from her bath, clean hair, and new gown and bedclothes. Still, a ten-year-old shouldn't be strapped to a bedframe. He held her x-rays in his hand and studied them.

"Papaw," Stacy said when she woke to see her grandfather sitting nearby.

Daniel rose and walked over and kissed Stacy on the forehead. He stroked her hand, watching for a response. Her little finger twitched, and he smiled. Maybe, there would still be hope.

"How's Mom and Dad?"

"They are good. They will be here this afternoon. Your dad needs rest to let his body heal."

Stacy didn't know about her grandmother and Henry yet.

"Where's Mimi?" she asked.

Daniel knew this time would come, and he had prayed for wisdom to tell this sweet girl her grandmother was no more.

"She's in heaven with Jesus."

Stacy cried out, "No! I need her!"

"You still have your mother." Daniel countered.

"No I don't, she's always mad."

A nurse stepped in the door of Stacy's room. "Dr. Holloway, a radiologist is calling you."

Daniel sat in his office chair and placed Stacy's x-ray on the viewer. "What do you think, Jim?"

"It's possible but tricky. The bullet is lodged close to her spine, but the spine is intact."

"I called Dr. Stevenson; he's the best neurosurgeon in the area. He agreed with our analysis."

The surgery took several hours. Trey and Hannah paced, napped, and waited in the waiting room. Daniel watched Hannah and Trey. They held hands and each other. He didn't know what happened, but he knew it came from the peace that passes understanding in a fretful heart.

After seven hours, Dr. Stevenson came out. He looked at Daniel and smiled. "We won't know for sure for a few days, we were able to remove the bullet, and the spinal cord is still intact."

On the way home, Daniel stopped to see Henry and give him the news. He rejoiced with his grandfather. Then he wept.

"PaPaw, I'm so sorry. I didn't know what I was doing when I shot—"

"It's okay, Henry, I know you didn't. Besides, your Mimi would rather be shot than for you to miss heaven."

"You think we will see her again?"

"I know I will, I don't know about you."

"How do you know?"

"I know Jesus is my Savior. Sin reigned in death, but grace reigns through righteousness to eternal life through Jesus Christ."

"I don't understand?" Henry shifted in his chair and leaned in toward his grandfather.

"Even when we are living in the deceptions of the dragons, Christ gave us the gift of eternal life with Him because of His great love. It's by grace we are saved from the eternal death in the dragon's lair."

"Still not clear, tell me more." Henry rested his chin on his fist.

"God wants a family. He wants children that love Him and love to be with Him. So, He gave us an earthly family to show us."

"My family sure failed in that respect." Henry leaned back in his chair.

"Your family revealed the dragons and their hate. Have you talked to your mother lately?"

"Yeah, she's been coming by every day."

"And?"

"It's been great. Dad comes with her most of the time unless he's in pain." Henry ducked his head. "I caused my dad all that pain, and he's so disfigured from it. He took the bullet. He saved me from killing myself." Henry buried his face in his palm and wept.

Daniel took a deep breath and sighed. "So did Jesus."

46
Regrets

HANNAH PLACED THE food on the table for a Christmas celebration. She knew there would be more food as her father, Daniel, aunts, uncles, and cousins joined them. Trey could eat soft food now as his face healed more and more. A couple of plastic surgeries built a new jaw for him and gave him a more human appearance. He would enjoy a meal of real food instead of protein shakes or blended food.

Hannah called to Stacy sitting in the den. "Do you need help?"

The swelling decreased a little each day, and Stacy pushed her body a little more. "No, Mom, just time."

The doorbell rang and the family arrived. Hannah's dad arrived with Henry beside him.

Hannah squealed and hugged her son. "How?"

"Mom!" His face clouded up as he tried to speak, his throat tightened. He took a deep breath, "PaPaw," was all he could say.

Hannah didn't ask any questions. She wanted Henry to tell his own story.

When Jason and Naomi arrived, they brought in a truck full of food, including a chocolate cake. Jason sat it in the middle of the bar. "In memory of Mom and Dad," he stated, and the family stopped and glared at the cake for a few minutes. Jason took Naomi's hand and raised it for the family to see her engagement ring. "She's one of us now and will join the family soon." Jason said with a broad smile.

Then Stacy broke the spell. "Is the cake still warm?"

"Of course." Jason hugged his niece. "It's the only thing I can cook." He winked.

Alyssa surprised the family when she brought a guest, Sid Long, the new doctor in town.

"Hope you don't mind me crashing your family dinner." Dr. Long said to Daniel.

Daniel gave an approving smile.

Sharon came behind Alyssa and Dr. Long, loaded with packages.

"You shouldn't have done that," Trey said.

Sharon smiled and answered, "Don't deny me the joy of giving; that's what the season's all about."

Trey placed the packages under the tree with the rest of the growing bounty.

Rance, Jenny Gale, Nathan, and Emily came bearing gifts and food.

Nathan kissed Hannah on the cheek. "How's my favorite cousin?"

"Almost human," she remarked

Belial roared, "I hate Christmas!"

"Of course, we do. Remember when He was born."

"Yeah, Herod was supposed to rid the world of Him."

"Why do our plans keep getting stomped on all the time?"

Lucifer stepped into the dragon's lair and took a seat on the high place next to the throne made of bones. The archangel whom the angels followed in rebellion against the Sovereign One shed a faint light upon the lair. The dragons once shared heaven. Now they lived in a scrap heap of maggots, worms, and rotting flesh. The dim light of Lucifer revealed his rotting corpse.

"There will come a time, we will destroy His little family! No one will love Him!" Lucifer bellowed to the dragons. The same message he gave every time he stepped before them. Even Belial the most fierce and loyal dragon of them all, ignored the empty words of Lucifer.

"I'll send you all to Tartarus!" he shrieked.

The dragons rested their heads on their claws. During the celebration of the Master's birth, there would be little they could do.

"You can prey upon their greed to get more." Lucifer suggested.

"They give to each other," Belial groaned.

"Then they cause disruption in the families." Ezequeel said.

"Take a look at the families. They are either a colossal mess due to our influence or they are protected by the Holy One."

Lucifer saw the hopelessness of his dragon army and wondered how they would be able to fight in the day of the Lord when the Chief Dragon Warrior came to destroy them. The lake of fire even made Lucifer cringe.

The bountiful table covered with all kinds of delicious foods found its beauty in the faces of the people around it. Laughter, conversation, and joy in each other's presence rolled through the house.

Buster, Barbara, Mrs. Waithe, Peggy, Paps, Michael, and a host of others bowed before the Christ who went to earth so they could be with Him and the Father. The joy of being in the presence of the Father, the Son and the Holy Ghost was the fulfillment of a life well lived through a short journey on earth. The family sat down at a bountiful table with each person enjoying their favorite foods.

"I'm grateful our families can have a small taste of the real party that awaits them," a man at one end of the table said.

"It won't be long now before we are all together," another said.

The guests at this banquet all spoke of the day when the Dragon Warrior would send all the dragons to the lake of fire, and God's family would rejoice together in the New Earth.

Henry asked to hand out the gifts. With each gift he gave, he offered an apology and a regret. After all of the gifts were distributed, he faced his family and said, "I'm sorry that I took our grandmother from us. I was released by a miracle." He turned toward his grandfather and Uncle Rance. "The psychiatrist determined I was temporarily insane, and I was. Uncle Rance employed a lawyer for me."

Henry choked up as he spit out the words that overwhelmed him. "I won't have to do jail time."

"How?" Hannah exclaimed, holding her hands together under her chin as if she were praying.

"I'll be tried as a juvenile instead of an adult, and until my trial, I'm in the custody of Uncle Rance and PaPaw."

"So, if he skips bail, I'm sending you the bill," Rance teased Hannah.

"It's a bill I would gladly pay," she responded with a smile. "Will he be able to stay home?"

"No, Mom, I have to stay with Uncle Rance."

Each family member forgave Henry and hugged him.

When he came to Hannah, she could feel the tears welling up in her eyes. She was proud of her son, and he showed her what she must do. Before the family opened the gifts, Hannah faced her family, the most difficult audience one can face.

"My dear family, I have been on a journey of examination of all things, especially my heart." She choked, knowing she had to continue. "I held unforgiveness in my heart."

The family nodded.

"My unforgiveness of my mother was a combination of many unforgiven acts." She wiped her eyes and continued. "I felt regret being born into such a family.

"Then I had to examine my own heart. I don't know all the details of your lives. I know the details of what I did to my mother, your sister, daughter, and aunt. I was cruel, vindictive, and unforgiving."

Daniel held Stacy as she sat weeping at her mother's speech.

"I say all this because I held unforgiveness in my heart, and Jesus said if we speak against Him, it will be forgiven, but if we speak against the Holy Spirit, it will not be forgiven.

"I have grieved the Holy Spirit with my hurtful words and in holding unforgiveness in my own heart. I didn't take the time to learn the details of the offenses I took. I put them in my victim narrative and focused on my feelings.

"It wasn't until everything precious was taken from me that I examined myself. I didn't like what I found, but in that exercise, I found a new relationship with my Lord. I stand before you, my family, and ask for your forgiveness for my dishonor of my mother. I don't deserve it, but I beg for it. I pray she will forgive me too.

Jason stood and made a confession, followed by the others. Everyone confessed his or her wrong-doings toward each other. Jason asked the family to join in prayer.

Heaven heard the prayer of the remaining Troye family.

Barbara wept with a smile of joy for her Hannah.

The Master held Buster and said, "You have come to your rest, you trained your family well. That's my army, they are now soldiers in my army, they are My dragon warriors."

Epilogue:

The Troye family is a representation of the family of God as we journey through this earthly life. These novels illustrate the attack on God's family by evil forces whose desire is to deceive and destroy humans. Perhaps it will help one to understand why there is evil in the world and why God allows His children to go through the fiery trials of the dragon attacks.

One answer for our suffering can be found in 2 Corinthians 1:3-5. "Blessed be the God and Father of our Lord Jesus Christ, the Father of mercies and God of all comfort, who comforts us in all our affliction so that we will be able to comfort those who are in any affliction with the comfort with which we ourselves are comforted by God. For just as the sufferings of Christ are ours in abundance, so also our comfort is abundant through Christ."

The glory and beauty of Heaven cannot be described in a novel, but I want to thank Randy Alcorn for his book, *Heaven*. It helped me greatly in writing these scenes. It helped to give a glimpse into the glory waiting for those in Christ. Scripture tells us we cannot even imagine the wonders of Heaven.

> "Yet we do speak wisdom among those who are mature; a wisdom, however, not of this age nor of the rulers of this age, who are passing away; but we speak God's wisdom in a mystery, the hidden wisdom which God predestined before the ages to our glory; the wisdom which none of the rulers of this age has understood; for if they had understood it they would not have crucified the Lord of glory; but just as it is written, **things which eye has not seen and ear has not heard, and which have not entered the heart of man, all that God has prepared for those who love him**" (1 Corinthians 2:6-9, emphases by author).

To the readers of the Dragon Series, I thank you for your support. This project has been a labor of love, first for the Word of God and its power to reveal, rebuke, and correct. (2 Timothy 3:16) and second, for you—the reader.

Jesus often spoke in parables, and those parables used the culture of the audience to whom he spoke. These novels are written to the culture of twenty-first Century Americans as an explanation of the events that occurred in 546 B.C. in the book of Jeremiah and are current to a modern audience. The dragons were the deceptions presenting false claims and the idols of self-fulfillment.

The Israelites struggled with false teachers and discernment, and so it is in modern culture too.

If you desire to know more about the Scripture reference for the events in the novels, I invite you to visit the website, *StonesInClay.com*, and request the study guide for the novel.

These novels are for your enjoyment and edification. I pray they encourage the reading of God's Word where truth can be found.

I would love to hear from you. Sincerely,
Deanna Cooner PhD
P.O. Box 1302
Newcastle, Ok 73065
coonergd@pldi.net

Notes and Further Resources:

Family Estrangement is a growing phenomenon among nurturing, loving Christian families. If you, the reader, have an estrangement in your family or you seek to help another with an estrangement, the following resources are recommended:

<u>For the Adult Child who has Estranged from their family</u>:

Estranged: Finding Hope When Your Family Falls Apart

by Julie Plagens

For the Parents of an Adult Child who has estranged

from them:

Abandoned Parents:

The Devil's Dilemma,

by Sharon Wildey,

There are two other books from this author on this topic:
First: to the estranged parents and
Second: to the adult child who has estranged from
    parents.

Done with the Crying

by Sheri McGregor

For information regarding Estrangement and the New Covenant:

Estrangement:

A Word that Spells Pain,

by Deanna Cooner

 This text gives the biblical background for the story in *Dragon Warrior.*

The reality of a family schism is that the one estranged must not dwell on what one cannot change, but rather pray for the other, keep one's eyes focused on Christ, and build a life without that family member. But always be open to reconciliation. The purpose of estrangement is to destroy the family unit so that the family of God is hidden.

Only the one who estranges from the family unit can initiate reconciliation. As seen in Dragon Warrior, an estrangement is hideous in the fact it injures so many people and is difficult to restore. It is truly a scheme of the dragon, that serpent of old, the devil. (Revelation 12:9)

Book Six: And Now the Judgment of the Dragons

Dragon Kings

By Deanna Cooner

Dragon Series

Buster Troye comes face to face with a horrid Dragon. Will he overcome the dreadful beast?

Barbara Troye is lured by her selfish needs into revolt? Can she be rescued from the Dragon's demon?

Dr. Zay Troye sees a Dragon carrying the secret of hell. Can science find the truth?

Rance Troye's wedding is cut short when the Dragon steals the bride. Will Rance's search save her or destroy him?

The pain of Buster Troye's Dragon bite grows from a family division. His final battle is fought by the Dragon warrior.

During World War II, military "Operation High Jump" explores Antarctica and finds the Dragon's lair.

www.StonesInClay.com   Stones in Clay PUBLISHING   www.AlongSideYou.org

Available wherever books are sold.

www.ingramcontent.com/pod-product-compliance
Lightning Source LLC
Chambersburg PA
CBHW061308190726
48288CB00002B/403